THE RENEGADE

Long ago, Jim Aherne had been adopted by the Sioux, he was given the name Warbonnet and had become a great brave. Rival tribes feared him. But when the soldiers came, the years with his adopted people slid away. Blood was talking for Jim Aherne . . . he couldn't kill a white man, could he?

THE RENEGADE

L. L. Foreman

GUNSMOKE

This hardback edition 2005
by BBC Audiobooks Ltd
by arrangement with
Golden West Literary Agency

ISBN 1 4056 8038 5

British Library Cataloguing in Publication Data available.

Printed and bound in Great Britain by
Antony Rowe Ltd., Chippenham, Wiltshire

CONTENTS

★

CONTENTS

INTRODUCTION

★

ONE CAN HARDLY PROWL THROUGH THE PLAINS INDIAN
Wars without coming upon the tracks of some white
renegade or other who fought on the side of the Red
Man. We speculate upon such unnatural behavior, particularly when we find that most of these men fought
on both sides in their times. What were the extraordinary circumstances that caused them to vacillate so
violently in their loyalties? What strong emotions impelled them? By what arguments did they defend themselves from their consciences?

Simon Girty, probably the most notorious of them all,
is represented as an inhuman monster, a fiend, an infamous traitor. But we learn that this same Simon Girty
held the affection and respect of those white comrades
who campaigned with him in Dunmore's War; that he
was never known to break his word; that when he fell
in love with Catherine Malott—whom he saved from the
savages—he behaved like a gentleman and won her
honorably for his bride. His friends called him fearless
and heroic.

How can we help speculating about such men?

The Renegade is my attempt at an answer to the rid-
dle, and Wapaha Jim is a composite of several authen-
tic renegades. In the writing of his story it became
necessary to make use of a few historical events—no-
tably the Powder River Fight and Custer's Last Campaign. In these, for the purposes of the story, I have
added a light touch or two of my own, but in the
main they stand close to the facts as history presents
them. In the matter of names I have where necessary
invented my own, but Custer and Terry and Sitting

Bull and Crazy Horse . . . men of such stature cannot be made to hide behind aliases.

However, those who have no taste for history have little to fear here. *The Renegade* is fiction—a story of those other days of tempest when the Man in Blue and the Feathered Warrior rode into battle on horseback, and of the women who loved and followed them.

L. L. F.

★

CHAPTER I

OFF THE TRAIL

IT SEEMED TO THE BOY THAT THE PRAIRIE MUST GO ON forever—that this green vastness must sweep on into the mystery of space and eternity, and could have no end. The long billows, furred soft and smooth by the fine buffalo grass, failed to break the deception of flatness, for the sun stared high and shadowed no hollows, and the horizon's purpled edge ran a bold straight line against the sky.

The boy clucked by habit to the mules, who continued their same steady gait, their quick little steps *sluff-sluffing* through the high grass, and the sway-backed Conestoga wagon creaked its familiar accompaniment, trundling cumbrously up another gentle swell. A patch of cottonwoods stood alone in all the emptiness ahead, and the boy idly tried to estimate how much longer it would take to pass them. You had to change your ideas about distances out here, he'd discovered. This morning from far off he had sighted the trees as a speckled clump, seeing only their tops. Now, as the wagon slowly took one swell after another, he could partly overlook the dip in which they huddled, and he saw more of them dwindling off in a scattery column, following the thin reddish scar of a creek bed hidden among the long billows. No antelope in sight anywhere, so he figured it was likely a dry bed, unusual for this time of year.

1

Somehow those cottonwoods made the prairie seem even bigger and emptier. He couldn't believe that they were tall and full grown. The straight trunks were toothpicks, and the foliage twinkled like silvered tassels in the light brushing of the wind. Lonely dwarfs. Tiny outposts of a world abandoned far behind to the east.

The thought vaguely disturbed a mood that had been solemn and pleasantly glorified by the strong sense of spaciousness. He shortened his wandering gaze to his father, riding in the lead with Old Moccasin, the guide that they had picked up back in Westport. James Alland Aherne sat his horse with a certain rakish ease and a large air of deep contentment. He was big and browned, quietly confident, a self-sufficient kind of man. It was hard to recall that his deep tan was no older than his short black beard, which he had let grow out during the past few weeks. The tentative uneasiness left the boy. He clucked again at the mules, settled back on the wagon seat with the lines loose in his hands, and invited back the solemn glory. This was a man's life and a man's land. He didn't care if they never got to Oregon.

Through the steady sounds of the wagon and team he caught a faint cry from the wagon following behind, and he guessed that Miz' Hathersall had just found another of her elegant dishes chipped or something. Seemed like it was always something, back there in the Hathersall wagon. She'd have that tight look about her now for the rest of the day, and poor Mist' Sam Hathersall would have to explain once more how it wasn't noways handy to pack thin china in a wagon without a piece busting occasional. Women.

Feet pattered alongside. "Hi, Whopper, let's ride with you."

"Climb on," said Whopper, and made his voice grunty, not because he was displeased, but because driving his father's wagon gave him a grown-up right to be gruff. " 'Nother Leemosh dish busted?"

Weston and Talitha Hathersall climbed aboard and he made room for them on the plank seat. West and Tally—that was what he called them, somewhat to the irritation of Mrs. Hathersall, who nursed a genteel abhorrence of nicknames and diminutives. "No, it's not the *Limoges* china this time," said Tally. "It's the Sandwich lamp." She sighed automatically, a fair copy of her mother's sigh, and pushed her tumbled yellow hair back from her ears. "Father couldn't have packed it properly."

"Packed it good as he could," West countered shortly. Being by two years his sister's senior he was in a position to dominate her, but he hadn't realized his blessings until he came under Whopper's wholly male-minded influence. "One of the prism danglers got broke," he remarked to Whopper, as between men.

"Broken," corrected Tally.

Whopper patronized them both with a glance. "When we bust something we just laugh and allow it saves washing, Pa and me. Git up there, mules!"

In his young way he was as large-minded as his father, and just as calmly intolerant of little things. He grew aware of Tally's considering regard, and turned his head to meet it. Tally, more introspective than her brother, more inclined to challenge cool presumption, pursued a middle course of private criticism and half-reluctant admiration of him. He sensed it. He grinned at her, and when he did that it always changed him, put a charm of engaging friendliness upon him, and the little girl glowed helplessly under the spell of it, her child eyes caught and quickly shining. Then his grin altered, grew mocking and scornful in the way that she hated. Furious, she went red, trying to ignore him.

"You and your Leemosh china," he jeered, and turned back to the mules.

In the overloaded Hathersall wagon, Elizabeth Hathersall carefully wrapped the flint-glass Sandwich lamp and reflected that beautiful possessions certainly were never intended for men. She looked at her husband slouched dispiritedly on the driver's seat, at the hairy back of his neck, and she drew a sad strength from resignation. This—all this—a woman could expect when she married beneath her station.

She squared her shoulders, pressed her rather thin lips together, and packed the damaged lamp away between the spare blankets. She was prepared to stand more loss than this, to gain a new life in Oregon, to grow rich with that new land, to be the wife of something more than a plodding bookkeeper. She had been a Chittendon of Massachusetts before her marriage, a marriage plunged into without heed in an insane year of youth.

It had not been easy to shift Samuel. James Aherne had helped her in that, and she was grateful to him. When he let it be known that he was going to Oregon she had begged him to persuade her husband to take the same step, and Aherne with his blazing enthusiasm had finally infected the dubious Samuel. He was only a schoolteacher, but she had always regarded him as something of a gentleman in spite of his peculiarities.

Undoubtedly, James Aherne had his peculiarities. His way of bringing up his motherless son, for instance —casually giving him a man's responsibilities and laughing it off when the boy made a mistake. Letting him use shocking grammar, yet insisting that he read classic literature that was far too advanced and mature for him. And giving him that unspeakable nickname of Whopper, when his name was James. Hazily she remembered some sort of anecdote told by Aherne, out of which the boy emerged with that nickname. She had missed the point. Something about the boy having told a monumental lie, and later boldly confessing that it had been a whopper. Well, she could easily conceive of that boy doing such a thing. A disturbing young animal, she found him, with his black hair, lean brown face and startlingly cool eyes. Dark Irish, like his father. And, like his father, with a hidden fierceness in him that flared up at rare times in a swift gust and was gone again.

"Samuel," said Elizabeth Hathersall, "I do hope Mr. Aherne's boy will not let our Weston try to drive their team again. He nearly wrecked it that other time, and might have injured himself. And Mr. Aherne only laughed!"

"I laughed, too," Sam mentioned unguardedly, wishing he could turn over some of his own driving to his son and ride up in front for a change, like Aherne. "Looks like we might be coming to water. Trees up ahead. Aherne and Old Moccasin are going on to take a look, reckon."

Trotting up ahead, James Aherne remarked that he hoped there'd be water, and Old Moccasin said he hoped the same. Neither man spoke of the question first in his mind, which was posed by the total absence of any trail and no sign of the big emigrant wagon-train that they should have overhauled and joined by now.

They had missed the trail five nights ago, when pushing on after dark to make up for time lost when young West bogged the Aherne wagon in a mud hole and broke a wheel. Next morning they had rolled on, rather than turn back to look for the trail, confident that they would come upon it soon. Old Moccasin had vowed he could strike it with his eyes shut and a cheek to the sun, but Aherne was beginning to suspect that the old drunk knew a lot more about the frontier grogshops than he did about the prairie.

To go striking off west out of Westport with only a two-wagon outfit was foolhardy enough to begin with, and the wise heads in Vogel's tavern had said so. Better to lay over for the next emigrant train to be organized. You didn't noways get ahead if you pushed in a hurry; not west of Westport you didn't.

But there was some bronco in Aherne, some of it brewed from years of bottled frustration, and a restlessness that had haunted him too long to pause now for niggling caution. Nor was he a man easily turned by advice, good or bad. He listened absently, his mind on his own affairs, and went along the course that he'd set from the first. "Thank you, gentlemen. I appreciate your interest. Mr. Vogel—a dram for me, please, and take these gentlemen's orders."

He was like that, a man of culture and yet a man of the crowd, courteous, independent, making friends easily. But you could see the seeking look in his fine eyes, a look of energy, of high-strung enthusiasm and a shade of brooding discontent. After two decent years of mourning for his dead wife, he had taken the step that he'd always wanted to take, and started west with his boy. Be damned to schools and the bored faces of young pupils. Far west in Oregon there was land for a man, good land to clear and farm, to test good muscles and bring out sweat. He had never been meant for a schoolteacher.

Old Moccasin, for his part, knew that he and the wagon party were quite lost, but he trusted to luck to bring him through. He had trusted to luck all his life, and as fast as it ran out in one place he drifted to another. He knew the frontier, knew it by its dram-shops and groggeries. The rest was a composite blur formed of misery and dryness, wherein he had sought no knowledge but only the comfort of rum. His speech, that had convinced Aherne of the old man's plains experience, was a reflection of many phrases heard and picked up from better men. He had hired out to Aherne because his luck had run dry in Westport, and he thought Aherne would be likely to carry a jug or two in his wagon. Destination meant nothing.

"I'm feered it's an *arroyo seco*, drier'n hell's bones," he mumbled huskily, peering on at the cottonwoods. "Happen it's so, we'll jest push on till we strike trail. If our stick floats thataway, shecks—I kin do 'thout water!"

"But not the mules," said Aherne, and stood up in his stirrups for a better look.

And then the band of Comanches, that had been patiently waiting half the morning in the cottonwoods, came out on the wild whoop.

★

It was a hunting party up from the south after buffalo, but when Comanches poached on Sioux country they came ready for fight, and for horses or hair or anything else they could take off in a hurry. This year, spring had come early after a mild winter. Not much snow north, and no rain in the south. The buffalo had migrated north early, seeking new grass, and emigrants started west weeks ahead of schedule. Aherne had missed the first wagon-train for that reason.

Aherne hadn't thought about buffalo, and not much about Indians, but he had his long percussion musket with him, slung across his saddle because he liked the feel of it. Old Moccasin had a battered and rawhide-mended Hawkins gun, too, but Aherne was quickest in getting off a shot and wheeling his horse for a hard run to the wagons.

"Whopper—fort in! Indians!"

To Whopper in that first instant, the Indians appeared as so many grotesque dolls mounted on toy ponies, small and distinct in the clear air, even their barking cries flattened by the unechoing vastness of the land. He swung the already nervously dancing mules in a cramped turn to bring the wagon about and angle it against the Hathersall wagon. A gasping little scream came from Tally, but West sat frozen and staring. In his reaction, young West had company, for Sam Hathersall wasn't doing much, either. Just sitting with his mouth open and the lines drooping in his hands, letting his mules stamp to a trembling halt. And Elizabeth Hathersall, for once forgetful of genteel moderation, screamed for her children.

Whopper ran the wagon alongside the Hathersall outfit and locked wheels. It was the best he could do in a hurry without cooperation from Sam Hathersall. Both wagons jammed together with a grinding smash that jerked the Aherne mules up short into a kicking tangle, and West fell off the seat with his sister. Whopper let go the lines and scrambled over the seat into the wagon for his father's new Colt pistol. When he dropped out through the rear end the Indians were riding up close, howling in a way that made his skin quiver. He couldn't see his father anywhere, but he caught a glimpse of his father's horse, riderless and running free, chased by some of the feathered men.

A shaking fury gripped him and he jerked the trigger of the Colt pistol, fired blindly into the thundering confusion of riders. "Pa! Pa—where are you?"

"Weston—Talitha! Oh, heaven—my children!" That was Miz' Hathersall, yelling her head off. It wasn't Pa. They'd got Pa, or he'd be here doing things.

They rode naked to their breechclouts, shaking tasselled buffalo lances and sounding off their choppy yells. The wind whipped fringed leather leggings and stained feather plumes, all wildness and terror, and the glistening copper bodies were the writhing devils of hell that the preacher had told about in the church-house. The boy cursed and fired again. A shrieking rider with the eyes of a madman whirled out at him and twanged a bowstring, and something slim and polished whispered briefly over Whopper's hair. It gave out two quick little slaps, passing through the wagon canvas, and sheer horror sent Whopper ducking away around the wagon.

He saw Miz' Hathersall leaning against the tail of her wagon, one hand on West's shoulder, Tally clutching her skirt and crying, and Mist' Sam facing her and taking no heed of the circling Indians. She looked sick and white, like maybe a whole lot more Leemosh dishes had got broke. Mist' Sam had a saw-edged hay cutter in his hand. It was like him to grab up a thing like that instead of his shotgun, which he should have had handy but never did.

Elizabeth Hathersall quit standing, quite suddenly, but she crumpled to the ground with a modesty of movement, like a lady fainting in public. She lay on her face, and then Whopper could see the bit of feathered stick in the back of her dress, and the stain. Tally screamed and West said something, staring.

Sam Hathersall just stood there looking down at his wife, and then he began cursing. Strange words, coming from him. He raised his head, but he didn't look at his son and daughter. He looked at the wild riders all around, and he walked out at them with the saw-edged hay cutter. Tally screamed again, and West called after him, but it didn't do any good. He slashed the heavy blade at three riders who bore down on him, struck a pony that had a red hand painted on its chest, and went down with a lance through him. All three riders jumped

down and hit him, each crying out something in turn,
their voices choking and hissing. The one who had
lanced him snatched out a short knife with a curved
blade. A scalping knife . . .

★

The mules were frantic and some of them had broken
away. A Comanche dashed in close and grinned horribly at the two boys and the girl, but he made for the
mules first. He cut them loose and began expertly herd-
ing them off for himself, but a metal sliver spun through
the air at him and he fell off his pony. An angry roar
went up, and Old Moccasin ducked in from somewhere,
afoot and without his Hawkins gun.

Old Moccasin caught the hair-rope bridle of the Indian pony, and retrieved his hammered knife from its
rider. "We gotta make a run fer it!" he shouted, which
showed he didn't know much about Indian fighting.
Turn your back on Injuns, said the wise heads, and
you're cooked. Safer to keep your face to 'em, if you got
a load left in your gun.

Whopper still had the Colt. "Gimme thet shooter,
boy!" Old Moccasin commanded hoarsely, fighting with
the Indian pony.

"Hell I will!" Whopper took a vicious shot at a riding
brave in high yellow moccasins and red rag headband,
a fellow far from home. An Apache, though Whopper
didn't know it. Injuns were Injuns, all bad.

The Apache took the load and tumbled. The angry
howl went up again, but the Comanches let their guest
lie there, and they rode a wider circle, wary, this affair
no longer a matter of sport. Soon they would gather
for the grand charge, but first they must empty that pistol. Young braves hungry for prestige began racing by
the wagons, enticing the shooter to waste his loads, rid-

ing off-side and hanging onto the hair rope braided into the pony mane, loosing off arrows from under the stretching neck.

"Got to save the wimmin," hollered Old Moccasin, all befuddled but stubbornly clinging to his role of veteran white warrior of the plains. "Gotta break through. Make a run fer it. Ya'll take this-yer pony whilst I stand off the cussed varmints—if ye gimme thet shooter."

"Get Mist' Sam's shotgun out his wagon," said Whopper. "I need this pistol. Got to look for my Pa. West—Tally—get on that pony."

"Ain't no use you go for your pa, boy," Old Moccasin told him, getting the shotgun. "He's a-layin' dead out yonder."

Whopper had known that his father must be dead, but to hear it said like that, so blunt and definite, made it terribly real. At this moment he could have done what Sam Hathersall had done. He fired at a passing rider, missed, and Old Moccasin shouted at him to quit wasting his loads. He swore back at the old man, glaring at him, eyes gone bright and savage, but cold hatred took the place of rage, and he counted his loads. Two left.

"Let's git," muttered Old Moccasin and started off, lugging the shotgun and leading the pony. West and Tally, upon the pony, and dazed into dumb obedience, kept shivering. Whopper moved into pace with Old Moccasin, though he didn't want to. It was insanity, and he half realized it. Away from the wagons there would be no cover.

The Comanches drew in their ponies, watching the pitiful little procession, suspecting a ruse. They had known some whites to do remarkably eccentric things, but nothing so utterly fantastic as this attempt to escape in the open with only one pony for four persons. They followed at a reasonably cautious distance, more in-

trigued than alarmed, prepared to make short work of
the matter when their curiosity was satisfied.

"We got 'em skeered, son," opined Old Moccasin, and
patted the shotgun. "Jest folly Ol' Moc'sin. He'll git
you clear. He'll show the cussed varmints!"

He got his chance soon enough. Three impatient
young bucks put their ponies to a lope, and came charging ahead. Old Moccasin turned on them and stood his
ground. There was some man in him, despite all the
sodden years. Perhaps he thought he could bluff off the
Indians. Perhaps he didn't intend to pull the trigger
and leave himself practically unarmed, when he swung
up the shotgun. But he did pull it, and the charge
roared from the barrel, and a pony shied off at a limping bolt. The pony's rider slid nimbly to the ground
and did a swift trick with his short-bow, standing with
his dark body thrown back from the waist. Old Moccasin murmured a word and dropped with an arrow in
him. The other riders yelled and came on. Some of the
main party turned back toward the wagons in a race for
loot.

Whopper heard Tally crying in a terrified, breath-
sucking way, and he did an instinctive thing, an unthinking thing. He hit the pony with the long barrel of
the Colt pistol. "Quit squallin' and go like hell!" he
yelled. "Run, you damn Injun horse!"

The pony took off. It was a good buckskin, lean along
the ribs, but with good legs. A Mexican pony, stolen
somewhere far south. As it stretched out and left him,
Whopper had a sick sensation of loneliness, standing
there, but his rage and hatred were too big to let him
down. He fired the pistol at the nearest Comanche, who
was bent on catching the buckskin, and a sense of
savage power swept up in him when the Comanche
screamed and rolled off his mount. The third rider rode
a circle and fell in with the rest of the coming party.

The painted ponies halted all in a jump, and the Comanches eyed the boy with fierce and sharp regard. They wanted to take him, and not dead. This small white boy had killed a grown warrior, and the friends and family of the dead man would desire to wipe out the humiliation. But he still had a load left in his pistol, for he held it cocked and his eyes said he was not bluffing.

Whopper backed away, a futile move in all that great sea of grassed prairie, gripping the pistol. The feathered men edged around him, closing in, tempting him to shoot and empty his weapon. They had him, and he was only a boy, but he was dangerous while he had a shot left. A daring young buck got off his pony and advanced on foot, crouched ready to leap for his life, a throwing club balanced in his hand. He growled as he slowly came on, growled to keep himself fierce.

Whopper stared at the poised club, fascinated.

CHAPTER 2

★

THE FEATHERED MEN

THE SIOUX WAR PARTY MOVED QUIETLY AFOOT ALONG THE muddy creek bed, stooping, leading their ponies. Where the cottonwoods grew thickest those in the lead paused and the rest caught up. They bunched, not too closely, and in silence they mounted their ponies and looked to their weapons. Then, for all their eager impatience, they looked to *Wambli-gi*, waiting his word.

Wambli-gi—Yellow Eagle— rode forward up the bank

until his eyes came level with the plain, and he examined what he saw. Being a man of high reputation and the leader of this war party, he did not hurry in his inspection. He was no longer young, though active, and a consciousness of dignity and prestige held him to a deliberation that was more seeming than real. With his notched coup-stick he touched the four yellow medicine bags that hung by a thong from his bared left shoulder, dutifully murmuring a prayer to *Wakan Tanka*, the Great Mysterious, for good fortune in the coming fight. He had his Sharps rifle in its buckskin scabbard, well oiled with marrow of deer's leg-bone, but he chose his beaded lance with the broad pan-iron blade. He was well armed. He had painted his pony with a red line on all four legs to make it strong and fast, and another red line around its jaws to make it long winded, so he was also well mounted. A Crow scalp dangled from its bridle, and three more stripes on its right foreleg gave its history. It had been ridden often against enemies, with success.

Slowly, grandly, Yellow Eagle turned his painted face to the waiting warriors. His head-feather swayed with his movement—a single eagle tail-feather, stuck upright in his black hair. He could have worn more, for his coups were many, but his pride and honor needed no such display. His world knew him. One feather was enough.

"*Hiyupo!*" He kicked his pony and was first over the bank. After him swarmed the warriors, patting their open mouths and sending out the quick staccato of the war whoop.

The sharp new sound almost caused Whopper to fire his last load. He shivered, baring his teeth like a cornered young bull-pup. Beyond the Indians crowding him, the others emerged as if erupting out of the earth after a running start from hell. This vast and brooding land was filling with howling devils, and he was their magnet. The pistol shook in his hand.

And then the solid phalanx broke from around him, the Comanches wrenching their ponies about, startled, dismayed, colliding in their frantic haste.

The Sioux thundered in at a headlong charge, riotous and magnificent, and at once everything burst into a chaotic anarchy. Whopper dodged, stumbling out of the way of fighting groups that swarmed and milled about him. The rearing, squealing ponies, the half-naked berserkers stabbing and slashing, the hideous howls, screams, the booming explosions of smoothbore guns— it dazed him. He had no understanding of what had come about, and he thought they had all gone mad. He had never conceived of Indians fighting Indians, or of tribal feuds and hatreds. Now he was forgotten and ignored, the fighters seeing only their ancient foes and all ablaze with the hot old urge to kill.

The fight was short. The Comanches were outnumbered, taken by surprise and off their own territory, and the wise heads could have told Whopper that Comanches never were a match for Sioux warriors in a stand-up fight. Riders broke out of the murderous ruck and went racing off, yelling sorry defiance and leaving their dead and wounded behind. A bloodied figure rose unsteadily from the ground, glared about him, and settled on the white boy for a last dying coup. He lurched at a shambling trot, knife in hand, too far gone to care for the danger of the pistol, and Whopper fired his last shot.

With the report, the fight reached its end. The Comanche pitched forward and lay quiet on the torn grass, and Whopper suddenly found himself the object of hushed attention. Here and there, dark-bodied men shifted their regard from silenced enemies, from knife and scalp lock, and surveyed the boy with eyes in-

flamed with fighting hangover. A deep voice called out
something, and the owner of it kneed his pony forward
and stared down at the boy. He wore four little yellow
bags under his left arm, yellow stripes on his face, and a
single feather in his hair. A big man, and well muscled.
Others joined him, all regarding the boy with that in-
flamed stare.

Whopper turned the pistol on them. When they
closed in around him he circled about, trying to scare
them off, but the pistol shook so badly he knew he
couldn't make the bluff stand. It was empty and they
could guess it from his face. He snarled at the one in
yellow paint, who slid off his pony and took an unhur-
ried pace toward him, and he tried to back off, but they
had him hemmed in. If he'd had a load left he would
have sent it into the chest of that big, yellow-painted
devil. The big devil pointed down at the dead Comanche and spoke a word, nodding slowly. Whopper
crouched, ready to lash out with the empty pistol, and
his back and stomach crawled with cold.

He was not to know that Yellow Eagle and his Minniconjou Sioux had been trailing the poaching Comanches
for five days, ever since coming upon the distinctive
tracks of their moccasins and rawhide horseshoes. To
those about him, Yellow Eagle said, "This boy has killed
an enemy. Now he would kill us if he could. His heart
is big."

Running Dog laughed, fingering his short-bow. He
was the son of Black Horn, chief of the band, who was
too old and fat to ride to hunt or war. "See the warrior
—wagh! See him shake like a pup that fears the stick!"

"He is afraid, but his heart is big," Yellow Eagle
stated gravely, and some of the others grunted agree-
ment. A brave man or boy might tremble without
shame. Cowards begged, or ran blindly like frightened

women. "Your voice is loud, young Running Dog. Save
your voice for counting coups."

Laughter rumbled through the group, appreciation of
the quiet irony. Running Dog had struck fourth coup
on a dead man, and no more. His lean face stiffened
sulkily and he turned away, knowing better than to en-
gage in words with a warrior of Yellow Eagle's standing. "He would like to wear the hair of that boy," put
in somebody.

"He could then count coup on a warrior," murmured
Yellow Eagle, and smiled, inspecting the boy. He admired the boy's stand, and was amused by it. That
empty pistol, against the pick of the Black Horn Minniconjou, made a grand symbol of hard-dying defiance.
Some of the hard-bitten warriors clowned fear of it,
begging the boy not to shoot, and laughter rumbled
again. It could have been fully loaded, and they still
would have clowned and laughed.

★

When the big devil came pacing deliberately at him,
Whopper swung up the pistol to strike. Running Dog,
on the outskirts of the group, slipped an arrow to his
bow-string, but an older warrior growled at him to put
it away. The spirit of the group was sportive now. The
boy was an antidote for the reaction of touchy irascibil-
ity and let-down that always came after a short and
bloody fight. A good joke or a comic accident would
have done as well.

The blunt end of a lance tickled Whopper along his
ribs. He jerked off-guard, and the next instant his pistol
was gone, plucked neatly from his hands. The big devil
had it.

"Ho, little crazy warrior!" A long and muscular arm
whipped around him, almost crushing his shoulders. In

calling him crazy, Yellow Eagle paid him a compliment, though not without sarcasm. It connoted wildness and an unsurrendering spirit of deviltry.

Whopper tried to struggle against that powerful arm, but gave it up. He glared up into the painted face of his captor, furiously hating him, and hating the laughter, too. Some of his fear left him when he saw the expression in the black eyes, but none of his fury. He would rather have been stabbed and scalped than this —being manhandled and laughed at as a child.

Perhaps Yellow Eagle sensed that. He had understanding, founded upon his own deep appreciation of dignity. He released the boy and quit smiling. The warriors, quick to follow a new mood, stopped their laughter and comments, watching curiously. Yellow Eagle drew himself up, made himself tall and impressive, and only the boy failed at first to detect the humorous mockery behind the respectful pose.

Yellow Eagle tapped a thumb against his own broad chest. "*Wambli-gi*," he introduced himself gravely. He poked a finger at the boy and raised his brows queryingly. Three times he had to repeat before the boy understood.

Whopper began to realize that he wasn't going to be scalped and roasted, not right away, and possibly not at all. Not by this big devil, anyway. He studied the black eyes, and found in them a dim likeness to those of his father, who had often gazed at him like that— gravely quizzical, understanding, and a shade humorous. There was a queer familiarity about that tolerant gaze, and it had its way with him. It did not challenge his self-respect. Unconsciously, he too drew himself up.

"Whopper," he stammered. "I'm Whopper. Whopper Jim Aherne."

It was the thrice-repeated nickname that caught the Indian ear. Yellow Eagle gazed a moment longer at him, and then around at the warriors. *"Wapaha,"* he said solemnly. "This boys calls himself *Wapaha."*

The laughter bellowed this time in an explosive shout. *Wapaha*—Warbonnet! A brave old Sioux name. A great warrior's name, endowed only when fully earned on many a reckless warpath. The boy had a big tongue. Had he been older they would have scorned such a braggart, but he was just a boy. A boy of big heart could be forgiven for boasting, and this one had killed an enemy, after all. Some of them wondered aloud if he really was a white. His hair was black like theirs, though not as straight. His skin was dark and ruddy. He had high cheekbones. Sometimes a northern Sioux turned up with eyes like his, too—a strange and changeable grey.

Whopper didn't know why they should laugh, and his rage leaped again. But Yellow Eagle, looking at him, saw the quick resentment and put an end to it. "He calls himself Warbonnet. Let it be so. His heart is big. Let him have the scalp and weapons of that one he killed, and a pony."

"Running Dog has taken them."

"Then let Running Dog give them."

Running Dog scowled. "My father, Chief Black Horn—"

"He is not here, and this party chose me as leader. Give Warbonnet those things that should be his. I shall tell Black Horn and let him judge." Yellow Eagle fixed his calm stare on Running Dog. The youth flung down his loot and stalked off, muttering.

Yellow Eagle, himself, picked up lance, knife and scalp, and offered them to their winner. He was a little irritated when the boy backed suspiciously away, not understanding his words or even his sign language. It was an honor that he was bestowing upon one so young, and to have it refused was a serious affront. But he remembered that the white men were a puzzling people, and he remained patient. He was pleased when the boy finally and hesitantly accepted the trophies, muttering a word in his alien tongue, but he had to show him how and where to fasten the scalp to the lance.

The watching warriors chuckled again when the boy attempted to mount a pony from its left side. Yellow Eagle recalled that he had seen the white men do that, at Fort Laramie. Always from the left, when everybody knew that the only way to jump on a horse was from the right, unless in a hurried pinch. The pony sidled off, rolling a wicked and scandalized eye, but his new master managed to mount him. After a moment of indecision the boy rode over to the burning wagons, the warriors trailing along and enjoying their own comments on his actions. But the boy passed the wagons and stopped his pony where a tall man lay on the ground with arrows in him. He slid off the pony and looked down at the dead man for a long time, saying and doing nothing.

"Why does he not wail for his dead?" asked a young warrior disapprovingly. Death of a friend or relative demanded loud grief. Such dry-eyed silence was unseemly.

Yellow Eagle saw the muscles working painfully in the boy's throat. "Perhaps he wails in his heart," he said.

The boy tramped back to the wagons for a spade, and didn't look at the faces following him. He knew vaguely that some kind of crisis had passed for him, that they meant him no hurt and were even ready to befriend him in their own manner. He knew, too, that the big fellow in yellow paint—*Wambli-gi*—had championed him and was a leader. There remained no fear in him now, but only a choking sorrow and a steady hatred of those other feathered marauders.

The wagons had been fired by the Comanches, and

were burning to the axles. Most of the contents, so carefully packed, lay scattered about on the ground. The raiders had been looking for whiskey, ironware, weapons and powder. Articles of no utility they had smashed as valueless. The ground about the wagons was littered with broken china, glassware, and pretty, useless knicknacks and women's dresses. Miz' Hathersall would have a fit if she could see this, he thought dully, and kept his eyes away from where she lay. Near the Aherne wagon were books, all lying thrown about, trampled on by feet and hoofs. James Alland Aherne had been going into the wilderness to leave forever behind him the schoolroom and the ordered streets of town, but he had brought along his books.

Whopper found a spade, Sam Hathersall's spade. He looked at all those strewn books and closed his eyes, and when he opened them again he saw his *Sayings of the Sages* lying among them. He had spent hours reading it, not too willingly, curling the shagreen leather cover in his hands, feeling its fine roughness, wishing he could make a sheath out of it for his jackknife. It was small, fat, well bound. Its full title, impressed elegantly in gilt script, was *Dr. Huitruff's Collected Best Sayings of the Sages.* His father had given it to him, and, not being an obdurate disciplinarian, had merely suggested that it would please him if Whopper would read it occasionally.

"You're a scampy young Arab, y'know, and a dash of the classics might do you no harm," James Aherne had remarked mildly, giving him the new jacknife at the same time. "Don't bury it in your bag. The book, I mean. Keep your knife sharp and your books well read, and the Devil will never get you."

★

Whopper picked up the little volume and crammed it into his shirt. To leave it lying there for the sun and rain to rot would have been like leaving part of his father above ground.

They helped him bury his father's body. Had the body been that of a Sioux they would have borne it off and given it proper rest in a high tree, lashed to a limb with weapons and food by it, and killed a good pony so that the dead man's spirit could ride his way handily off to the happy land. But the boy gave no sign of wanting such things done, and they let him have his way. Yellow Eagle explained tolerantly that this was what the white men did, and that they believed their *Wakan Tanka* visited the grave later on and took the spirit away with him. The white men had many strange beliefs and habits. They smoked without first offering their pipes to the sun, but they worshipped a colored rag on a long pole, which they invariably took in at night as soon as the sun quit shining on it. The rag was painted with stars and straight stripes, although the stars were never allowed to shine on it, and music was played when it was brought down from the pole. Also, they were very careful not to let it touch the ground. Yet they buried their dead in the ground. Queer.

Yellow Eagle had been one of those who attended the Indian nations assembly at Fort Laramie for the great treaty, twelve years before, riding better than three hundred miles to get there. He had seen few white men, and was curious. The Black Horn Minniconjou had generally been satisfied to keep to their hunting grounds away north along Grand River, as long as the buffalo were plentiful, and were not overly interested in what went on elsewhere. When word came of the treaty-making down at Fort Laramie, Yellow Eagle and a few cronies rode in just to see the crowd.

There on the Platte they found encamped the repre-

sentatives of the seven Sioux tribes: Hunkpapa, Black-
foot, Two Kettles, Sans Arc, Oglala, Brulé, and some
distant cousins of their own Minniconjou. And Cheyennes, friendly but tough; and slippery Arapahos; and
those hereditary old enemies, the Crows; and Shoshoni,
Mandans, Hidatsas, Rees. . . .

They were all there, eight thousand of them. The
White Commissioner had his tent pitched near Horse
Creek, and all around stood the camps of the traders
and agents, and the white soldiers of the Dragoons and
Mounted Rifles. Nothing like it had ever before been
seen along the Platte. The treaty, such as it was, after
interminable councils was signed with much ceremony,
with all its tall provisions and contrary clauses.

Yellow Eagle carried home some gifts, and tales
enough to last him through many a campfire confab.
One of his lasting impressions was that white men wore
a lot of hair on the face and not much on top of the
head. Like hairy dogs. There had been gifts passed out,
but nothing fit to eat. No buffalo meat. Only white
men's cow beef, tasteless stuff with an unfamiliar sweet-
ish smell. The Indians nearly starved. Dark red buffalo meat was what they wanted. Roast hump and
scalded back-fat, raw heart and liver. *Meat.* The wild
white trappers chuckled when they heard of it. What
did soldiers and commissioners know about feeding
Injuns! These wasn't poor tame agency beggars. These
was *Injuns.*

But the whole thing was an experience, and Yellow
Eagle made new friends there. He met an Oglala Sioux
by the name of Red Cloud, and another young warrior,
a Hunkpapa, called Sitting Bull. Both good company
and of honored families. Comparing notes, these three
modestly agreed that they were at least as good as any
white man they had seen so far, and certainly more
handsome. No hair on *their* faces.

James Alland Aherne was buried. Buried as far from
a schoolroom as he could have wished. They buried the
Hathersalls, too, while they were about it, although it
was a good deal of trouble to go to for strangers. Whopper felt that he ought to say something over his father's
grave. It looked kind of lonely and it was going to be
there a long time. He'd heard the burial service when
his mother died back in Massachusetts, but he couldn't
recall a word of it. So, remembering his *Sayings of the
Sages* and what his father had claimed for it, he fished it
out from under his shirt and thumbed through it, while
the Sioux watched interestedly.

He found what seemed suitable. It contained just the
right note. His father would have liked it, he was sure.
He cleared his throat.

" 'Cowards die many times before their deaths;
    The valiant never taste of death but once.
    Of all the wonders that I yet have heard,
    It seems to me most strange that men should fear;
    Seeing that Death—a necessary end—
    Will come when it will come.' "

He blinked his eyes clear again, and read the last ap-
pended word. "Shakespeare," he said. "Amen."

Riding off with the Sioux war party, it didn't occur to
him to try a bolt. He was no more afraid of them now
than if they had been white men. They had helped bury
his dead. They were different from those other feathered
devils. These were men. He felt wholly at ease among
them.

Yellow Eagle watched the boy shove the shagreen
book back under his shirt. "What is that thing he has?"
asked Iron Breast, his close friend. "Does it speak to
him?"

"I think it must be a holy book, or a charm, such as I
saw the Black Robe Man talk to at the great soldier-

house on the river, during the treaty-making," responded Yellow Eagle. "It is his, and we will let him keep it."

"And what will we do with *him?*" wondered Iron Breast.

Yellow Eagle, not quite prepared to answer, didn't. He kicked his pony. "*Hopo*—let us go home!" he called.

Far to the east, and clinging to the running buckskin, young West Hathersall squirmed around in the Indian saddle and looked back; but now he could see nothing but the buckskin's long dust-trail and a faint smear of whitish smoke which he knew must be rising from the wagons. His sister was in hysterics, crying and screaming, and he had to hold her on. A sort of wakefulness came over him, dissipating the hazed numbness that had held him stupid, and with it came a slow prod of shame, a dull knowledge that he had been inadequate in a time of desperate need. Then fury—fury at those painted killers, and fury at himself.

"I'll kill 'em when I grow up—I'll kill 'em all!" he raged impotently, tardily. "They murdered Mother an' Pa . . . an' Whopper. I'll kill every Indian I find, when I grow up! I'll kill 'em—you watch! You watch! I'll . . ."

CHAPTER 3

★

WARBONNET

THEY CALLED HIM WAPAHA JIM—WARBONNET JIM—OR sometimes just Wapaha. He had grown lean, and long in the legs, all brown smoothness and long black hair.

It was an idle day and he sat on his heels by the river with the camp at his back, reading the shagreen book, pondering, frowning when meanings eluded him. Many of the lines were friendly old enemies that allowed themselves to be committed to memory while refusing to yield their cores of concealed sense. But even these were of value. He amused himself by translating them into Sioux as best he could, and springing them at opportune times upon Jumping Calf and Sleeper and other friends. Sometimes he was overheard by his elders, who puzzled in private over such profundities.

Now he was fifteen, and for three years he had been one of the tribe, accepted and taken for granted. It seemed much longer in his mind, a much more solid and real part of his life than that which lay in the past. So big and near that it overshadowed that other life, making it distant and difficult to recall in detail. This life was full and active, constantly moving, giving off unexpected flashes of color and fresh experiences, and he had little time or inclination to linger over the past. One did not live for last year or for the next, but for today, for today's pleasures and possibilities. On the surface, at least, and in surface thought and philosophy, Wapaha Jim was Indian.

Playing and squabbling with other youngsters around the camp, he had soon learned their ways, their language, their games and aspirations. He had fast feet, cool wits, and a ready daring that matched theirs. He could hold his own with them, as well as awe them with odd bits of strange white wisdom.

Jumping Calf and Sleeper, his two best friends, were proud of him. They never missed a chance to bring up the fact that he had downed a Comanche, whenever boys from visiting Sioux and Cheyenne parties mixed with them. Then the scalp and weapons of that conquered enemy would be brought forth, and Wapaha

Jim would relate with all the fire and relish of a veteran warrior the story of that coup.

"... And he came at me—Wapaha Jim—with his knife. He was a fighter, that one, and had counted many coups. He wore five feathers. But my heart was big. He and his people had killed my people. So I—Wapaha Jim—killed him. Wagh!"

Old warriors, listening, smiled and nodded approval, and visitors were properly impressed. Few youngsters could brag of even having ridden out with a war party yet, let alone counting a coup. Wapaha Jim felt very big and dangerous at such times, with his head flung back and a fist thumping his chest, and gloried in it.

It was fine. Even the stirring up of his blazing hatred of the Comanches fired a savage enjoyment in him, and his hearers thoroughly understood. They, for their part, young and old, lived and dreamed war, although they usually thought of the Crows, their hereditary enemies, in connection with it. But the prowling Comanche poachers were fair game, too, and often had better horses to be captured, for they came up from the southwest and Mexico, where they had the best opportunities for stealing fine animals.

To the Sioux, Wapaha Jim learned, war was a sport, and glory the incentive. The rating of a warrior depended upon the number of his coups, and every man who called himself a man was a warrior. To strike an enemy in battle was a coup, and it wasn't strictly necessary to kill him. It was still a coup, even if the fellow got up and ran away, although it was better to scalp him and make sure of him. Between times, during precarious periods of peace for trade or hunting, warriors of enemy tribes often met and compared notes, checking up on doubtful claims. They made grimly sinister jokes at one another's expense, examined the other fellow's wounds, and promised to do even better at the next meeting.

War was a sport. But not to Wapaha Jim. Not when he had Comanches on his mind. Yellow Eagle agreed with him that the skulking Comanches were a low order of animal akin to wolves, for they went out on their raids primarily for loot and captives, with glory only a secondary consideration. But so far he had forbidden Wapaha Jim to ride off with a war party. Too young, he said. But he promised that the time would soon come when he could begin on the Crows, who were stealing altogether too many Sioux horses lately and needed a lesson.

Outside his tepee, Yellow Eagle painted the finishing touches on a shield. He had cut it out of buffalo-neck hide, and after repeated applications of fire and water it was shrunk thick and hard as a board. It, and a nicely balanced lance which he also had fashioned, were gifts for his adopted son, Wapaha Jim. Soon the lad must be allowed to have his way and go off to war, and Yellow Eagle had no intention of stopping him when the time came. Men were made for war—what else?

While he painted a rainbow all around the edge of the shield to discourage arrows and bullets, he considered the news that was going through the land: War against the white soldiers had broken out again.

White Swan, one of the six powerful Scalp-Shirt chiefs, had had a vision. Dying, he warned his people that the white soldiers were building more big forts and intended to wipe out the Sioux. "Kill them, or they will kill you!" he had said. "Now I die."

Just about that time, some troopers at Fort Kearney committed the error of firing on some Cheyennes who happened to be whooping by. So, believing that White Swan must have known what he was talking about, Sioux and Cheyennes from the Tongue River camp rode against the fort. They lured a troop detachment out of the fort to chase them, then turned on them and wiped them out. The whites were calling it the Fetterman Massacre, and they were out for vengeance. Red Cloud, now a great war chief, was calling on all the Sioux nation to rise and help him run the white soldiers clear out of the country. The whites had no business here, anyway, building roads and forts, and killing off the buffalo herds. What would this land be without buffalo? Nothing but a barren land of starvation.

Iron Breast dropped by at Yellow Eagle's tepee, and admired his old friend's handicraft. "A fine shield and lance you make for Wapaha," he complimented, and added mildly, "Who will he use them against?"

"Against enemies," responded Yellow Eagle absently, giving the formal reply.

"Whites?"

Yellow Eagle paused to consider the question. "Wapaha is my son, for I have said so, and therefore our enemies are his enemies," he answered finally. "He is eager to fight."

"He is eager to fight," agreed Iron Breast. "To fight the Comanches. His heart does not forget that they killed his people. Does his heart forget that his people were white?"

"Wapaha is my son," repeated Yellow Eagle stubbornly, but the friendly hint laid a cold fingertip upon his own uncertainty. He was a warrior, not a thinker, and he had a warrior's impatience of anything that did not run a simple and direct course. "On the next warpath my son will ride with me, wherever it may lead."

"I like Wapaha, and you and I have taught him many good things that he did not know," said Iron Breast. "But my eyes are clear." He rose, gazing off. "He will not want to fight against his own people!"

"You talk like Running Dog, who hates him," growled Yellow Eagle.

But his friend's words still itched his mind when he gave the shield and lance to Wapaha, and that made for an unwonted stiffness between the man and boy. He spoke briefly of the war, eyeing the boy sidelong and trying to read his reaction. But Wapaha Jim had learned to wear the Indian mask. He stroked the smooth haft of the long lance, and took refuge in a hastily compounded miscellany of cryptic jargon filched from the little sha-green book, as he sometimes did when he wanted to be noncommittal. Yellow Eagle walked slowly away, and Wapaha Jim looked after him with miserable eyes.

★

That night Chief Black Horn called a council, and the leading men of the band gathered in the big lodge of their warrior society to discuss Red Cloud's call to war.

Such a call held no compulsion. They could join Red Cloud or not, as they felt inclined. Each tribe and band ruled itself and owed no rigid obedience to any great chief. When a chief was obeyed in major matters it was largely because his wish ran in line with the popular will, and even then organization was loose, cracked by jealousies and internal feuds. A touchy and quick-tempered people, the Sioux guarded their independence even among themselves. Even in battle, each warrior fought as an individual for his own glory. At any time, a noted warrior might take a notion to quit and go home, and nobody thought to throw it up to him later. Perhaps he had lost his war charm, or he might have had a bad dream last night. There were so many good and sufficient reasons. Only a fool ignored a warning from fate.

It was late when Yellow Eagle returned to his tepee

and quietly shook Wapaha Jim awake. "Come," he murmured. "Put on the warbonnet and best moccasins that Pehangi made for you, and come with me to the lodge."

Yellow Eagle wore his swagger warbonnet trailing to his heels, and red breechclouts fore and aft, beaded buckskin leggins, and elkskin moccasins trimmed with stained porcupine quills. He was all dressed up for the council, befitting a man of his standing. A magnificent figure, his stomach still flat and hard, his broad cheeks not yet shrunken by his years. Wapaha Jim always felt proud whenever he saw him dressed in all his splendor. Yellow Eagle was a comparatively modest man, and seldom took the trouble to don his best finery.

Such a summons was extraordinary. No other lad of Wapaha Jim's acquaintance had ever been allowed to attend an important council of the elders. He blinked himself awake and fumbled for his clothes. From her couch across the tepee, Pehangi, squaw of Yellow Eagle, silently rose and got out the warbonnet, fine moccasins, soft leggins, and the other things that she had made for him. Lastly, she laid on his couch the little wooden knife with the red-painted blade and tuft of hair for him to carry, so that all should bear in mind that this was a boy who had taken a scalp. She was proud of her adopted son, the more so because she had never borne a son of her own. Only a mere daughter—Luta-ho-ota.

Luta-ho-ota, lying very still and modestly pretending sleep while Wapaha Jim dressed, watched from under the darkness of her buffalo robe. She was much impressed by his being called to the council.

Wapaha Jim caught the shine of her eyes in the gloom, but paid no attention. He had grown to regard her as a kind of handy maid around the tepee, a maid who neatly mended his clothes and helped old Pehangi with the cooking. She was pretty, he knew, for some of the younger bucks were already noticing her, and he liked her, but she was just Luta-ho-ota. Just a girl. Anyway, right now his mind was in a whirl over this summons. He stole a look at tall Yellow Eagle, but the inscrutable dark face told him nothing. A trickle of uneasiness crept into him, for he had never seen Yellow Eagle so sternly impassive, but he walked steadily with the veteran warrior out of the tepee into the night.

The head men and leading warriors sat around the council fire, wrapped in unfathomable silence, Black Horn in the front position of first honor and precedence. Black Horn was getting on in years, and had long given up physical activity. Enormously fat around the middle, he retained a ponderous dignity, although his mouth was petulant and his eyes round and small. His subchieftainship had come to him through heredity, and Running Dog would inherit it in due course.

The old chief said nothing as Yellow Eagle entered the smoke-filled lodge with Wapaha Jim, but merely raised a sour stare at the boy. He disliked Yellow Eagle and resented his influence among the warriors. He held a grudge against Wapaha Jim for beating his son out of a Comanche scalp-coup.

Nobody said anything. They went on smoking their long pipes, seemingly aloof and indrawn, actually taking in every detail of the boy warrior's attire and waiting alertly for what was to come. Running Dog, seated behind his father, half rose to his feet but slowly sank back again, glowering.

Yellow Eagle made his way to his own place, but remained standing. "I have brought him—Wapaha, my son," he announced, and the slow gaze that he ran over the contemplative faces was haughty and forceful. In this moment, with his feathered head arrogantly high and his big shoulders squared, he was consciously posing for effect. Wapaha Jim didn't know what to make of it, but he sensed a tension, an impact of silent force against force.

"You all know him—this Wapaha, my son. He is yet a boy. But you have heard him speak words old with wisdom." Yellow Eagle raised his knotted right arm and pointed to Wapaha Jim. "I say he has in him a spirit that speaks through his mouth. An old and wise spirit. Today it spoke to me of war, and now it shall speak to you."

Running Dog leaped up. "A boy! A boy in council, and he not even of our people! Are we old women, to listen to—"

"Silence! I am speaking!" thundered Yellow Eagle, and his imperious anger cowed the younger man. He turned again to Wapaha Jim. "My son, today I spoke to you of war against the white soldiers. Say now what you then said to me."

Wapaha Jim held himself stiff and straight to keep from trembling, and his mouth was dry. What he had said to Yellow Eagle had been a jumbled evasion, constructed on the spur of the moment. Now it suddenly loomed big with a heavy significance that almost unnerved him. He worked saliva into his mouth, mentally scrambling to recall just what he had said to Yellow Eagle, and trying to remember the Sioux translation. They were waiting. He had to start it, somehow, and struggle through.

"Those who—who stay away will live to fight some other day. . . . For Crows are blackest when seen against —uh—white. Fight the good fight. . . ."

He stumbled into silence, a silence made thick by the voiceless men around the fire and the intent stares of quickened eyes. He had botched it horribly. It hardly resembled what he had said to Yellow Eagle that morning, when he had misquoted a hodgepodge of Goldsmith, Du Bartas, and the New Testament.

But Yellow Eagle, if he was dismayed, didn't betray it. He gazed around him with an oracular air. "Is this not a warning?" he intoned hushedly. "Is this not wisdom that is old—older than the mouth that speaks it? What is this that has been said? Where does it come from?" He flashed his eyes. "We must stay away from Red Cloud's war with the whites! Thus we may live to fight the Crows, who are the blackest! It is the good fight!"

He turned abruptly and stalked out, forestalling all argument from Black Horn and Running Dog and their faction. At the entrance to his own tepee he paused and laid a hard brown hand on Wapaha Jim's shoulder.

"I have done what I could," he said gruffly. "The white soldiers have not harmed us here, and I know you do not want to fight against them. But the young men are eager for war, for there has been much war talk. Very soon we go on the warpath—perhaps against the whites, perhaps the Crows. The council will decide. I would like you to ride with me, wherever we go. That is why I gave you the lance and the shield today. My son, do not bring shame upon me."

★

They rode the warpath, the Black Horn Minniconjou warriors, each with his best pony and his full accoutrement for battle. It meant little that they had a long and uncertain trail ahead, as long as there was the prospect of a good fight at the end. They rode in lusty spirit, some singing, some exchanging broad jokes, others content to grin and listen.

"Ho, Bear Man! Do not hope to capture a woman

this time, for I am here! Nor will they run too hard
when they see me coming!"

"You talk with a big mouth, Spotted Horse, for one
who lives alone! A young squaw waits to welcome me
home to my tepee—the same Crow girl that I captured
from under your nose! She cried when I left, and will
sing when I return! Wagh!"

Wapaha Jim rode with Yellow Eagle, and behind
rode Jumping Calf and Sleeper on their first warpath—
trying to appear not too eager and green, dreaming of
many coups and captured horses. Jumping Calf, stocky
and short, had his ugly, good-humored face set in a
fixed and grim smile. Crazy brave, cheerfully belliger-
ent, he had fought Wapaha Jim five separate times before claiming him as his fast friend. Sleeper, tall and
slim, almost girlishly modest and soft spoken, never
fought with anybody unless forced. Then he was a
wildcat.

There were over fifty in the party. They paraded along
in careless order, a tumultuous and noisy mob, lance-
tips flashing in the sun, feathered warbonnets waving
and nodding, all filled with a barbaric zest for living
and a fierce pride of arms. They paid homage to nobody. Self-reliant, quick to laugh or scowl, capable of
hot cruelty and a strange tenderness, touchy as any
blue-blooded Spanish grandee of the far south. . . . In
their own opinion they were gods of the earth. Fighting men.

Wapaha Jim felt good. It was gloriously satisfying
to be riding in such grand company, with the clear air
brisk and cool against his skin, an eagle plume flaunting upright in his thick black hair, his long lance in his
fist and a good pony under him. He was glad just to be
alive, sharing life with tough and masculine men who
figured they knew how to live it. For it was war against
the Crows.

The Black Horn faction had been beaten in council by the will of the majority and the mysterious wisdom of the little shagreen book. Let Red Cloud handle his own fight, it was no affair of the Black Horn Minniconjou, said the warriors. The unregenerate Crows had been stealing too many Sioux horses and women lately, and they'd soon get to thinking they ruled the earth if not put in their proper places. It hardly seemed good sense to travel away off to make trouble for the white soldiers, when there were plenty of Crows handier to home and spoiling for a fight.

Sleeper edged his pony up alongside Wapaha Jim's, and the two young warriors exchanged brief smiles. It was unusual for Sleeper to make conversation. "I shall take a Crow scalp, or die," he murmured without any preliminaries, and for the moment his quiet eyes glittered hard and dangerous. "And I shall capture horses, many horses. One—perhaps more—I shall give to Luta-ho-ota, your sister."

"Huh? She's not my sister."

"She is Yellow Eagle's daughter, and Yellow Eagle is your father. Does that not make her your sister?"

Such simple reasoning was difficult to refute, though it ignored all details of blood and birth. "Why will you give her your horses?" Wapaha Jim asked, honestly surprised.

Sleeper eyed him gravely. "I shall be a man and a warrior when I return, and shall be given a man's name. Why does a man make gifts to a maid?" He was very much in earnest. This was a confidence that he was giving to his friend. It was also a hint, an unspoken wish that Wapaha Jim might mention the matter to Yellow Eagle and pave the way. He nodded and dropped back beside Jumping Calf.

Wapaha Jim mused over it, and found himself thinking of Luta-ho-ota, thinking of her in a mood that was new to him. She had come to him as he was about to ride through the camp with the rest in a dashing parade before leaving, and she gave him the little shagreen book, packed in a beaded and quilled buckskin pouch that she had made for it. Yellow Eagle had paid the medicine man a pony for a war charm for his adopted son, but Luta-ho-ota didn't appear to think that sufficient protection.

"Carry this with you, Wapaha," she said. "You know it is big medicine, and I have seen you talk to it. See— I have made a bag for it."

She looped the thong of the bag around his neck and he bent his head for her, so that her hair touched his face and one of her smooth young arms brushed his ear. He had wanted to thank her, but while he searched for words of fitting condescension she turned and ran back into the tepee. He saw her once more, during the wild gallop through the camp, peering out, and her eyes were brighter than he had ever seen them. Bright and wet. Then old Pehangi moved in front of her, grim and taciturn as ever, nodding a brooding farewell to her man and her boy in the dust of departure.

Now he touched the buckskin bag, lifted it, looked at it, and saw that the beadwork was fine, the quills small and exact in their pattern. Luta-ho-ota had clever hands. She was a good girl. He was fond of her. He would bring her back a pony, if he was lucky. She loved white ponies. He would look out for one. Luta-ho-ota—he thought of it as suddenly a pretty name. Luta-ho-ota on a white pony—that would be a pretty sight. Yes, he certainly would look for one. He turned and nodded to Sleeper in the rear. It didn't occur to him that Sleeper might also be thinking of Luta-ho-ota on a white pony.

"We will make camp at the low rain-road, and scout from there," Yellow Eagle told Iron Breast. "I think we will soon meet up with some Crows. My dream was good last night."

★

Luta-ho-ota rode up from bathing in the river, and trotted into camp. She had dried and combed her hair in the sun, and it was blue-black and glossy. Her fine teeth flashed white when she smiled to a slim young male who turned to watch her ride by, and the silver bands on her round arm struck a small jingle as she waved to him. Being a modest girl, she wore a robe around her waist, hiding the tightness of her soft doe-skin skirt. Above that nothing more was required or expected, and her healthy skin shone smooth and clean. She rode a white pony.

Wapaha Jim waved back, and admired that which he had helped to bring about. She was as pretty on that white pony as he had thought she would be—prettier—and he was glad he had given it to her. He and Sleeper and Jumping Calf had raced to catch it, during the first whirlwind skirmish with the Crows, and he had got his hair rope on it first. Coups and reputations had been made in that fight. Sleeper and Jumping Calf had earned the right to discard forever their boy-names.

"Ho—Bad Buffalo! Come and eat with me!" Yellow Eagle had called that night in camp. "Bad Buffalo—you that were once called Jumping Calf—come and eat with me!" And Jumping Calf, that cheerful young slaughterer, rose with glowing eyes, big with the honor of his new name.

And then—"Where is Long Mane?" called another with mock impatience. "It is a good name, Long Mane. Why does he not answer when I call it?" And Wapaha

Jim, grinning, shoved Sleeper forward. "Here is Long Mane!"

Bad Buffalo and Long Mane. Good, honorable names, the names of many old warriors now dead and gone. Never again would a stocky, ugly-faced youngster answer to the name of Jumping Calf, nor a soft-spoken stripling to Sleeper. Now they were young men.

Silenced settled around the small fires, nobody yet eating, all waiting. Iron Breast rose, doing the honors for the son of his friend. "There is one who called himself Warbonnet when a boy, and we laughed, for that is the name of a man. Now we do not laugh. It *is* the name of a man. Warbonnet, my friend and the son of my friend, come and eat with me!"

Wapaha Jim now wore four eagle feathers in his hair, three upright for first coups, one at a slant for second coup, and a red stroke on his buckskin shirt to show where an enemy lance had gashed him. When he talked with men they did not interrupt him, but gave him the respect that they gave each other.

"That is a fine young horse," he observed to Bad Buffalo and Long Mane, as Luta-ho-ota lighted from the white pony before her tepee. To brag a little about one's gifts was pardonable.

"Finer than the two brown horses which I gave to her," said Long Mane, and his voice was not soft. "She does not ride them." He turned and paced off.

Wapaha Jim looked at Bad Buffalo. "Is he angry?"

"His heart is sick," answered Bad Buffalo. "Luta-ho-ota does not ride his horses. She rides yours, and puts a fine saddle on it, and pets it as if . . ." He paused. "She is your sister, and Long Mane is your friend."

"But she's not—not really my sister."

Bad Buffalo looked down at the ground. "You are wise in many ways, Wapaha. Often you speak words that are *wakan* and old. Now you speak like a fool. Do

not let Long Mane hear you say that Luta-ho-ota is not
your sister, or perhaps you will lose a friend. I would
not want Long Mane for my enemy. He goes mad and
knows no fear."

Two things occurred later that summer to induce
Wapaha Jim almost into believing that there really
might be something *wakan* about the little shagreen
book. An Oglala Sioux rode into camp with news, saying Red Cloud had run into more than he could handle and had lost prestige. A mere handful of white soldiers, trapped on an island over toward Fort Kearney,
had fought a desperate battle from behind a barricade
of wagon-boxes and beaten off Red Cloud's army. A
most amazing fight—thirty-two against three thousand,
and the thirty-two had won. Many good warriors had
been killed. There was mourning in many a Sioux camp,
and Red Cloud was in disgrace.

That disaster of the Wagon-Box Fight, it was generally conceded, certainly bore out the *wakan* warning of Wapaha Jim not to go to war against the whites.
The fight with the Crows, on the other hand, had been
highly satisfactory from the Sioux viewpoint—the good
fight that he had predicted it would be. Even Black
Horn looked somewhat queerly at the youth. The camp
medicine man, a good enough shaman in his way, swallowed his professional jealousy when he saw the popular drift and sought to lead it. He announced that the
benevolent spirits of all the departed Warbonnet warriors, due to his own personal influence with them,
were in constant attendance upon the present bearer
of that honorable old name. Wapaha thanked him for
it, and Yellow Eagle gave him another pony.

So, when game grew scarce and camp had to be
shifted again, and the shaman was called upon to decide the direction of the move, he publicly consulted

Wapaha Jim. Perhaps he privately hoped the lad would guess wrong this time and cease being a competitor.

Wapaha Jim thumbed through the shagreen book. Meanwhile the camp kept up an interminable and hopeful buffalo dance to make buffalo come, just to be on the safe side. The noise was terrific, but he was used to that. He sought inspiration, and got it when he remembered that the Sioux symbolic color for the south was red. It was toward the south where he wished to go, buffalo or no buffalo. South, down along the big river, where there likely would be an occasional band of roving Comanches to wipe out. He came upon a neat and gory bit of Macaulay that fitted well enough and was not too elaborate to translate.

" 'Oh, therefore come ye forth in triumph . . . with your hands and your feet and your raiment all red. . . .' "

In the grey morning the cavalcade marched southward, leaving nothing behind but a bare area to record the abandonment of one more campsite. Loose colts frisked among pack horses that plodded sedately under their loads of parfleches, tepee poles and indiscriminate baggage, dogs quarrelled and barked, and old men made the most of their waning authority to scold the women. The warriors rode the flanks like herders of the flock, singing endlessly, clad in all their masculine splendor of plumes and paint, preening themselves when coy maids glanced their way. And Wapaha Jim, on a fine Crow pony, rode as a man among men.

He thought that there could be nothing better than this. No cares. No nagging problems or inner conflicts. These were his people and so were the whites, and he was proud of both, for both were of the fighting breed. He had listened, all warm inside, when the Oglala told of that amazing Wagon-Box Fight; yet he need not have kept silent, for the Oglala and the Minniconjou

gave frank and admiring credit to those hard-bitten
thirty-two on the island.

This was his country, this splendid land, and he shared
with the Sioux their almost sensual love of it—a pas-
sionate, personal love. It was right to fight for such a
land, but surely there was room enough in it for everybody. It was a generous land, the prize of all lands.
Game—buffalo, deer, antelope, elk. Cougar and grizzly
away up yonder in the Big Horn Mountains. Beaver
and birds along the numerous, fish-rich rivers. Berries
and wild fruits. Prairies and mountains, thick-wooded
bottomlands and fertile valleys. If game grew scarce in
one spot, a light-hearted trek took you blithely to another where there was plenty. *This* was the Happy
Hunting Land. There could be none better.

He saw the future as a brilliant reflection of the heart-
satisfying present, sparkling with promise. Let the years
come.

"We run away from the white soldiers!" harangued a
grumbling old man up ahead. "What happens when
you run away from an enemy? He comes after you!
The whites build long trails and great soldier-houses—
for what? *Nyah!* Better to fight them now, before they
are too many and strong. White Swan was right. You
will see—you will see!"

Wapaha Jim grinned, disbelieving such nonsense.

★

CHAPTER 4

FORT LINCOLN

ALWAYS AT THIS SUNDOWN HOUR THE GIRL LIKED TO STAND alone, facing west across the parade ground, and watch the last rituals of the day. The fluttering descent of the flag and the melancholy lingering of the trumpeter's call; the soldiers of the guard all rigid at attention, and the boom of the sunset gun—these things saluted the dying day while the retiring sun exploded silent bombardments of color into the sky. The swollen Missouri River reflected the reddened bluffs, but the long buildings of Fort Lincoln below the bluffs were black in a valley of purple-tinged shadow.

The girl had a fancy that the fort shrank into itself at this hour, and she saw it as a small and lonely guardian in a large world of broodingly alert enemies.

The door of the Adjutant's Office opened behind her, and she recognized the voices of the two officers who stepped out. Half consciously, she also recognized from their tones and their rapid strides that both officers were still on duty, and therefore expected no leisurely pleasantries. She merely turned her head toward them as they came up to her, and let a smile do for greeting. She had fair hair of a deep shade, and to her medium tallness she coupled a peculiar slow grace and a directness of gaze that most men found pleasantly disturbing.

Her uncle, Major Philip Chittendon, saluted her ab-

43

sently and passed on, but Captain George Vaugant broke his measured West Point stride to get in a few hasty words. "Lovely evening, Miss Talitha, but don't stand out too long. Getting cold."

"I won't, Captain. Yes, lovely, isn't it?"

Vaugant saluted, smiled his best, and lengthened step to catch up with his superior. He glanced aside in time to catch a slight frown on the thin, bleak face. Major Chittendon was of the old Army school that never unbent to social amenities until the last duty was finished for the day. Also, he had been speaking, and he liked full attention to what he had to say.

"Do you think it wise to send out a detachment at this time, sir?" Vaugant asked respectfully, taking up the subject where Chittendon had broken off. "Fine open weather for this time of year, of course, but they say there's heavy snow in the west. Might have trouble with the horses."

The major did not answer for the space of a dozen strides, conveying a silent rebuke and a hint that the point was hardly worth discussion. Vaugant flushed. Privately, he detested the major's waspy dryness and stolid efficiency, and was quite aware that the major, in his turn, did not care for him. In the rare moments when Chittendon loosed off a personal opinion, he had made it plain that he regretted the Civil War for what it had done to the Army. Too many brash youngsters had won brevets and come out with ridiculously high ranks. He had no abiding faith in big-muscled young officers of the dashing horse-and-sabre type. Such men made excellent troopers and useful noncoms, but his ideal for commissioned officers was more conservative.

"I suggest," he said finally in his driest tone, "that you take your thoughts to the general, who will doubtless be greatly influenced by them."

Vaugant swallowed that without comment. "May I

choose my own second-in-command for the detachment?" he requested crisply. "I'd like to take Second-
Lieutenant Hathersall. He's been with us nearly six
months and seen no action. I've told him I'd take him
along if anything like this turned up."

"Indeed?"

"Er—yes. Hathersall is very anxious for action. His
parents were killed by the Indians when he was a boy,
so . . ."

"I know," said Chittendon shortly. "His mother was
my sister."

"Yes, of course. I forgot Hathersall's your nephew, sir.
May I take him?"

The major's face grew a trifle more sharp and cold.
"Captain, let me remind you that—ah—personal feeling should never influence military judgment," he remarked. "That was proved in the Fetterman Massacre
at Fort Kearney nine years ago, when Red Cloud and
his hostiles wiped out a whole detachment commanded
by rash and incompetent officers. Your second-in-command will be named by the general, and I trust he will
pick an officer with more experience than the one of
your choice. I suggest now that you begin listing the
men for your detachment. Please use your best judgment. Take special care in seeing that their horses are
in good condition. Good evening."

Vaugant saluted and strode off, silently damning the
elderly martinet. He was in such a temper that he aimed
a kick at one of the general's hunting dogs that ambled
across his path. The dog backed off surprisedly and
set up a barking, and Vaugant hurried for the stables
before the general should come out to investigate. General Custer thought a lot of his dogs.

★

Blackness was driving the color from the sky. Windows came alight around the hollow square of the parade ground, and here and there a cigar glowed on the dark porches of Officers' Row. Masculine voices ran a comfortable undertone to the occasional murmur and light laugh of women, and there was the usual evening drift of unmarried men toward the sutler's store and billiard room.

Now the fort grew big again with the coming of night, and the tautness of the military day was relaxed. Off duty, men laid aside their absorption in routine, and allowed themselves to lounge. Even their manner of walking subtly changed. One could always tell if an officer or trooper was off duty, regardless of dress, by his movements or the timbre of his voice. Talitha Hathersall sauntered on her way to Major Chittendon's married quarters, but she knew she would not be allowed to retire so early to her room. Groups along the porches would call her to join them, and somebody was certain to dart off and fetch her mandolin. Music was as scarce and gratefully appreciated as female company, and she was one of the very few unmarried ladies of the fort. Young officers were chronically lonely, notoriously gallant and hard to resist.

When she first arrived, less than three months ago, she had been bewildered and a little shocked by the frank and pressing attentions crowded upon her. But she soon grew to understand and accept it all. They were like boys, these young officers, when they took off their swords and gloves; high spirited and gay, shamelessly rivalling one another in paying extravagant court to an unattached and pretty girl. Any time she slipped off for a ride alone, they somehow materialized around her in twos and threes, their faces carefully grave, eyes twinkling, until the return to the fort took on the nature of an unofficial parade. She found it all rather marvellous.

And the regimental and company dances . . . they were miracles. The most matronly matron present could be assured of more demands for waltzes than she could handle. There were so few women in the fort, and so many men—tanned, handsome men with the Army swagger and masculine elegance, carrying an air of quiet danger with them. And so young, many of them, behind their drooping cavalry mustaches and stern parade faces. The arrival of a feminine visitor took on more real importance than a general order, and her departure ranked as a military defeat. To allow a girl to leave the fort, still free and single, was a reflection on the whole Seventh Cavalry, no less.

Talitha knew the speculations of the major's wife and the other married women. With the best wishes in the world they waited for her to be captured by some tall young officer, and by this they showed that they fully approved of her and liked her. They wanted her to come into the family of the fort and be one of them. Most of them had been through the same whirlwind experience, and Army women counted themselves as something very special. There was hardship in their lives, and constant moving with the regiment from post to post; and the stark but hidden terror when their men rode off on campaign against the hostiles; and the loneliness, the makeshift quarters, the outdated dresses that had to do for year after year. But they all were quite convinced that the best luck that could come to any sister was to become an Army woman, married to a soldier—a cavalry officer, naturally, and preferably of the Seventh. Army caste could go no higher than Custer's Cavalry, and the ladies of the regiment proudly wore the forage cap when in riding habit, with its crossed sabres and "7."

Talitha had begun by feeling challenged, and soon after she arrived she had decided firmly that life in an isolated Army post was not for her. Nice as an experience, but not as a permanent thing. But the Army, she found, had an insidious way of getting into one's blood, and she loved the informal family atmosphere of the fort. Its members had their arguments, but no serious quarrels, for they knew the risk of allowing a feud to develop where everybody had to live in close contact. Private argument invariably had a way of becoming public property, thoroughly discussed by everybody and finally brushed aside after its conversational possibilities were exhausted. By that time the original disputants usually were comparing horses or recipes for buffalo-berry jam.

"That you, Tally?"

"Hallo, West."

Second-Lieutenant Weston Hathersall came striding through the darkness, slim and fair and young, not even the night completely hiding the evidences of his recent emergence from West Point. By daylight the signs of his newness were much more evident. It would take the sun more time to fade the shoulders of his blue service coat, and his Jefferson boots hadn't a crack in them. "I'm on stable duty tonight," he said hurriedly. "Want to come along and see the horses? Better get a heavier wrap, though, or you'll be cold."

"I'll get warm enough, trying to keep up with you."

She walked fast beside him, smiling a little at his long gait and purposeful gravity. West took everything he did with such intense seriousness, and yet with impatience, as if these small duties were irritating preliminaries that he must attend to in order to reach a main objective. She knew the nature of that big objective—it had taken root near some cottonwoods on the trail to Oregon, twelve years ago. It was an obsession with

him, and she knew more than one reason for that, too.
Hatred had its place; hatred for Indians and a craving
to take vengeance on them for what they had done. But
that was not all. He had to prove to himself that he
was man enough to take that vengeance when the
chance came. Some kind of self-doubt stayed with him,
secretly mocking and belittling him, torturing him, driving him on. It was because of this, and her knowledge
of it, that Talitha had come here to Fort Lincoln. A
cough had been her excuse for a long visit. The Dakota
air was getting famous for curing coughs, and more
than one restless girl had used no better excuse for
visiting Army relatives stationed in the West. The cough
vanished even before arrival at the fort, but nobody
mentioned that. They spoke of the need for rest and
recuperation, nicely ignoring the fact that she was as
healthy and clear-eyed as any one of them.

But it was because of West that she had come, and
perhaps others guessed it. She had to be near him, to
try to temper his driving urge with humor and understanding. They had always been very close, particularly
since the death of their parents, and she knew West
liked her being here.

They drew near the long stables. "What's this I hear
about a special detachment being sent out on scouting
duty?" she asked. "Don't answer if it's an official secret."

"It is," West said curtly. "Those women hear too
much."

"*Those* women? I'm a woman too, West, and just as
much interested in what's going on around here."

"You're not Army. You're a guest. Have to marry or
be born into the Army before you rank as an Army
woman."

"It's too late now—about my birth, I mean. Are you
suggesting that I should marry into the Army?"

"You could do worse, Tally. They're all mad about

you, and they're all fine men." He laughed shortly. "It's wonderful how many friends I've found I've got, since you showed up—every one of them wanting to do me favors! Too bad Custer is already married, although I do like his wife. If one of the unmarried had command —Vaugant, for instance . . ."

"West! I do believe you're getting a sense of humor."

"I never lacked it," he retorted. "And don't try to change the subject. You know Vaugant's in love with you. Sure, and a dozen others. But George is in earnest. He asked me to call him George. I like him. He's a real soldier, and you know you'd never find a more handsome man. When he's on mounted parade, Tally, I swear he looks like—like . . ."

"Like a god," she finished for him. "A rather red-blooded god with curly brown hair and a sort of sullen grimness that I suspect hides an awful temper. Yes, I've seen him on mounted parade. Very handsome. Now get your mind back on your horses!"

West shrugged. "I must say you're mighty particular. Or is there somebody back East?"

"No. I just don't seem to fall in love easily, West. Like you. Oh, I'm fond of your dashing Army men, all of them. I think I could love General Custer if he had black hair."

"What's the matter with his hair as it is? Oh—I know. Sorry. I forgot for the minute." The tightness returned to West's face. "Jim Aherne. Black hair. Queer. You were only a kid then, too. Whopper Jim. May hell take all Indians! He was only a boy, and they killed him like—like . . ."

"Yes, West, they did. But let's not go on cursing every Indian in the country for it. We're grown up now, or we're supposed to be. There are bad white men, too. But we won't fight over that again. Do you know we've marched right past three of these stable doors? Looking for a lucky one with a horseshoe over it?"

"I'll start inspection from the far end. Hello, what's going on in there?"

An oath and the noise of somebody falling came from the stable they had just passed, and West wheeled on his heel and entered. All the stables were lighted, waiting for nightly inspection. Tally followed, and she heard West mutter an exclamation.

Then the voice of Captain Vaugant, harsh with anger. "The drunken damned half-breed . . ."

The captain saw her then, pausing in the doorway behind the lieutenant, and he closed his mouth on the rest. His flushed face and hard eyes made an ugly picture in the lantern light, but only for that instant. He cleared his throat and bowed to her with forced self-possession and quick apology. "I beg your pardon, Miss Talitha. Didn't see you. This trooper attacked me, and I'm afraid I lost my temper with him." His breathing was noisy, but he conjured up a smile for her.

Horses stood in their swept stalls, heads raised, gazing backward inquisitively at the disturbance under the lantern. Their manes and tails had been combed and fussed over by their masters until they fluffed out like the hair of a girl, and every animal was covered carefully with a blanket against the cold night. The smells of fresh hay and well-groomed horses were pleasant and clean.

The man who rose from the floor was grimy, bleary eyed, and bits of straw clung to his shirt and rumpled hair. He had the dark and dull skin of mixed race. He dabbed the back of one dirty hand against his broken lips, and held it out, and he narrowed his eyes at the red smear on it.

It was not so much pity as disgust that brought a sharp protest from Tally. "Captain Vaugant, isn't there an Army law that prohibits an officer from striking a trooper?" she asked.

Vaugant looked at her for a moment longer, and he still kept some of his smile, but restraint of temper made his eyes a little glassy. "There is, Miss Talitha," he said. "There most certainly is. You're right. But a man must protect himself." He spoke very carefully, rounding out each word. "This fellow attacked me when I accused him of being drunk on stable duty, you see."

"I didn't," mumbled the man. "Jest fell 'ginst you, was all. Then you hit me."

Vaugant snapped around. "Stand to attention when you address an officer! Report at the guardhouse in the morning. I'll be there with charges against you. Now dismiss."

He glanced at West as the man reeled out. "Scum," he commented. "One or two of that breed do get into the regiment sometimes, but we weed them out. I've been waiting a chance to get rid of him. I want no mutinous drunkard like that with me when we go after that band of hostiles on the South Fork."

Tally stepped aside to let the man pass. She heard him stumble outside, and from where she stood in the doorway she could see him. The glint of his eyes turned her cold and made her think of Indians glaring in the darkness and contemplating murder. She stepped farther into the stable, hurriedly, and found Vaugant talking again, his voice now regretful and friendly.

"Sorry, Weston, old man. I'd like to have you with the detachment, but there it is. The major refused in the blankest way. You might talk to him yourself. After all, he's your uncle."

"I'll go to the general," said West, and spoke with a strained voice. "He's not a relative."

"Do you think you should?" Tally put in swiftly. "I

mean, West, do you think it right to go over Uncle Philip's head like that?"

West turned an angry face to her. "Major Chittendon," he said distinctly, "has made it fairly obvious from the first that he is not pleased to have me in the same regiment with him. He was even against my going to West Point, as you know. If I expect to receive decent opportunity in the service, it's plain that I must look to somebody else for it. Thanks for speaking for me, George, anyway."

Vaugant graciously waved away the thanks. "Go along and beard the general. He's a fair man, and I think he'll give you your chance if you mention I want you with me. And he'll be in his best humor after dinner. I'll do stable inspection for you. Perhaps your sister would like to make the rounds with me—eh, Miss Talitha? Help me kiss the horses good-night? No? Oh . . . Well, good-night. Good luck, Weston."

He watched them both leave, and after they were gone he shoved his hands deep into his pockets and scowled at a horse that nickered coquettishly at him. "Damnation take my rotten temper!" he muttered, and went moodily on the rounds.

That night a man went over the hill. He took with him an Army horse, carbine, pistol, and some food that he'd stolen from the Commissary, and he struck southwest. North would have suited him better; north to the Black Hills and the mining camps; but that was just where they'd look first for a deserter. He wasn't going to get caught that way. Soldiering on the frontier was a hell of a life for a man who liked his drink and women, and he'd seen enough of that guardhouse. Before he turned off from the river he peered back at the tiny lights of the fort, and spat, and growled an oath he'd do that bucko captain dirt if ever the chance came his way.

★

"You gentlemen know why I've requested you to join me privately here tonight, I think," said the general in his pleasant, rapid way, and the three officers seated around the table with him nodded. A good host and congenial commander, the general had supplied cigars and coffee, but no whiskey. It was said that he had been a noble drinker in his younger days, when his extraordinary energy needed some outlet after the close of the Civil War, but Mrs. Custer had deftly changed all that, and the general scrupulously kept his promise to her.

"Vaugant, you've been chosen for a certain piece of work which I'm sure you're well qualified to perform. My brother Tom would have liked the task," he added with a smile, "but I turned him down, poor fellow."

"I appreciate your confidence, sir," said Vaugant. "Colonel Tom and I have already exchanged condolences and congratulations on the matter." Actually, Colonel Tom Custer had called him a lucky dog and remarked that his curly brown hair would look very tasteful on a Sioux lodge-pole. To be sent out on detachment was a prize for any man, after being cooped up in the fort all winter.

The general nodded. His keen, forceful face, still youthful and seldom in repose, contrasted oddly with the wooden inexpression of Major Chittendon on his right. The general whipped one of his lightning glances at West Hathersall, the youngest of them there. "Colonel Tom is in an unfortunate position, being brother to his commander," he mentioned. "Rather than lay myself open to the charge of favoring him, I'm afraid I lean the other way. But I suppose that's natural, eh, Major?"

"I am sure the colonel sensibly understands the situation, sir," answered the major, not looking at anybody.

With quick hands the general spread open a map on

the table, changing the subject. "As you know, gentlemen, we've had orders to remove all Plains Indians to within the limits of their reservations, and I don't think the folks back in Washington will listen to any excuses if we don't get it done." He stabbed the map with a finger. "According to our Crow scouts, Sitting Bull and his followers are camped somewhere along there, and Crazy Horse is still in winter camp on the Rosebud, not far from them. They have defied the Washington order and said they'll fight. That means a campaign this year, but first we want to round up the smaller bands before they move to join the hostiles. Our Crow 'friendlies'—save the name!—insist that there's a fairly large Sioux camp on the South Fork, and I judge that they're particular enemies of the Crows. Some notorious fighters among them, evidently. The Crows speak of them with respect. I believe the camp is—let me see—yes, just about there. I'll mark the spot, Vaugant, and you'll take this map with you."

"Yes, sir. When shall I move out?"

"As soon as possible. Take ammunition packs, rations for two weeks, and medical supplies. This band will probably fight. When you find their camp you will demand their surrender and removal to the reservation. If they refuse, you will arrest the lot and bring them in. If they resist, you will regard them as hostiles and act accordingly. They're dangerous, so don't take the slightest chances with them. Hathersall, you will go as second-in-command. Everything clear?"

"Perfectly, sir."

"Good." The general drew out a slip of paper. "The Crows gave me the names of some of the leading warriors of that band. If you make your arrests, check up on these. We don't want any of them to slip away. I may not have spelled all of them correctly, and some of them are not translated, but here they are: *Wambli-*

gi or Yellow Eagle, Iron Breast, *Wapaha, Tatanka Hinto,* Bad Buffalo, Long Mane. . . ."

West Hathersall left the conference with shining eyes, profoundly grateful to the general for giving him this almost certain chance of action against hostiles. Major Chittendon caught up with him and fell into stride. They paced together, saying nothing, and West felt awkward, wondering how his uncle would show his displeasure. The major paused at the door of his quarters. He fumbled in his pocket and thrust a cigar at him.

"Better than the general's," he said gruffly. "Good luck. Don't get yourself killed, boy."

CHAPTER 5

★

THE DESERTER

THE HUNTERS HAD MADE GOOD. THEY CAME RIDING HOME into the winter camp on the South Fork, singing their own praises, leading spare horses loaded with fresh meat that had frozen on the way, and the camp turned out to greet them. And among them rode a stranger, muffled in a bearskin overcoat, a black slouch hat pulled down over his cold ears. He wore boots and spurs, and his big horse was equipped with a white man's saddle and bridle. The saddle cloth was blue, with a yellow band of stitched tape following the edge, and a yellow "7" at the corner. The man's dark face was gaunt and stiff with the cold, and his eyes were frightened. He was a prisoner.

The camp eyed him curiously, but the real attention was for the fresh meat. Many hunting parties had returned empty-handed this winter, bitterly denouncing the white hunters who were killing off all the game in the country, and hunger had begun to make itself known. Bear Standing, the leader of the party, modestly accepted the congratulations and called to the eager women to come and cook meat. He noosed a rope around the captive's neck and tied him to a stake. Then he and the tired hunters sought rest and warmth in their lodges.

After the feasting that night, Bear Standing pointed to the prisoner, now sitting and eating with them. "He was camping alone last night when we saw his fire and crept up on him, and he did not fight. He had a long gun and a pistol. Now they are mine. He is a soldier. What shall we do with him?"

Chief Black Horn, gorged and sleepy, stirred his fat bulk by the fire. "Kill him!" he grunted.

The prisoner, paling under their unwinking regard and perhaps divining the drift of their talk, squirmed and slowly got to his feet. "I'm your friend!" he gasped. "Your friend—don't y'unnerstand? Me *amigo. Sabe amigo?*" He stared around at the dark, fire-lighted faces, and the last shred of his nerve broke under the strain.

"For God's sake—don't none o' you talk American? Quit lookin' at me like that—I tell you I'm your friend!" His hoarse voice went throaty, and they saw with disgust that he shuddered.

To Wapaha Jim, sitting with the brothers of his warrior society, it came as a strange shock to hear the language of his own race spoken. He was ashamed, too, ashamed of that frightened man, and he stared into the fire and said nothing. Bad Buffalo, beside him, grinned wickedly and started to say something funny, but he changed his mind and kept silent after a glance at the

face of his friend. Long ago they had gone through the
solemn ceremony of blood-brotherhood, and a brother
could insult a brother in jest without offense; but there
were limits.

Running Dog spoke up across the fire, dragging his
voice to a sneer. "What says the shivering woman-sol-
dier? Does nobody know? You, Wapaha?" He nudged
his father, and the chief clumsily entered into the play
of barbed sarcasm.

"Wapaha, yes—he should know. Or has he forgotten
the tongue of his white people? Wapaha, what says
this brave white brother of yours?"

There were men who chuckled under their breaths
at the broad malice. Black Horn and his son had their
favored clique. There were others, warriors and friends
of Wapaha Jim and Yellow Eagle, who frowned. Wapaha Jim stood high in the band as a warrior and man
of council, and to jab at his dignity did not sit well
with his friends. The prisoner stared about him, fearful
and uncomprehending, until Running Dog drew his
knife and ran a thumb along the sharp blade, blandly
studying the man's hair. That brought on another
chuckle.

Wapaha Jim rose. The active, untamed years had
given him a tall and muscular body, splendidly propor-
tioned and without the thin limbs of most Indians. His
skin was brown and there were wound-scars on his body
that he did not bother to enhance with daubs of paint.
He wore his hair long and knotted at the nape of his
neck, adorned with one red feather. To wear the single
plume was an act of such extreme modesty that it
would have been arrogant presumption in most young
warriors, but his prestige was big enough to carry it
without challenge. He was Wapaha—Warbonnet—a
fighter known as a clever and daringly impudent raider
of Crow horses, and a relentless scourge of Comanches.

They talked about him in other camps. His fame was rising.

"I know the man's talk," he said, and fixed a long stare on Running Dog until the son of the chief reluctantly put away his knife. "He says he is our friend. Perhaps he is a messenger from the big soldier-house."

He turned to the man, hesitated, and had to frame his query in his mind before he put in into English. "Are you a messenger from the fort?"

The man gave a start of relief. He peered at the browned face, saw the grey eyes, and let out a gusty breath of wonder. "Goddlemighty—a white man! Ain't you white? Sure, I see y'are. A white renegade, by—! Man, I'm sure glad to see you! Listen, you tell these cussed hostiles . . ."

"These what?" The expression was new to Wapaha Jim.

The man flinched at the barked interruption. "Your friends, I mean. Tell 'm I'm a friend, like you. Naw, I ain't no messenger. I went over the hill, *sabe?* Skipped the Army. Deserted. I got news for 'em, though, you tell 'em that. Soldiers are comin' here! Some o' the Seventh Cavalry an' a bucko captain I'd like to skin alive."

"Soldiers coming here? Why?"

"Hell, you know why. Your bunch is hostiles. Sioux, ain't they? Well, then. The troops is comin' to bust up this camp, an' if they catch you—or me—huh! You powwow these Injuns an' tell 'em they better move *pronto.* Hell, tell 'em I was lookin' to join their bunch when they caught me. Wouldn't mind, at that. You look fed an' healthy. Plenty to eat, huh? Likker? An' women?"

Wapaha Jim turned to the curious faces around the fire. "This man ran away from the soldier-house. He says soldiers are coming to attack us here. I do not believe him! He is a coward, and he lies because he hopes that we will feed and hide him. I say give him his horse and let him go. He is bad."

"Perhaps he is a spy," suggested Iron Breast, but Wapaha Jim shook his head.

"Why should the soldiers come against us? Have we ever harmed them? Did we not refuse to join Red Cloud when he made war on them, nine summers ago?"

Perversely, Black Horn took the other view. "I think the man speaks with a straight tongue," he declared, and nodded, heavily important. "The white soldiers have sent out word that all our people must give up this land and move away. This we know."

"We have heard such things before, but nothing happened," spoke up Yellow Eagle. He was getting old and shrunken in the face, but his eyes still held fire and his blunt force had not waned. "Sitting Bull and Crazy Horse have said that they will fight, and that is good, for we should not give up our hunting grounds. Our fathers and their fathers have lived and hunted and died here. Our boundaries are marked by the graves of our men and the bones of our ancestors, who fought to hold this land. But I think like Wapaha, who is my son. I think that it is only more talk, and nothing will happen."

"Has Wapaha talked again with spirits, then?" sneered Running Dog. "Has he taken council with his *wakan* war-charm that he keeps in the pretty beaded pouch—the pouch that was made for it by the girl he has said is not his sister?" He looked directly at Long Mane, and laughed. For nine years the situation had teetered between joke and scandal, mentioned guardedly with sly grins by men, whispered over behind hooding blankets by women.

Long Mane shot to his feet in one lithe movement. He seldom voiced himself upon any matter, and was known as a man who shunned friendship. Whenever he did speak, others listened because of the rarity rather than the quality, for he had a stinging way of thrusting through the crust of a matter and dragging out something unpleasant. He had the dour face of an embittered poet, soured by frustrations and thoughts that had brewed too long in him.

"The white men are our friends, for they have many times told us so," he began, and pointed barbs edged through his thin mockery. "In our treaties with them they told us that our people may live forever in the Black Hills—also that we may hunt without harm as far south as the great river, as long as the buffalo lived. Their soldiers would protect us from other white men who might seek to take our land or spoil our hunting. Thus they pledged their friendship, and there was to be no more war. This was the treaty that Red Cloud agreed to when he stopped fighting."

His hearers grunted assent. Long Mane sank his voice to a soft crooning, his large eyes on Wapaha. "But white men found yellow metal in the Black Hills. They dug holes in the ground, and built villages there. They built an iron road across our land, for their iron horses. They hunted our buffalo, first for meat and then for the hides, and where is the buffalo now? Our people tried to stop them. There was fighting again. Then the white soldiers came, as they had promised us. *Ma-ya*—they came! But it seems that these soldiers were not the ones who made the treaty. It seems that the white men have many chiefs, always changing, never thinking the same. These soldiers made a mistake. Perhaps they had not heard of the treaty. Or perhaps they forgot."

His pseudo tolerance was the essence of sarcasm. He paused, smiling gently, letting his words sink in, cleverly timing the next. "The chiefs of these soldiers spoke of new laws of which our people had never heard. But they protected our people. Yes. In a strange manner.

They protected our people by driving them off their land and punishing them for killing white men!"

"*Ho!*" growled a warrior, getting stirred up. "*Ho—*this is true!" Many eyes took on a glitter around the fire, and blanketed men began swaying restlessly.

"Do not be angry," soothed Long Mane. His lean body swayed gently with the rest, his cavernous eyes glowing. For the moment, at least, he had them under his spell, flaying their fierce pride, whipping up their strong sense of injustice. "Do not be angry at the white men. They are your friends! Now they are coming to protect you again! They will take you to the reservation, and give you cow-beef and flour to eat. You will not have to hunt any more, so they will take your weapons away, and perhaps your ponies. What use is a lance if there is no hunting? What use is a pony if you stay in one place? You will not need such things. You will forget that you were once warriors and men, and when you are old you will squat by the fire and mumble your stories to the children of your children, who will laugh behind your bent backs and call you liars, for they will never have seen any such things and will not believe in them. But perhaps they will believe you when you tell them about Long Mane, who stayed away to hunt and fight, and never crawled in to die of old age on the reservation!"

He was prophet and devil-man. At last the passion broke through the thin shell. His lips stretched and he flung up both arms. The hissing, choking syllables of his Fox Warrior brotherhood song came chanting forth, and now his voice was high and harsh.

> "*Tokalaka miye ca—*
> I am the Fox, always the Fox!
> Fighting, fighting—though alone;

> Fighting, standing—falling, dying—
> Then this Fox shall be no more!
> *Nakenula waon welo. . . .*"

He broke off and brought his bitter eyes to bear again
on Wapaha Jim. "May *Wakan Tanka* curse the white
man for his crooked friendship!" he rasped, and glided
off on swift, light-stepping feet.

★

Luta-ho-ota trotted her pony over the hump to the
river, but as she crossed the hump she slowed and
looked back at the camp, wishfully, as she had done a
thousand times before, her hope never quite dying. But
Wapaha Jim did not come out to follow her, although
she had ridden openly across the *hocoka* past his lodge,
as she usually made a point of doing whenever he was
in camp. And, as usual, she tossed her head and called
him names under her breath.

"Man of stone! Blind one! Man who sees no woman!
Man of no love! *Sunka*—dog. . . ." She sighed, soften-
ing. "*Sicé, wan mayak uwé*—Beloved, look upon me!"
She went on down to the river out of sight of the
camp, and sat with her knees cuddled, absently watching her pony drink from the cold, clear stream. The
white pony had attained age but no sedateness, and
drank delicately, cocking its ears at its reflection in the
water and pretending a mild startlement. It snorted,
hoping to gain some petting attention, but Luta-ho-ota
was in a reverie of wonder at the stubborn stupidity of
men. Just because they had once been friends, both
Wapaha Jim and Long Mane scrupulously avoided her
rather than precipitate a duel to the death. Silly! Wapaha must know that if it came to a fight, she—Luta-ho-
ota—would certainly be on hand to slip in an arrow

where it would do the most good if needed. *Ma-ya,* what a fool he was!

She did not see or hear the man in the bearskin overcoat come stepping quietly along the bank. The question as to the coming of the soldiers had not been settled, but rather confused by Long Mane's declaration, and it had made a minor split in the camp. Some, siding with Black Horn and Running Dog, were for trekking north at once to join Crazy Horse. Others, cleaving to Yellow Eagle and Wapaha Jim, argued that the Army deserter was a liar and that there was no real danger.

Wapaha Jim had staked his prestige on an opinion and a promise. "The man lies," he told them. "White soldiers would not attack a peaceful camp where there are women and children. If they do come, it will only be to tell us that we must move to the reservation. Let me talk to them, for I talk their tongue. I shall tell them that we do no harm here, and I think they will ride away and leave us here in peace."

So, in a mingled atmosphere of uneasy distrust and hopeful faith, the camp left the matter to the future. In the meantime, the Army deserter was allowed the freedom of the camp, within limits. Nobody cared much whether the man ran away or not, but he'd have to do it on foot. Bear Standing, after appropriating the cavalry horse and weapons as his just dues, took no more interest in the man.

The deserter paused. His eyes sharpened on the white pony. To attempt stealing a pony from the hundreds belonging to the camp was too dangerous, guarded as they were. Too fraught with terrible consequences if he failed. But he had to get one somehow, and get away from here before that Fort Lincoln detachment came jingling in with the bucko captain at its head. He studied the back of the girl speculatively, and touched his tongue to his lips. She was pretty. Damned

pretty. He'd noticed her before. Maybe she'd run off
with him; why not? He was a man, and white—well,
white enough for an Injun wench to feel mighty proud
to be his woman, anyway.

He moved on toward her, treading with care. Mustn't
scare her too soon, or she'd be off like a shot. Let him
get his arms around her, though, and it would be all
right. Women were all the same. She'd soon quiet down
and go along, happy as a dog with its master. He took
a rapid look about him. Nobody in sight. The hump
hid him and the girl from the camp. Nobody would see
them ride off on that pony, and they wouldn't be missed
for hours.

The pony backed leisurely from the stream, snuffling
its nose against a foreleg, and its noises drowned out
the cautious advance of the man.

When the two reaching hands touched her from behind, Luta-ho-ota screamed a little and jumped. She
nearly got away, but the arms closed around her too
fast, and her thick red blanket kept her from wriggling
free. It slipped down around her own arms from off her
shoulders, and the man held it tightly with one hand
and pulled her around to face him, grinning down at
her. She could read all that was in that grin, for men
found her desirable and she had more than once had to
cope with a too ardent brave. So, wasting no strength
in useless struggling, and too proud to scream for help,
she stood quiet and passive, gazing steadily at him.

The man's grin broadened. This was easier than he
had even hoped for. The girl was downright meek and
willing. "All right, *querida*," he muttered huskily. "*Sabe
querida?* You come with me, huh?" He groped for the
few Sioux phrases that he had picked up. "*Ku*—uh—
with me, *yutonkal*, huh? On *tasunke*, there." He drew
her very close to him. "My *squaw*, huh? *Hiyupo!* Say,
you're as pretty a lil' *squaw* as . . ."

The point of Luta-ho-ota's little knife pierced the blanket, down low, and jabbed him in a thigh. He let out a yelp and knocked her down. The pony stamped a hoof, but didn't leave. Luta-ho-ota jumped up, furious, pulling her blanket into place. No man had ever gone so far as to resent her little knife so crudely. On other occasions it had been accepted as a straight answer, the recipient of the jab departing hurriedly and trying to recover his poise. So she was not prepared for a blow to follow, and she didn't dodge when the man hit her with his fist.

The man was in a rage. He cursed as he struck her, and his fist cracked on her forehead. The girl dropped with hardly a moan, and lay tangled in her red blanket. Then terror filled the man. He caught the bridle of the pony. Nobody had seen him. The hump was empty. He had a good pony and a clear road out. Some of his courage returned. He looked down at the senseless girl.

"Damned lil' wench!" he muttered, and picked her up. She was light, and the pony was powerful. "My woman, like it or not!" He mounted, took a last scrutiny about him, and headed the pony across the river in a splashing lope.

Toward evening he looked for a place to hide, where he could rest the pony. All afternoon, chill fears icing his spine, he had kept it to a punishing gait, but he took on more confidence as night drew near. He would rest the pony a spell, push on all night, and hole up somewhere tomorrow. In a day or two he could be out of the Sioux country. The girl rode behind him now, never a word out of her, meeting his eyes with silent hatred whenever he twisted to look back along his trail. He had taken her knife, and this was the only weapon between them. He knew that she was only biding her chance, and he feared her, and hated her because of it.

On their right ran a narrow stream bordered with timber and brushwood, and off to the left the valley of the stream was bounded by rolling hills with here and there a patch of snow in the shaded hollows. The deserter reined aside to a hollow between two hills, but before entering it he drew in and took a long look back. Nothing moving showed anywhere. The sun had not yet gone down, and he thought that by the time it was full dark he could push on again.

"It's goin' to be a hungry camp," he said to the girl, "but if I can do without eatin', so can you. Git off."

He was afraid to start a fire for warmth, although the air was getting cold. After unsaddling the pony and tying it out, he huddled in his bearskin coat and stared sullenly at the girl. "I reckon I'll tie you, you lil' she-devil. What you lookin' at? Come here!"

The girl said something, and a kind of tired horror came over her face. She stood looking past him, and the man said again, "Come here!" But he turned to see what she might be looking at, and then he saw them. He was much too late to do anything, and too paralyzed by fear to try. He sat huddled and staring.

In the light of the sinking sun the string of Comanches appeared like red ghosts on horseback, and their wiry little mounts made not much sound as they came on at a walk in single file down into the hollow. Riders and ponies were accustomed to furtive travel. There was no shouting, not a war-whoop, and not any special hurry. The situation did not require any. The Comanches had seen that the man and girl were unarmed. They merely walked their ponies down until they formed a ring around them, as if going through an unsmiling clownery of a slow attack, and they wheeled their ponies inward to the circled pair and stopped.

The girl stood unmoving. She knew what to expect, and stoic courage rose to aid her. It was not in her nature to do a useless act, so she did not scream or try to break through the ring.

The man shivered, getting stumblingly to his feet. "*Ho!*" he whispered, and swallowed, and tried again. "*Ho!* Me friend. *Amigo. Sabe amigo? Kola—*me *kola!*"

They knew some Spanish. For generations their tribesmen had raided down into Mexico. They had no friends there. They knew a word or two of Sioux. The Sioux were warriors who killed any Comanches they caught poaching on their lands. But the deserter could have spoken in fluent Comanche, had he been able, and done no better. He was a stranger, therefore an enemy. Also, he possessed a horse and a woman, sufficient incentives for murder in themselves.

He plodded shakily to the one he took to be the leader, a man with a flat face and broken nose, wearing a ragged and filthy blue tunic and a Mexican sabre. "Me *kola!*" he gasped, and took off his bearskin overcoat. "Here—for you!"

The Comanche slid a lazy look at the coat, the man, and around the circle, and Luta-ho-ota sensed silent laughter rippling around her. The deserter dragged a tobacco can from his pocket. "Here—this too. Smoke. Yours."

Casually, the Comanche took the tobacco. He took the bearskin coat and laid it across his pony. He reached down and plucked off the deserter's black campaign hat. With cold laughter in his eyes, he drew the Mexican sabre from its tarnished scabbard. . . .

The sun had not quite vanished when the Comanches trooped back over the hill, among them a white pony ridden by a girl in a red blanket. Down in the hollow behind them they left a hacked and scalped bundle that had once been a man.

★

CHAPTER 6

THE HOSTILES

"COMANCHES!"

Those with Wapaha Jim grunted corroboration, examining in the moonlight the tracks of ponies and moccasins.

They gathered around the hacked body in the hollow, and inspected it. "Fourteen," said Bad Buffalo. He had counted the tracks. He squatted on his heels and pointed with his chin. "They went that way and took the white pony with them. It is unlucky that we are so few."

There would have been only the three of them, but Running Dog and five friends, happening to be starting out on a hunt at the time, had joined them in the pursuit. Wapaha Jim had been in no mood to dally and organize a large party after discovering the loss of Luta-ho-ota and the deserter, and neither had Long Mane, while Bad Buffalo was never one to give much excess time to preparations. The signs in the earth down by the river told them all they needed to know, and they had hoped to catch up with their quarry before nightfall.

Long Mane swung onto his pony again and started off, saying nothing. He had not spoken all the way. Running Dog, looking at all the tracks, called after him, "Wait! We must send back for more men before we go farther."

Long Mane didn't even glance back. He rode on up
the hill, following the tracks, and Wapaha Jim loped
after him. Bad Buffalo rose and vaulted onto his pony
with shambling agility, and caught up with them. He
had never gained much height, was still short and
chunky, so ungraceful that the women laughed at him
behind his back; but few men could match his enormous
strength and bewildering swiftness of movement. Running Dog brought up the rear, muttering with his
friends. "Those three are fools! We should let them go
on alone. To risk death in the darkness, and only because a woman . . ."

It was getting close to dawn when with one accord
they halted their ponies and sat motionless. The tracks,
not more than two or three hours old, had brought them
through a series of rolling hills to a valley. They were
in unfamiliar country, avoided by their hunting parties
because of its dry barrenness—but here lay a sheltered
valley with a grassed and timbered floor and a narrow
stream winding through it. A perfect site for a snug
winter camp, for men who wished to live unseen and
undisturbed, and did not mind riding far abroad for
game.

And the camp was there, down there on the level
floor and handy to the stream. A big camp. The startled
watchers counted over thirty lodges, and looked down
on a pony herd that covered a large meadow just north
of the camp. They had stumbled upon a hidden Comanche stronghold, the headquarters of some marauding band that, raiding this far north last year, had
elected to remain through the winter for reasons best
known to itself.

Running Dog was first to utter a whisper. "Quick—
let us get away from here before their dogs smell us and
bark!" He began edging his pony back along the shallow draw through which they had come.

"They have no dogs, or we would have heard them earlier, howling at the moon," murmured Wapaha Jim. "Long Mane, do you see a white pony? Down there, see? Not with the herd. Her pony never would stay with the others. She petted it too much."

"I see it. And she—?"

"I don't know. Those who brought her here are tired and sleeping. Later they will make the scalp-dance, and she will be painted and brought out. Bad Buffalo and I have spied on Comanche camps and seen them do these things."

"And turned their stamping into a death-dance, with arrows, before we slipped away!" grinned Bad Buffalo. "I see a dark lodge. Is it red? Perhaps the medicine lodge. In there?"

"Perhaps. I go down to find out." Wapaha Jim began taking the saddle off his pony.

"*I* go down!" said Long Mane.

"Fools!" hissed Running Dog. "I say we go home and make up a big war-party. Obey me!"

Wapaha Jim finished stripping his pony of everything except the hair rope braided into the mane. "It will be too late, after they make the scalp-dance," he pointed out. "And you are not the leader, Running Dog. I am the leader, and I am the man who has first right to seek Luta-ho-ota." He looked at Long Mane, and added simply, "She is my sister."

Long Mane moved impulsively to touch him, but his habit of reserve checked him. His large eyes turned young and eloquent. "Yes, Wapaha," he said muffledly. "She is your sister. We hear you. Tell us what we must do."

"The ponies?" suggested Bad Buffalo.

Wapaha Jim nodded. "Yes. You, Long Mane, and you, Bad Buffalo—creep down to the meadow. If I get into trouble, then stampede their ponies and run them off. They will come out and chase you, and perhaps that will give me a chance to get away if I find Luta-ho-ota. You, Running Dog, and you others—I ask you to help us. You have guns. We shall come back this way, if we come at all. Shoot those who come after us. Drive them back and keep them from shooting at us. We rely on you."

Softly he chanted the song of the Dog Warriors, making his vow of devotion and demanding their vows in return. *"Kola, taku otehika . . . Imakuwapilo . . . Waon welo!"* He looked questioningly at them, and Running Dog nodded.

"Hiyupo!" breathed Bad Buffalo, and went snaking off on foot with Long Mane.

Wapaha Jim climbed onto his saddleless pony, lay flat along its back, and let it drift idly down toward the camp. Its unshod hoofs set up little sound on the grass and sandy soil. Any Comanche sentinel, noticing it but not its flattened rider in the darkness, might think it a pony of the camp that had strayed and was now returning.

The pony was brown and inconspicuous. It ambled on down the slope, choosing its own footing, but unobtrusively guided by its rider toward the grazing white pony below. The white pony lifted its head and nickered, sniffing a familiar scent. This was the initial risk, and no way to guard against it. Wapaha Jim eased over onto the hidden side of his plodding mount, hung there with his left arm through the braided hair rope and a toe hooked along the backbone, and cocked the loaded Army pistol that he had borrowed from Bear Standing.

The white pony nickered again more loudly, stretching its neck and stepping daintily to meet an old friend. It snuffed at the brown, shivering with pleasure. It pricked its ears at Wapaha Jim and nuzzled his hair. Wapaha Jim hung motionless, peering under the neck of his mount. He caught a movement among the lodges: a dark and blanketed shape, noiseless and suspicious by life-long habit, prowling out to investigate the noises of the pony.

The man halted less than thirty yards away, hooded face turned toward the two ponies, and both animals broke off their nuzzled greetings to eye him at first in mild curiosity. The brown, catching a foreign whiff, snorted and sidled off with its ears laid back. The presence of strangers always brought out its meanest disposition. The white caught the alarm of the brown; it planted its legs apart like a colt, provocative and skittish, ready to wheel off and bolt if the man approached too closely. For a full minute the man scrutinized them. At last, after a long look at the quiet pony herd farther up the valley, he paced off back among the lodges.

Wapaha Jim slowly let out his held breath. Dawn was on the way, but he allowed more time to go by before putting his feet to the ground. He laid a carefully gentle hand on the white pony, patting the sleek neck. He ran his palm down the nose and rubbed the soft muzzle. "*Ho*, petted and foolish beast," he whispered into the twitching ear, "you know Wapaha, don't you? Are we not old friends?"

The white pony shivered again self-consciously, arching its neck, coy as a kitten, thrusting its muzzle into the fondling hand. The brown pushed in, jealous. Wapaha Jim slipped the hair rope over the neck of the white, loosely attaching both animals together before they knew it, and left them. They stood quietly together, comforted by each other's presence, gazing after him as he crept in among the high, narrow-topped lodges. Had he used less tact they would have been nervous, all keyed up to bolt at the first frightening sound.

He heard occasional sounds within some of the lodges

as he tiptoed past. The camp was beginning to stir awake. He dropped to a crawl and came up to the red lodge. The buffalo-hide flap was laced shut from the outside, and a tufted red lance leaned against it to warn off anybody from entering the forbidden place. Such signs were conclusive, and Wapaha Jim breathed deeply again. He did not disturb the flap or the lance of the medicine man, but crawled on around to the back, and with his knife he punctured the stiff hide. He cut a rough half-circle, bent back the section, and crawled through.

It was dark inside the lodge, but a small fire smoldered feebly in the center of the floor, and he made out the shapes of several big kettles ranged around it. Drying bundles of herbs hung from the walls and slanted tepee poles, and the close air was heavy with odors. Something moved with a muffled rustling, and he heard breathing. Lying crouched on the floor, he picked the location of the sounds as being somewhere on the other side of the dying fire. Whatever it was that made them, it was awake and listening.

He raised the cocked pistol and put his chances on a low whisper. "Luta-ho-ota—is it you?"

The answer came in a gasp. "Wapaha—oh, Wapaha —you!"

She lay between robes on the floor, and when he darted around the fire to her he tripped over a rope. She was staked out under the covers, wrists and ankles attached with ropes to stakes too far off for her to reach. Wapaha Jim used his knife again, and lifted her to her feet. She shook badly, her muscles cramped, and clung to him.

"Oh, Wapaha! I prayed that you come before the day and the dance! I made prayers to *Wakan Tanka* and to . . ."

He hushed her swiftly with a hand over her mouth,

and they stood listening together. He saw terror in the dark shine of her eyes. His own were glittering, narrowed. Somebody was outside the lodge, unlacing the flap and being quiet and deft about it. A strip of rawhide rasped softly, and the flap rippled, a thin sliver of grey dawnlight appearing near the bottom.

A respectful voice uttered a morning greeting, and moccasined feet padded on by toward the river. The unknown one answered with a grunt that sounded annoyed, and worked with less quiet care at the flap.

Wapaha Jim hustled the girl across the lodge to the gap that he had cut. It was nearly light outside now. "Your pony and mine—under the big cottonwood near the path," he whispered. "Hurry!" He pushed her through.

The flap folded open, and a heavily wrapped figure ducked into the lodge, drawing the flap shut behind him. He took a step to the pile of robes, and stopped, his attention taken suddenly by the hole in the rear wall. A growl started in his throat, and his eyes widened in an amazed glare at the crouched shape of Wapaha Jim, who was backing out. There was nothing else for it, and Wapaha Jim pulled the trigger of his pistol. After the brief spurt and loud report, the wrapped figure whirled totteringly and plunged out of the lodge, and he screamed as he fell outside.

There was no period of wondering aftermath, no shocked inaction. The camp burst alive with a roar. Comanche reactions were always immediate. But even before the first warrior erupted from his lodge the pony herd was in motion, scared mad by the howling and waving of Long Mane and Bad Buffalo. Everything happened with the explosive suddenness of a stepped-on tomcat, and Wapaha Jim felt again the grim relish of setting off a thunderbolt among men who considered themselves masters in the art of surprise. A warrior,

wearing nothing at all and clutching a carbine, slid to
a halt in his bare feet and changed his mind about running to help save the ponies. He threw up the carbine
to fire, but the pistol spat and beat him to the shot, and
Wapaha Jim plucked up the falling carbine on his running way to the cottonwood.

Astride her white pony, Luta-ho-ota held the brown
from bolting in the noisy confusion. Men, most of them
naked from their couches, were obeying the first impulse of the raided, racing to protect their indispensable
ponies. Long Mane and Bad Buffalo were doing good
work. They could be seen tearing back and forth on
stolen mounts, waving their blankets and driving the
mass of ponies in a thundering stampede up the valley.
Bad Buffalo raised himself up on his pony, bouncing
and weaving, and anxiously looked back. Wapaha Jim
waved to him as he leaped onto the brown, and even at
that distance he saw Bad Buffalo flash his big teeth in a
grin and shout across to Long Mane. There was no real
hope that they could get away with the herd, but at
least they could keep the Comanches worried and busy
chasing them for awhile.

"*Hopo*—let's go!" Wapaha Jim called to the girl, and
put his pony to a dead run for the path up through the
hills. The Comanche camp boiled with commotion, and
some women began a wail for the dead, but so far no
shooting cracked from the hills where Running Dog and
his five friends had been left posted.

A piece of flesh flicked off his left shoulder with a
sting of pain, and Wapaha Jim hipped around. He let
Luta-ho-ota ride by him up the slope, and he tried a
shot at a small group of men coming along fast after
them on foot. One dropped out, limping, but the rest
took to running a zigzag course and came on, and he began to wonder about Running Dog and the others. This
was their task, to turn back pursuers and discourage

close shooting. He sent a Sioux yell of taunting defiance at the group and caught up with the white pony,
but a premonition rose uneasily in him. If Running
Dog and the others were not on hand it would be bad.
There were many Comanches able to wear down a
pony in a long chase on foot, and they seldom quit
easily when their prideful desire for vengeance was
as aroused as it was now. The brown and the white
raced on, side by side, and their hoofs cut sand in a
tight wheel into the draw between the hills.

"Where are the others?" called the girl.

"Ask the wind!" Wapaha Jim rapped back. "Gone,
that great warrior of the big voice—that son of a chief,
Running Dog! May he die in darkness!" He thrust the
pistol to her. "Take this. I have the carbine and my
knife. Save your pony. We have far to go, and we
make no stops."

"*Tziksu weta tariruta, Sicé,*" responded the girl obedi-
ently, happily. The words were not words commonly
used between sister and brother. "My faith is in your
power, Beloved." Her shining eyes said that the devot-
edly desperate act of saving her from the Comanches
had been beyond that of a mere brother, giving her the
right and glory to speak such intimate words aloud,
where before she had only whispered them in secret
loneliness.

But Wapaha Jim's mind was on Bad Buffalo and
Long Mane, back there in the valley and making a running fight of it, expecting help from Running Dog and
not getting it. "*Ho, Wakan Tanka,*" he prayed, "give
speed and good luck to my two friends back there, and
place your curse on those who abandoned us!"

When next he looked back the group of Comanches
had strung out, settling down to an all-day dogtrot, following the two ponies with relentless patience.

★

Running Dog said angrily, "Are we fools who must be led by fools?" He said it in reply to one of the five riding home with him—Blue Beaver—who had remarked that bad luck might come of this.

"What shall we say when we are asked where they are, those three?" queried Blue Beaver uncomfortably. "They are surely killed or captured by the Comanches. We live and are without wounds or trophies. How shall we talk of this?"

"We shall say that we do not know," growled Running Dog. "We shall say that they left us. Let us pick up that dead soldier on our way and take him back with us. We shall say that we caught and killed him, but Luta-ho-ota was not with him, and those three were not then with us and we do not know what became of them. The dead one will be our proof and our trophy. Wagh —leave all that to me, and let any man beware who calls me a liar! Come, let us hurry. The Comanches may be hunting us."

In the afternoon they sighted the trees fringing the narrow stream, and came upon their own tracks leading away from the hollow. Blue Beaver threw up a hand for a halt, and pointed. "Smoke! Somebody is there!" He gestured widely. "Let us go around and cross the stream."

They struck the stream at a point well below the curling drift of smoke, crossed it, and warily worked their way up along the brushy bank until they were opposite the hollow where the dead deserter had been left. Blue Beaver at once slipped an arrow to his bowstring, and a warrior beside him thoughtfully thumbed back the hammer of his musket.

"Soldiers! He spoke straight words, that one. They come to hunt our camp and to attack it! Horses—they have good horses! Big, like the one that dead coward rode. And guns!"

"Wa-aa-agh!" A warrior pinched in his lips and glared hatred across the stream. "Could we steal some of those fine horses? Look, they dig a hole for that dead man."

Eight troopers took turns at digging the grave, using tin mugs and knives. The rest of the detachment rubbed down the horses and aired saddle cloths, or stood around the fire making coffee. The sun was warm, and most of them had peeled off their thick fur overcoats. They were a tough and seasoned bunch of men, taking long riding and short rations in their stride. Their faded and casual smartness was not that of the city barracks and newly brisk recruits. The yellow cavalry stripes against the blue, and the wide-brimmed campaign hats, added to an air of rakishness that fitted well into the raw country. They were aware of their toughness. Prided themselves on it. The Seventh Cavalry was a tough outfit, a crack outfit, and if anybody didn't know it he was soon informed.

Captain Vaugant straightened up from inspecting the body. He hitched his belt and tugged the creases from his coat. "I guess it's that half-breed, all right. Hard to tell. They chopped him up pretty bad."

"Ghastly," said West Hathersall. "The damned fiends!" He felt a little sick and looked away. "George, you've got your hands—ugh—dirty."

Vaugant glanced at them, and at his second-in-command. "M-mm, somewhat." Because of the troopers within hearing, he kept to military formality. "Mr. Hathersall, a man has to develop a—well, call it a protective philosophy. Doctors have to have it, too, or they'd break down. It may be a form of callousness, but it's very necessary. And after all, this fellow was a deserter."

"He wore our uniform, didn't he?"

"True—true," Vaugant conceded. "He could have been a loyal and capable trooper, and they'd have done the same thing to him. The hostiles are not discriminating in their murders. Sergeant, send a man down to the stream for some water, will you? I want to wash my hands."

"This certainly seems to prove that the Indians along this country are hostiles," he went on musingly, and shrugged. "No surprise, that. They're all on the warpath. It's spreading like grass-fire." He picked a broken feather out of the trampled dirt. "Looks like a Sioux head-feather, doesn't it, Sergeant? The Sioux did it, of course. Probably some of the same band we're looking for. Say, what's the matter with that man you sent down there? Hey, soldier—I'm waiting for that water!"

The trooper down at the stream dipped in his canvas bucket and came back at a smart pace. "Something over there on the far bank, sir," he reported. "Might be a buffalo calf or the like, caught in the brush. Sounded like it. Kinda bawled one time, real low."

"Yes? Hope you're right. Sergeant, ride over there with a couple of men and look around. We could use some fresh meat."

They watched the sergeant and two troopers trot their horses down to the stream, riding bareback and carrying their carbines. Men left off rubbing down their mounts to look, and others cheerfully began building up the fire and cutting sticks in readiness for the roasting. The three riders splashed across the stream and climbed their dripping animals up onto the far bank.

"Spread out, Sergeant," Vaugant called, and strolled down after them, drying his washed hands. "It may be a bear. If it is, you better give it plenty of . . ." He didn't finish. His right hand smacked his holster.

The sergeant, who had turned around to acknowledge the command, fell off his horse without speaking,

and his booted feet followed his head into the thick
brush. There was no sound to account for it. His horse
halted at once, dipped an inquiring nose down at him,
and snorted, backing away. The two surprised troopers
closed in to see what was wrong. One of them sat up
straight with a spasmodic jerk that lost him his carbine,
and this time the watchers in the hollow glimpsed the
brief shimmer of the arrow. The other trooper fired into
the brush while he swung his mount around, and another
shot answered him. His horse leaped, unseating him,
but he kept hold of the reins when he tumbled, and
then it was a struggle between them, the animal out of
control and kicking.

Vaugant broke into a run, barking a short command.
He was cool; emergencies never flurried him. Only personal emotions could wreck the hard calm of his Army
ego. His men grabbed their arms and came pelting
after him, but before they could reach the stream it was
all over on the other side. Two copper-brown men rose
from nowhere and jumped the trooper struggling with
his wounded mount. The horse got away, but the other
two animals were seized by three more dark men. One
of them snatched up the sergeant's carbine and took
quick aim at the runaway horse, preferring to kill it if
he couldn't capture it. Vaugant, far in front of his men,
loosed a pistol shot at him. The Indian fired and
dropped the horse with his first shot. He changed his
aim promptly and fired again, and crowed like an exultant boy when Vaugant pitched headlong into the water.

Then, like bizarre puppets tugged neatly off-scene at
the conclusion of their allotted act, the Indians were
gone, and the steel plates of the two captured Army
mounts beat loudly through the drumming of unshod
ponies. West Hathersall got to Vaugant and hauled him
out of the stream, half drowned and senseless.

"Easy, there, men—stay together! What? Yes-yes, go

get the sergeant and those two men and bring them back here. Unpack the medical kit. Get back and guard the horses, some of you! Watch the ammunition packs! Trumpeter! Where's that trumpeter?"

It was half an hour before West Hathersall quite realized that the raid had not been the preliminary to a grand attack, and that all emergency was past. By that time Vaugant was lying on his back and quietly swearing, paralyzed by the splitting agony of a bullet-chipped skull.

"Sergeant M'Gill's dead, sir," reported a corporal. "So's Bucknell, an' Morris is in a bad way. Three mounts an' three carbines lost. They took Mac's hair, too, the devils."

"Help me up, Mr. Hathersall," muttered Vaugant. "Damnation! Not more than half a dozen of 'em, and look what they did to us. From that camp we're looking for, I'll wager. Well, we'll know what to expect when we—we . . . Hell, I'm going to faint again!"

He fainted, and West and the corporal caught him. The corporal cocked a meditative eye at his lieutenant. "Shall I give orders to break camp an' start back for the fort, sir?" he suggested. "The captain needs doctoring. Maybe his head's busted."

West wanted to push on in search of that Sioux camp. He hadn't proved himself yet. "If the captain is no better by tonight we'll return to the fort," he granted at last. "Meantime, post lookouts and tell them to keep sharp watch."

Along toward sundown the corporal hurried down to the fire and saluted briskly. "Two horsemen coming this way, sir, from over yonder. The lookout on the hill says they're Injuns."

Men within hearing passed the word, and there was general movement. Vaugant, sitting up and nursing his head, automatically drew his pistol. Pain had made his facial features prominent, and his eyes were bloodshot. "Good!" he said, and blinked unseeingly at the corporal. "Let 'em come. Keep everybody below the skyline. If they're Sioux let me know."

Minutes later the corporal returned. "I guess they're Sioux all right, sir." Eagerness flattened his tone. The sergeant had been popular. "They're making straight for here, so I reckon they didn't sight our smoke before we put the fire out. Act like they're on the prowl."

"Coming to find out if we're gone yet, the brazen blackguards," commented Vaugant. "Mr. Hathersall, hold the men in hand and don't let them fire unless I give the order. We want to make sure of this pair. May get some information from them."

The detachment waited in dead silence, and kept that silent immobility when a head bobbed into sight up the hill, followed by another. Both riders jogged into full view, topping the hill, and instantly reined their ponies half around and stopped, peering down at the soldiers in the hollow. Obviously they were startled. The smaller rider, muffled in a red blanket and seated on a white pony, moved to take flight. The tall one with a feather in his hair put out a hand, restraining his companion. He rode forward a few steps and held out his hand again, this time above his head, the palm turned outward to the soldiers, and he sat there waiting for his gesture of peace to be returned.

Even to the bitterly prejudiced eyes of West Hathersall, the man made a striking picture, all red and black against the sky and the sinking sun shining on him. His brown pony drooped a little tiredly, but he sat as straight as a guardsman, and although his features were too far off to be plainly visible he appeared to be smiling. His calm poise was impressive, but the troopers saw it as an astounding arrogance, particularly when they noted that he carried what looked to be an Army carbine. Two troopers by the picket line adjusted their sights and took careful aim. The corporal warned them in a low voice not to fire yet, and they nodded. Vaugant shifted his pistol to his left hand, to leave his right free to beckon the pair on down.

The movements could be seen by the alert eyes on the hill. The tall warrior shook his head urgently. His companion took more direct action. A high little cry of alarm, a kick of heels, and the white pony took off. The brown spun around to follow, and then every trooper threw butt to shoulder.

"Aim for their horses, men!" Vaugant called, and his pistol rapped quick reports in the flurried discharge of carbines.

The white pony swerved and lost its head. It had never been trained as a war pony, so it didn't know what to do, and it was frightened. It was frightened at the shattering noise and the strange behavior of its rider, who slumped over its neck and tried to hang on, both arms hugging it. It ran a circling course around the top of the hill, and stamped to a trembling halt only when its rider slipped off and rolled over on the ground.

The troopers, shooting, saw the tall warrior wrench his brown mount in a slithering curve and come tearing back for his fallen companion. Some of them had seen such acts of devotion before among the hostiles, and it no longer astonished them, but they could still admire the suicidal courage of it. The warrior dragged his mount back onto its haunches and leaped from its bare back. He cried out in a deep and savage voice as he picked up the limp body in his arms, and he laid it with swift care over the white pony, while bullets dug up dirt around him. He tied the red blanket with a tug, fastening on the body, and he slapped the white pony on its way.

"Get him—don't let him get away!" Vaugant barked,

and cursed because his legs were too shaky to stand on.
"Go up there after him and bring him in!"

Half a dozen troopers started up the hill ahead of the
rest. The warrior turned on them with a snarl. His carbine cracked three times, and he didn't stand still while
he fired, for he was vaulting onto his pony and charging
down at them, but three of the troopers quit.

"Damnation, give me my rifle, somebody!" Vaugant
clawed his way to his piled belongings. "I'll drop him!
Why, look at that devil! Look, he's—!"

The warrior made his lone charge and descended
upon the remaining three of the forward group, and he
wasn't bluffing to strike a coup. He was gripped by a
deadly cold rage, utterly unlike anything they had ever
seen. He struck one trooper with a sweep of his carbine,
rode down the other two and bowled them over, and it
looked likely that he would keep on coming and attack
the camp, single-handed. He looked capable of trying
it, and the total unexpectedness of his berserk charge
had already set the whole detachment back on its boot-
heels, but he fired one last shot into them and whirled
back up the hill. The last they saw of him, he was
pounding off after the white pony, and as he rode over
the hill he looked back and shook his carbine high in
the air. Then the mad apparition was gone.

West Hathersall found himself futilely clicking an
empty pistol. "Good Lord!" he breathed. "If the Indians fight like that—!"

"They don't, thank the gods—not often," muttered
Vaugant, himself somewhat dazed. "That devil! Take
a squad and go after him. I don't expect you to catch
him, but you can try. Turn back when it gets dark.
Phew! Never saw anything like it!"

A trooper came limping down the hill, helping another who sagged in the middle. "Mahogany Christo-
pher!" he blurted. "What kind of Injun was that?"

"Wasn't Injun," mumbled the wounded man. He raised a sick and shocked face to Vaugant. "His eyes wasn't Injun. I saw 'em! Grey, they was, like a white man's. Like a crazy white man. A white renegade! He was crazy, I tell you!"

"So are you," grunted Vaugant. "Somebody give this man a drink. Bring the injured here, and hand me that medicine kit. Great gods o' war—wait'll Custer hears about this!"

West Hathersall rode back in with his squad long after sundown. "Lost him in the dark," he said briefly. He looked uncertainly at the wounded men around the fire, and lastly at the captain. "Corporal Dunnington thinks one of them was a woman. The small one. The one we—uh—that got hit. I hope he's wrong."

"You do, eh? Well, so do I. Come to think of it, that one did act like a woman. Too bad. But take a look at that." Vaugant nodded at a cavalry dragoon pistol lying on his blanket. "The trumpeter found it right where that wild man made his stand. Must have been dropped by the one we hit. It's a late issue and one of ours. Taken from the fellow we found chopped up, of course. Those two had a hand in the chopping, so don't get to grieving too much about the woman—if it was a woman."

West nodded. "I suppose you're right. Still . . ." He gazed up the hill. "I hate Indians, but I can't get over the way that one risked his life to save the woman. And she was dead, you know. It—it must have hit him hard to make him act like that. He went mad."

"I've known of white men who went mad that way, too," said Vaugant harshly. "White men whose wives were killed—or their parents—by Indians. Sorry. I didn't mean to bring that up."

"It's all right." West turned his paled face away. "Yes, a man does go mad when that happens. Or whenever he thinks about it. That fellow had some revenge on us, and that's something. I wonder if that'll satisfy him, though. Oh, damn! It's a rotten business when women get caught in it, isn't it? Or kids. There was a boy who was killed along with my parents, and his father too. I liked him. So did Tally. If he'd lived, I'd never have wanted a better friend. There was something about him that—well, you know how it is. Once in a lifetime you meet somebody like that, and you're friends for life. Unforgettable. Tally feels just the same way. His name was Jim Aherne. Whopper Jim, we called him. . . ."

CHAPTER 7

DEATH AND DEPARTURE

IT HAD SNOWED IN THE NIGHT, AND THIS MORNING THE wind brushed up drifts against the tepees and kept the old people huddling around the fires. Winter, that had struck only lightly so far, now threatened to come in late and break its mild promises. The river was freezing over; it would have a solid coat before long, for the sky was sunless and the wind came moaning out of the north.

Somebody set up a shouting and ran through the whitened camp. "Ho, Yellow Eagle! He comes— Wapaha comes!"

Even the shivering ancients turned out with the rest, mumbling and incredulous. Black Horn, waddling from his warm lodge, sent an agitated look at Running Dog, who wrapped his robe about himself and stood silent in the crowd. Running Dog had told a convincing story that had left few hopes for the lives of those who had not returned with him and his party.

Expectant eyes scrutinized the pair of ponies coming plodding through the snow, and a hush fell slowly over the crowd. The ponies were played out, staggering along with dragging hoofs and hanging heads. A red-blanketed bundle hung across the back of the white one. The man on the brown rode with bowed head and shoulders slumped, like a dead man propped up. Here was no warrior returning in triumph. Old Pehangi uttered a long, low wail, and Yellow Eagle did a rare thing; he put an arm around the shoulders of his woman while he kept his eyes on that red bundle, and he drew her close to him.

When the two ponies shuffled to a standstill before the hushed crowd, Wapaha Jim raised his head with an effort. He was half frozen, so stiff with the cold that he could not dismount. His blued lips cracked when he moved them, and bled, and at first he could not speak. Then his wind-inflamed eyes blurred, and he could not see Yellow Eagle come to his side, but he felt the hand touching his arm, and heard the voice.

"Wapaha, my son . . . you are home."

"She is dead," said Wapaha Jim. He stared blindly before him. "They killed her. Soldiers. They did this thing. I led her to their camp, and told her not to fear. We went in peace. But they fired on us. White soldiers. Where is Pehangi? Take her, Pehangi . . . she is cold. I brought her home to you. We saved her from the Comanches before the scalp-dance . . . but the soldiers killed her."

He heard the growl of the crowd, and old Pehangi's wail. "From this day let no man call me white," he mumbled. "Help me, Yellow Eagle. My hands and my feet . . . I must save them. I must live and be well, to fight the soldiers who come to kill my people. We must join Crazy Horse, and fight. . . ."

They carried him into the lodge, and Yellow Eagle and the shaman worked over him and the agony poured into his limbs. He gave out no sound, and closed his eyes. They brought in Luta-ho-ota and laid her down, and there was angry talk going on around him. He heard a shouting outside, and then heard no more.

He opened his eyes later and found a familiar stocky figure bending over him and examining his feet and hands. Bad Buffalo had his face frozen on one side, giving him a hideous leer. He still wore furs and he was dirty from the trail, and smelled strongly of blood and horse. Behind him old Pehangi sat on her heels and cried, rocking to and fro, at the same time attending to a cooking kettle at the fire. Yellow Eagle, lighting his own best pipe, handed it to the stocky warrior and gestured toward the steaming kettle. The law of hospitality took precedence over grief. Bad Buffalo had no woman of his own to care for him.

"You will be well again, Wapaha," Bad Buffalo said between grateful puffs at the pipe. "You and I will ride and hunt and fight together again. We got away with some of the Comanche ponies. When we were cold we killed two and cut them open, and put in our hands and feet to save them from freezing. *Ma-ya*, they were good ponies, too, but they had to die. We ate some of them. We worried about you and Luta-ho-ota."

"She is dead, Bad Buffalo. Soldiers . . ."

Bad Buffalo nodded, warming his hands around the bowl of the pipe. "We have been told. When you are well, you and I will go and pay them—*lo!*"

"Long Mane—?"

"He is here." Bad Buffalo shifted to let him see. He shook his head at Yellow Eagle, declining the food offered him. "I do not eat until I have done that which shall cool my heart."

Long Mane stood at the foot of Luta-ho-ota's couch, his back straight, shoulders sloped and head sunk forward, his large eyes fixed steadily on the reposed face of the dead girl. He seemed in a trance, like a man living in remote and visionary thoughts. His lean face was slack and haggard, as lifeless of expression as that one on the couch, and when Wapaha Jim spoke softly to him he remained silent and oblivious.

Bad Buffalo got up and went to him. He laid a square and dirty paw on his shoulder and offered him the pipe, but left him alone after a moment of waiting. "His heart is dead," he said simply, and handed the pipe back to Yellow Eagle. His frozen face twitched horribly. The battle-glare entered his eyes. He worked his dirty hands and stared about him, and by the blind look of him Wapaha Jim knew what was coming.

"Wait, Bad Buffalo! Help me out there. Let me fight that crooked-tongued dog! It is my fight! Yellow Eagle—!"

But there was no stopping Bad Buffalo. There had never been any way of stopping him when the killing rage rose up in him. He snatched up the nearest weapon at hand—Yellow Eagle's short and heavy lance —and shambled out of the lodge, growling. Wapaha Jim rolled from his couch and hobbled to the door, but Yellow Eagle caught him and held him in his arms. "Give him this fight. He has sworn to do this. If he fails, then you and I will take his place."

Bad Buffalo lumbered through the crowd outside, and those he shouldered out of his way turned to stare after him. With comprehension of his purpose, the crowd drew back, retreating to watch him from the outer boundaries of the *hocoka*, the hollow center of the camp. He took the first pony he came to, and swung up onto its back, the lance in his right fist.

"*Ho, sunka!* You who ran away from the Comanche camp and left us to be killed! Hear me!"

His hoarse voice boomed through the sudden hush, hurling the insult of all insults, the charge of cowardice and betrayal. "He who ran home, and lied—where is that whining *sunka?* Where is that cowardly dog and spawn of a dog? Does he hide with the women? Does he fear to come out and show himself? Wagh! Must I drag him out from his father's lodge and beat him around the camp? *Ho*, he comes—he comes! I call to the dog and he comes! Get your lance and a pony, *sunka,* and face me!"

Running Dog emerged from his father's lodge, muttering, twisting his lips, his face purplish and a red glow under his eyes and over his cheekbones. He stepped forward, one slow stride at a time, until he stood in the *hocoka* facing the squat challenger. He flung off his robe behind him with a sudden whisk of his elbows, and then it was seen that he had his seven-shot carbine with him.

"*Waya-ta-nin makah*—may you eat dirt!" he howled, and fired. He fired again as the pony came launching at him, and laughed to see the pony crash down and turn over in a kicking somersault.

Bad Buffalo bounced on the ground, flipped over, and was on his feet, running forward with his lance upraised. He threw the lance as the muzzle of the carbine steadied on him for a third shot, and this was a fighting trick that he could do better than most. Any weapon in his hands was worth three on the enemy side. The lance slipped through the air like a live thing, stopped with a jar, and the thud of it was audible all around the camp.

Running Dog fell flat on his back, the shaft pointing upward, and he scraped his heels in the ground. A bellow came from the chief's lodge. Bad Buffalo left his lance where it was. He picked up the carbine.

The carbine cracked, short and sharp. Black Horn, coming blundering out of his lodge with a smooth-bore musket, dropped very heavily. A low moan of horror went through the watching crowd. Bad Buffalo had shot down the chief. He didn't appear to be shaken by any aftermath of the deed. He wheeled slowly, running his glowering regard over the crowd of faces, deliberate as an executioner.

"Blue Beaver—you were there! You left with him!"

"Yes, Bad Buffalo, but I . . ."

Crack! It was fine shooting, deadly shooting. He didn't waste time in his aiming; just swung the carbine and pulled the trigger.

"And you, *Maza-ska—!*"

Maza-ska—Flat Bone—thought to make a fight of it. He wrenched a gun from the hands of a neighbor, but never got its butt to his shoulder. After he fell, the owner of the gun made no motion toward retrieving his weapon.

"Enough, Bad Buffalo—enough!" Yellow Eagle strode out onto the *hocoka*. "Let this be enough killing!"

"*Nunwe*—so let it be," grunted the berserker. He tramped over to the dead chief, kicked dust at the body, and tore the feathers from the hair. "Our chief is dead," he announced loudly, belligerently. "He lived long— too long—but now he lies dead. Let us now have a man for our chief, not a fat and lazy *ratawe!* Do we not go to war soon? Then we need a warrior to lead us."

Some of the younger braves, thinking he was casting out a hint for himself, began calling, "Bad Buffalo—let him be chief!"

For the first time Bad Buffalo evinced some abashment. He rubbed his nose with the back of his hand, self-conscious as a boy. "No, I can never make a chief," he disclaimed embarrassedly. "I am not wise nor good, and I shall never live to be a wise old man. It is Yellow Eagle I think of as chief. He is brave and wise. He is a great warrior. He has many friends."

A rumble of approval gave plenty of foundation for the last statement.

★

That night Chief Yellow Eagle held an emergency council with his leading men. "We must move away from here," he warned. "The soldiers are coming to make war on us, and there are not enough of us to fight them off. We must take our women and children out of their way. It is winter all over the land, and colder in the north. Some of the old ones may die on the trail. We will lose ponies. The soldiers will come fast after us, and we must hurry. But these are things that must be suffered. I am for joining Crazy Horse in the north, and fighting with his men against the soldiers!"

Wapaha Jim got to his feet a little painfully. The shaman had done well with his herbs and potions, but his skill was not magic, and Wapaha Jim's feet were still tender and raw. "In another council I talked against war with the soldiers," he reminded them. "I said they would not attack us. Now I know that my tongue was foolish. I was wrong. My eyes were blinded because I thought of them as my people. They come to kill! Let us go to the camp of Crazy Horse, and fight when the time comes! I am ready!"

"And I!" growled Bad Buffalo.

"And I," came the low voice of Long Mane, and every man present gave his assenting grunt.

Iron Breast rose and waited his turn to speak. He faced the new chief, his life-long friend. "You have said that the soldiers will follow fast after us. They will, and they ride big horses. We shall be heavily loaded. We shall have our women and children, and the old ones to care for. If the snow stops and they find our trail, how can we hope to escape from them?"

That strong eventuality already lay in the minds of most, and they nodded. Yellow Eagle, no master of strategy, eyed his old friend reproachfully. "Should we stay here till they come?" he demanded. "Should we wait and let them kill us? You grow old, Iron Breast!"

The old warrior smiled. "Old," he agreed. "But it is the cunning wolf that lives to old age. Listen. Often the soldiers have Crow scouts with them—but what does a Crow know of Sioux country? The soldiers would like to have a Sioux for their scout—a Sioux who had turned against his own people. And that Sioux, telling them that he was leading them after his people, could take them somewhere else and lose them, while his people hurried safely on to the camp of Crazy Horse!"

It was something of a novel idea to all of them, an innovation in war strategy that left them struggling to grasp its possibilities. They frowned, thinking it over, and one by one their faces brightened. Bad Buffalo jumped up, grinning his crooked grin. "Good!"

"And," finished Iron Breast, "*I* am that one!"

Wapaha Jim had been thinking hard along a reluctant course, but his conclusion was definite. "No," he said soberly. "Not you, Iron Breast. They would not trust you. They could see what you are. Would a brave old warrior betray his people? They know he would not. They would shoot you and come on. *Ma-ya*, they shoot Sioux on sight, as I know! But if a white man went to them—a man they think is . . ."

"Wapaha—not you!" cried Yellow Eagle.

"Who could do this better?" Wapaha Jim countered. "I know their talk. I remember many of their ways. When I wear no feather and no paint, men can see that

I was not born a Sioux. I can tell them that I know the Indian camps. I can show them that I know the country well. I can guide them far away from your trail. Later I shall slip away from them and join you in the north."

Yellow Eagle kept shaking his head. "Mad—mad! You will be killed!" But the rest were nodding admiringly. Any kind of daring impudence appealed to them.

Bad Buffalo strode over and faced Wapaha Jim. "It would mean that you go alone, without me," he complained aggrievedly. "Are we not blood-brothers? Have we not sworn to die together when the time comes? No —let Iron Breast go!"

"I go." Wapaha Jim touched him briefly. "We shall be together again, after this is done. Perhaps I shall find a chance to avenge Luta-ho-ota before I leave them. Perhaps I shall learn which ones of them killed her. Will you lend me your gun? I broke mine on a soldier."

"Anything I have, Wapaha. . . ."

"Take mine," cut in Long Mane in his soft and tone-less voice. "It is a good gun, and I have plenty of bullets for it. I took it from a Crow. If you find those ones, Wapaha, use it. Use it for me. . . ."

Next morning in a near blizzard they struck camp, piled bag and baggage onto the patient pack-horses, and moved out. There was no singing, no noisy wrangling among the touchy old men, no lusty joking among the young. The very old and the very young rode muffled against the biting cold, their faces blue, whimpering quietly. The women were silent, the men grim. They had a long, long way to travel, up there to the big armed camp of Crazy Horse, warrior chief of the Sioux nations. Up there in the country of the mighty Yellowstone River. Up there where winter came from.

Wapaha Jim had made his farewells. He watched the

riding column and the drove of spare ponies go winding
off through the snow, and loneliness ran through him.
The abandoned campsite had a brooding air of desola-
tion and emptiness, and he had to shake off a heavy
sense of foreboding. The last group of riders, Yellow
Eagle and Bad Buffalo among them, turned and raised
their right arms in a last farewell to him. They were de-
pending on him. The whole band looked to him to see
that they got safely out of the country without running
afoul of the soldiers who sought them. From habit he
touched the beaded pouch that hung under his left arm-
pit, for luck. As an afterthought he removed it and
tucked it into his buckskin shirt. White men did not
wear war-charms.

He reined his pony around and rode eastward, following the river. The distance widened between himself and the travelling column, and at last, when he
looked back, he saw only the snow and the empty land.

CHAPTER 8

★

ATTACK AT DAWN

THE ARMY DETACHMENT RODE WESTWARD. "IF I TAKE THIS
command back to the fort and admit we never got a
sight of the enemy camp, Custer'll disown me," Vaugant had said that morning. So he made his decision
and disregarded his head injury. The dead and wounded
were started back for the fort, escorted by a dozen
troopers and a corporal who bore with him Vaugant's
report to the general.

The report was terse and written in haste: *All Indians hereabouts evidently hostile. Have had some trouble from raiders and spies probably from South Fork trying to delay us while main band escapes. Am pushing on to find camp. Will pursue if band has fled.*

He still had sixty-three men left in good shape and well mounted and armed, all hot to square accounts, but he regretted the loss of Sergeant M'Gill. "He knew this country better than any other man in the regiment," he told West Hathersall. "Used to be a guide for the emigrant trains before he joined us. But we'll come up with that bunch sooner or later, with all this snow on the ground. They can't hide their tracks, and they can't make fast time unless they abandon everything but their horses. They won't do that, not in this weather."

West Hathersall, being fairly fresh from West Point, was about to venture the opinion that the detachment was none too well equipped for a long pursuit, but the corporal riding behind broke in with a surprised oath and Vaugant snapped his reins tight. The detachment came to a halt. Everybody, all at about the same time, noticed the stranger on the pony, and at first look they took him for an Indian.

He sat his pony like an Indian, erect, unmoving, on the far side of the shallow river, gazing without expression at the cavalrymen. How long he had been sitting there, watching them as they advanced, they didn't know. Nobody had seen him appear. There were trees back of him, leafless and black against the snow-covered bank, and his total lack of movement helped make him invisible until they were almost directly opposite him. He could have come from anywhere, could have spied them long ago and calmly made his way here unseen to wait for them. Such a cool display of skill was an unspoken and irritating reproach, and it mutely charged the soldiers with blundering like greenhorns in the wilderness.

The corporal ungloved his hands in a hurry and slid his carbine from its saddle-boot. The action drew a warning command from Vaugant. "Take it easy. Damned if I don't believe he's a white man. Hey, you there! Where the devil did you crop up from?"

The stranger sent back no reply, but he pressed his knees slightly. His pony stepped carefully down the bank onto the frozen river and made its dainty way across. It wore an Indian saddle and bridle, very ab-breviated, designed for light and fast travel rather than comfort. The rider was garbed in plain buckskins, fur moccasins and a buffalo robe, and his black hair hung to his shoulders. He was tall and long-legged, but thick around the shoulders and neck. His eyes were a star-tling shade of grey, lightened by contrasting dark brown skin, and arrested immediate attention. They confirmed Vaugant's first impression that this was no Indian, or not a full-blooded one, at least.

"*Ni-ho . . .*" began the stranger, and closed his straight lips. But the slip passed, barely noticed. White trap-pers and hunters often used Indian phrases, dressed like Indians, even adopted Indian habits of thought. When next he spoke it was with slow care, as if the words did not come readily to him, and his speech construction was a little strange. "Do you look for the Indian camp?"

They regarded him in some bewilderment. For a lone white man to materialize casually in this hostile-haunted wilderness, and in winter, was unusual enough —as unusual as the enigmatic character of the man him-self. But for him to make his first remark a matter-of-fact question, dispensing with any kind of greeting, took them aback. He had an austere dignity, too, that by its cool aloofness discouraged at once any warm expressions on their part. His shaggy pony sniffed the foreign odors suspiciously, and rolled a wicked china-eye.

Vaugant stiffened, matching his manner to that of the stranger and trying to out-do it with a clipped curtness. "We do. You know where it is?"

"Yes. Follow me."

"Just a minute. Who are you? Where'd you come from? How do you know where it is?"

"My name is . . ." Wapaha Jim checked himself again. "Warbonnet," he said. "I can take you to the Indian camp." He gestured briefly. "That way."

"Across the river? You sure?"

"Yes. We can reach it tonight."

"You haven't told me yet where you came from."

"No," said Wapaha Jim, and looked through him. He knew that these were the same soldiers who had fired on him and Luta-ho-ota.

Vaugant studied him. He motioned to West and rode off with him a little way. "What d'you make of the fellow?" he inquired. "I've come across some queer birds here and there, but nothing to beat him. He's hiding from the law, I guess."

"That name he gave you." West shook his head. "Warbonnet!"

"Oh, a name means nothing out here. I don't hold that against him. Half the men you meet have had nicknames so long they've forgotten their own. But he's a mysterious cuss. Not a bit friendly, eh? I've got a feeling he'd like to knock out my teeth, damned if I haven't! Well, what's your opinion of him? You're my second-in-command, you know, and I'm supposed to confer with you occasionally."

West couldn't keep his eyes off the stranger. The man had something—a compelling quality and something else less easily identified—that fascinated him. "Why not let him prove what he says?" he suggested. "You don't downright distrust him, do you? After all, we can always keep a close watch on him. But I think he's straight. I like him, somehow."

"Can't say I share your taste," said Vaugant. "But we'll take him up on his offer. Can't lose more than a few hours, if it turns out he's faking us. I'll tip the men to keep their guns handy and their eyes on him, just in case. Frankly, I don't care for him a bit. Inasmuch as you like the fellow, you might drop a gentle word in his ear. Let him understand that if he's fooling us he'll never live to comb that long hair of his tomorrow morning!"

★

In darkness the detachment wound its way through a series of jumbled hills, every man on foot and leading his mount for quietness' sake. The troopers were tired and getting disgusted with the foot-work. West kept glancing doubtfully at Wapaha Jim, for no trail was anywhere visible in the snow and their course appeared to lead nowhere. Even to his inexperienced eyes these barren and deserted hills held no promise of Indian habitation.

Vaugant, who half leaned on his horse as he walked, and whose head kept falling forward, finally went to his knees in deep snow. He was in no condition to go on, and had not been for hours, but the responsibility of his command had kept him going. He waved West away when he tried to help him up, and he dragged his pistol from its holster.

Kneeling, holding with one hand onto the stirrup-leather of his horse, he moodily regarded the stranger who had volunteered as guide. "I ought've known better," he grumbled. "Knew the fellow was up to no good, minute I saw him." He levelled his pistol. His eyes were hard and bloodshot. "Damn it, Hathersall, stand out of the way!"

"If you shoot," said Wapaha Jim quietly, "the Indians will hear it." He made his glance purposely contemptuous, in the expert way of an Indian who desired to convey insult to one whom he especially disliked.

Vaugant held back the hammer of the pistol with his thumb. "What? You mean they're near? You lie!"

Wapaha Jim drew in his lips. "If you were not on your knees," he said in his careful manner, "it would be foolish of you to say that!" He shifted his cold look to West. "Come with me, quietly. Leave the others here. Or are you afraid?"

The cold contempt and the direct challenge took West off guard. He stuttered, stared. He remembered that he was an officer, and drew himself up. "Lead the way!"

"Keep your voice low," Wapaha Jim warned him in the same tone that he might have used to an inept youth on his first warpath. "Leave your sword behind. And take those noisy things off your boots."

He led the way, walking upright and noiseless until he passed through a fold that funnelled out onto an open downward slope, and then bent low, with a curt gesture for the officer to follow suit. He stopped, on hands and knees, unmoving, peering downward.

West crawled up beside him and uttered an exclamation. "By Joshua, you were right! Look at all those . . ."

Wapaha Jim motioned him silent. "Perhaps they keep watch," he murmured. He turned his head, smiling grimly. "There are your Indians, soldier—two hundred or more! They sleep, but they can wake fast, and they can fight. Send some of your men around to the other side of the . . ."

"I must report to Captain Vaugant. He's in command."

"A sick man in command? He is weak and his thoughts are not straight. He is not fit to lead."

"As long as he's got his senses he's in command," said West, and crawled back.

But when they rejoined the detachment, the troopers were bundling blankets around Vaugant, who lay shivering, his eyes shut and his teeth clenched. West bent over him and spoke to him, without getting any response. Vaugant's last resources of stubborn strength had run out. He was a little out of his head, mumbling parade-ground commands behind his teeth. The troopers looked worried. The captain was a tough man to soldier under, but he was able and he had their confidence. The lieutenant was a green hand and an unknown quantity. Grudgingly, they looked to the dark stranger and listened for what he might have to say. Civilians were lesser mortals and did not belong to their Army world, but this one knew his way around and they instinctively recognized him for a man with latent fighting ability.

West straightened up. He gave his belt a hitch, and just by the way he did it he got the full attention of the detachment. It was the unconscious action of an officer who had come to a decision. "What were you going to say back there?" he asked Wapaha Jim. "Frankly, I'd appreciate your advice. This is my first experience in active command, and I don't want to fail."

A reluctant respect for the young officer tempered Wapaha Jim's hostility toward him as a soldier. "Send some of your best shooters around to the other side of the valley," he said. "They must be careful and not be heard or seen. They must creep down as near to that little river as they can, and hide themselves along the bank. We will give them time to get there. Then we ride down from this side, and they shoot when the Indians come out of their lodges."

West nodded. "A good plan. But we don't attack unless the Indians prove themselves hostile by refusing to surrender."

"Surrender?" echoed Wapaha Jim. "How can you make them surrender without fighting them?"

"By demanding it, under threat of attack," replied West. "Our orders are to call on them to surrender, and not to take action unless they refuse. Those were the general's orders. We'll carry out your plan. When we've got it ready we'll wait for early daylight, and I'll go down and talk to their chief. His name is Black Horn, I believe."

He saw Wapaha Jim's queer expression. "You don't quite understand," he added, and smiled with some friendliness and a certain tolerance. "We're Army men. Our orders are to round up these people and shift them onto the reservations. To be frank, I hope they'll give us cause for action. But we must give them a chance to surrender, before we attack. You see?"

Wapaha Jim didn't see. This amazing precept didn't fit in with his opinion of white soldiers at all. It didn't fit into the normal Indian behavior, either. To give warning to an enemy before attacking him, after going to all the trouble of arranging a surprise, and particularly when he outnumbered you, was a thing unheard of. It was unreasonable. To amble into his camp and suggest that he meekly give up without an armed contest was simply the ludicrous act of a madman tired of life.

"They will kill you, of course," he pointed out. "Do you *want* to die?"

"No, I don't," West admitted. "But that's a risk that must be taken. I can't hang back and send in one of my men. Do you speak their language? I was hoping you might come with me and act as my interpreter."

"They know me. I could do you no good." Wapaha Jim shook his head. "They would kill quicker if I went with you. Do you know Spanish? Then you need no interpreter. But they will not give you time to speak."

★

It struck Wapaha Jim as the most foolish action that he had ever seen, and perhaps the most wastefully gallant, the way the young lieutenant paced his horse at a parade walk down into the valley of the Indian camp. The man was throwing himself away. The camp was astir with the dawn. There would be no smashing surprise for sleeping men.

The blue-uniformed horseman made a trim showing, with his sword and gilt buttons, his black campaign hat at just the right West Point tilt, his left hand gloved and gauntletted and his right resting lightly on his thigh. A correct figure. He could have been paying an official call upon a neighboring Army post. Such misgivings as he felt, he kept shielded behind a calm West Point mask. Orders were orders. Captain Vaugant, perhaps, would have thought twice before riding down alone into that armed camp; would have combined some independent initiative with his orders and made his explanations later to the general. But the captain lay tossing and mumbling in a cocoon of blankets, guarded by four troopers, and Lieutenant Weston Hathersall retained a very clear memory of the general's instructions. They had been explicit. He would obey.

His lack of hurry enabled him to continue his descent unnoticed until near the bottom floor of the valley. Then somebody shouted.

It was queer how the single shout altered the whole aspect of the camp. For a short moment there were flitting movements of dark figures over the snow, and some noise. By the time the horseman reached the outskirts of the camp he had before him a mob of armed men. He misunderstood their astounded hush. Not knowing Indians, not knowing that these were marauders by trade and killers by choice, he was encouraged by the reception.

He looked them over. These were fairly reasonable savages, after all, despite appearances and tales to the contrary. Possibly it was his uniform that impressed them, he thought. He had always known that the Army uniform was a potent factor in giving its wearer a domination and an advantage over other men. This was going to be no real trouble at all. He would shepherd this bunch to Fort Lincoln, and the general would no doubt publicly commend him for handling the matter so efficiently. A bit of action would have suited him better, but judgment told him that was best avoided, seeing that there were so many well-armed warriors in the camp.

He raised his right hand. "*Dondé está . . .*" He voiced in halting Spanish the request that he had mentally prepared as he rode down. "Where is your chief? I wish to speak to him."

Perhaps they understood his school Spanish, perhaps not, but it made no difference, as Wapaha Jim had well known. Nothing that he could have said in any language had the power to stave off the inevitable. He was a white man and a stranger. He wore a dress of white authority, and there was an irrational air of placid arrogance in his manner. He was condemned from the start.

"I am an officer," he added, and that settled it.

They jumped him. So many of them enthusiastically lunged for him at the same time, they swamped him and got into one another's way, and from up in the hills it looked something like a live animal suddenly caught and heaving under a ragged blanket. Parts of him and his horse could be glimpsed, slashing and rearing about, but not much of him at any time. The Indians were not paying him the compliment of running him through with spear or knife. They were beating him to death, and enjoying it.

Wapaha Jim heeled his pony over the slope, and his high, ringing whoop was automatic, as natural as breathing. The trumpeter, with orders from nobody, pealed out the charge, and the troopers followed the wild man in a rush. The horses took on speed and abandon, thundering down the slope, and every man raised the long cavalry yell, while down in the valley and across the stream a volley of gunfire ripped from along the hidden line of dismounted sharpshooters. The aspect of the camp underwent another shift.

The Indians were caught by surprise, but their recovery was swift. They melted from the shouting, striking melee and raced for cover, to shoot from behind trees and any obstruction they could find. Some of them made for the river and the low bank, but the furious fire of the soldiers hugging the ground on the other side drove them back. It was left for the shrieking women to run to the pony herd up the valley; the soldiers picked off every man they could get their sights on, running that way.

West Hathersall lay under his killed horse, his hat gone, his sword and belt stolen from him, and his face clawed and bleeding. But he still had his pistol, and he squirmed around with it in his hand, trying to stand off a homicidal pair who skuttled crab-like over the ground to get at him from the blind side of the dead horse. Wapaha Jim slung a rifle shot at the pair, and he had long ago mastered the Indian art of shooting accurately while at full gallop. One of the pair slapped a hand to his chest and stood up howling. The other discarded all caution and made his leaping run for the

pinned officer. The pony clattered abreast of him and
a muscular hand grasped him by his knotted hair. Wapaha Jim hurled him ahead and rode him down.

He dragged to a halt by the dead horse. "Soldier, you
wanted a fight," he called. "You got one!"

West strained to free himself. "Sure have! Pull this
horse off me, will you? Thanks. Where's the trumpeter?
Oh, trumpeter! Sound the rally! Curse it, I can't stand
on my legs."

The troopers were all spread out, fighting without a
leader, every man for himself, and this was the kind of
fight made for Indians. The tribesmen darted in and
out, back and forth in small groups, attending to one
enemy at a time, and they quickly learned to avoid the
fire of the shooters across the stream. The trumpeter
heard the lieutenant's command and did his best to
sound the rally, but a bullet hit his trumpet at the
mouthpiece and knocked it spinning. He ducked, a hand
clapped over his mouth, glaring resentfully about him.
A corporal began yelling and beckoning to the scattered men to close in, but his voice was lost in the uproar.

West got up as far as his bruised legs would let him,
and added his shouted commands to those of the corporal. The attack was a failure, but he knew what might
still be done to save the detachment, if he could only
do it. "Get together—form defense! Warbonnet! Get
them together, for God's sake, or it's a massacre!"

Wapaha Jim tried no such thing. It was too hopeless
a task. Half the men were already cut off and would
have to fight their way to any gathering point, no matter where it might be. Most of them had their hands
full, trying to stand off personal disaster. He took to
the river and raced his pony along the bank, snatched
the blanket from a snarling old woman on his way, and
made for the pony-herd. Dividing hatreds were for the

time forgotten, and the issue of the fight was his one concern. He launched across the flanks of the disturbed herd, dodging the screaming women who struck at him, and waving the blanket. Not much of that was needed. The ponies, with a hang-over recollection of a recent terrifying experience with waving blankets, lit out in a mass bolt up the valley, and Wapaha Jim crossed the stream and turned back.

He rode down the line of sharpshooting cavalrymen on the south bank, who couldn't see more than a fraction of what was going on over on the other side of the camp. "*Hiyupo!*" he shouted to them, and they understood his gesture, if not his imperative Sioux call to battle.

They rose and followed him at a foot charge across the stream and into the fight, and somebody raised the cavalry yell again. When they stormed through the camp they were a unit, a hard core that could not easily be split apart. West Hathersall barked commands as they roared past him, but right now they were following the lead of somebody else, and they didn't hear him. The brush and cottonwoods spilled tribesmen ahead of them, and isolated troopers who had been fighting for their lives joined the charging squad. It became a moving focal point, gathering strength in numbers as it advanced, scouring the coverts of Indians and breaking up one nest after another.

But it was the stampeding of the pony-herd that took the Indians' minds off victory and discouraged them from continuing the fight. Soon the troopers were shooting at long distance up the valley at Indians chasing ponies, and Wapaha Jim rode over to West Hathersall.

They looked at each other, muddied and war-torn, and both grinned. "Joshua, that was a scrap!" said West. "You certainly know this business, don't you? Thanks.

Vaugant couldn't have done better. Anything wrong?
Lost something?"

"Yes, I lost . . ." Wapaha Jim closed his lips. It would
hardly do to tell this white officer that he—another white
man—had lost his war-charm. "It is nothing," he
amended, but he kept his eyes searching over the
ground.

"Where'll those hostiles go, d'you think?" West asked.

"They will come back here, if we leave their camp
standing," answered Wapaha Jim absently, still searching. "Destroy it, and they will go back south where they
came from."

West puzzled over that for awhile. "South, you said?
I didn't know there were Sioux in the south."

Wapaha Jim glanced at him. "These were Comanches," he murmured. "Were you looking for Sioux?"

CHAPTER 9

★

ARMY SCOUT

THE GENERAL STOOD UP AND SHOOK HANDS VERY WARMLY.
"I want to assure you of the thanks and compliments
of all Fort Lincoln, Mr.—er—Warbonnet," he said, and
went on to quote from the reports of the detachment's
officers. The report of Captain Vaugant was necessarily
brief concerning the fight at the camp, but his second-
in-command had handed in a full and stirring account
of it.

" '. . . Not only did he successfully guide us to the
hostile camp. When our men were without leadership,

due to the incapacitation of both Captain Vaugant and myself, he took over command and by his masterly handling and personal bravery undoubtedly saved the whole detachment from disaster,'" read the general aloud. "'After destroying the enemy's camp, I persuaded him to continue as guide and adviser until we should reach the fort, as we had several wounded and we wished to avoid further action. It is my opinion that Mr. Warbonnet should be offered some position in the Army, in a responsible attachment commensurate with his ability, for he is an extremely valuable man.'"

The general put down the report, smiling. "It would appear that you have made a very deep impression upon Lieutenant Hathersall," he observed.

For the first time that name plucked a chord of dim memory in Wapaha Jim. "Hathersall?" he echoed, and then it came back to him and he remembered. Those people who had started out for Oregon with his father and himself . . . Mist' Sam, and young West, and that kid girl—Tally—and Miz' Hathersall. The name gave him a tiny shock. Queer, to come upon it again so soon after meeting white men. Perhaps the officer was a relative of those other Hathersalls.

The general eyed him curiously. "Did you know beforehand that it was a Comanche camp?"

"Yes."

"Didn't you know that the detachment was looking for Sioux?"

"Captain Vaugant said he was looking for Indians. I guided him to the nearest camp. Comanches are Indians."

"And hostile!" agreed the general. "The fact that they weren't Sioux by no means detracts from the value of the action. I'm glad to get the devils out of this territory before we go out on campaign. Could I persuade you to accept a position as special scout? There's a big campaign coming up, and sometimes one good plainsman is worth a regiment. Lord knows we need reliable scouts." He ran his eyes over the worn buckskins and moccasins. "I presume you're pretty well acquainted with the tribes and some of their camp locations?"

"I know Indians," Wápaha Jim admitted. "Is your campaign to be against the Sioux?"

He wished to know for certain. Why he had come all the way in to the fort he hardly knew, but it had been with no thought of engaging as a permanent scout on the payroll. He had told himself that it might enable him to pick up a little information that would be of use to the Sioux in avoiding any trap set for them by the soldiers. But now, true to his Indian training, he stood ready to shape his future course according to change of circumstances. He waited for the general's reply.

The general nodded. "Sioux and Cheyennes, mostly. They're getting ready for the warpath again, as perhaps you know, and they've defied the order to move to the reservations. I can't say exactly when we'll move out. General Sheridan is supervising all operations. General Crook will take to the field first, from Fort Fetterman. He'll probably ask to borrow you, when he hears about you and what you did to those Comanches. Well, can I sign you on as special government scout?"

"Yes, General."

"Fine! And your name is . . ."

"Jim Warbonnet."

He turned to leave, and an icy touch flicked him when he found a soldier at the door. It was a new and unpleasant sensation for him, and he knew that it stemmed from inner guilt. But the soldier was an orderly and he opened the door respectfully for the stranger that all Fort Lincoln was discussing. Wapaha Jim left the general's quarters, angrily bludgeoning his unreasonable conscience. Weren't these soldiers the enemies of his

Sioux friends? Hadn't they come to drive his people from the land of their inheritance? Invaders, all of them. He was exasperated at having to convince himself that he was right and justified in what he was doing. White men could later call him a renegade, but his own people would honor him and that was all that mattered.

But the sense of guilt refused to be placated by logic, and he presented a forbidding demeanor when he stepped out onto the gallery. It was getting dusk, and the chairs along the galleries of Officers' Row were filling with the usual evening groups idling before the dinner hour. Feminine eyes, old and young, regarded him obliquely with lively interest. The men sent him friendly nods, hid their curiosity until his back was turned, and wagged their heads at the whispering women. They had all seen him come riding in with the battered detachment, and Hathersall's story had gone the rounds. He cut a strange and striking figure, tall and dark, long-haired, a knife and pistol belted to his flapping buckskins, walking with a peculiarly soft stride. He didn't turn out his toes as white men did, and he balanced his weight on the balls of his feet, giving an impression of springy energy held in reserve. Many of them recognized it as the stride of an Indian.

"If it weren't for those eyes and a few other details, I'd swear the man's an Indian," murmured the adjutant of Company B. "And a hostile, at that! Wonder how many scalps he's taken in his time?"

A lady shuddered delicately. "I consider that in very bad taste, and most unjust. He's not an Indian savage."

"He's a white savage, dear lady, make no mistake about it," drawled the adjutant. "When a man like that throws off civilization he's pretty thorough. I'd like to know his story."

"You'll never know it," put in somebody. "Hathersall says you can't get him to spill a word about himself. He

tried. Why, even the name he gives—Warbonnet—think
of it! He's a mystery. You come across them occasionally, here and there. But he may be just a trapper playing a lone hand and hiding from an indiscreet past.
That's what Vaugant thinks. Vaugant, I suspect, doesn't
like him. He's glum about missing the fight and losing
his Sioux. Hard luck, all right."

A trooper clicked to a halt before Wapaha Jim. "Lieutenant Hathersall's compliments, and he invites you to
join him for dinner in his quarters," he rattled off, and
after a second's indecision, ". . . sir," he added, and
saluted.

It was a gratuitous gesture of respect, rather than a
required formality, and Wapaha Jim realized it. He was
no officer and rated no salute. These white soldiers, in
their conservative way, were making much of him for
what he had done with the detachment. He considered
that Hathersall had quite overrated that fight and given
out entirely too much praise. It reminded him of a time
when he and Bad Buffalo had ridden home from a raid,
bringing sixteen captured Crow ponies, and Bad Buffalo had announced to everybody that it was his good
friend—Wapaha—who had done it all.

It brought to him the same warm and embarrassed
feeling.

★

West said seriously, "Tally, if you'd rather not go
through with it, I won't mind."

"Didn't you invite me to dinner?" inquired Tally.
"And got me to cook it for you!" she added.

"Yes, but it's just that I'm wondering if—well—you
may find him a little unusual. He's obviously lived an
outlandish kind of life. He may not be—er . . ."

Tally took pity on his stammering earnestness. "You

mean his table manners may be slightly unorthodox?"

"Well—yes."

"Does he growl when he eats meat?"

"Really, Tally—!"

She laughed at him. He lay on the couch, and she went and sat by him. "You like him, West, don't you? So do I, what I've seen and heard of him. I saw him from the window. He looks capable of anything. There's a wildness about him that sort of takes your breath away. But he doesn't strike me as crude. Put him in some civilized clothes and cut off some of that long hair, and he'd pass for a gentleman anywhere. A handsome one, too, I might add. You're not going to frighten me away with his table manners. I want to meet him."

West was worried. There was a streak in Tally that he didn't quite trust, and it came out at unexpected times in a bubble of high spirits that contrasted oddly with her usual quiet reserve. It was as if a pagan and provocative fire smoldered in her, well tamped down until something happened to fan it, and then at such times West feared that almost anything might happen.

She ruffled his hair, and he knew that this was one of the times. "I'm going to get him to talk about himself," she said. "It'll be a lovely evening. I'll exert my softest charms on him and melt that wild heart of his. Or do wild hearts get wilder when they're charmed? What a picture! Maybe he'll let out a whoop in the middle of dinner, and jump into a stomp-dance like those Indians up at . . ."

West uttered a strangled grunt and said loudly, "Oh —hello!"

Wapaha Jim, standing stiff and silent in the open doorway, looked at the girl. He watched her go white and then blush crimson, and he thought that he had never seen anything so lovely, nor anything that angered him so deeply. To knock on the open door simply had not occurred to him, and he had heard what she said about him.

So this was the extent of white people's hospitality. In their impudent assumption of superiority they would attempt to trick him into making a show of himself.

"Come in, old man—come in!" cried West, desperately trying to be hearty.

Wapaha Jim entered. The cult of Indian good manners demanded that he betray nothing of his feelings, but there were ways and manners of delivering stinging rebukes without stepping beyond the bounds of cold courtesy. This fort, crude and restricted enough in its graces and conveniences, to him appeared royally splendid, and it had put an uneasiness upon him. He had vaguely resented what it did to his inner poise. Now his resentment crystallized, and he let it have its way with him. The place was foreign, and these people were aliens.

He groped back in memory for the teachings of his father, recalling what he could of white manners. Gravely, he bowed to the girl, his eyes chill and gazing through her.

"M-my sister," West stammered, red-faced. "Sorry I can't get up. Legs still sore. Wrenched 'em when my horse fell on me, y'know."

Wapaha Jim merely nodded. He drew a keenly malicious pleasure from their horrible discomfort, and did nothing to help them out of it. Deliberately, he added to it with his stony silence, and now he was master of the situation. They were awkward; he was poised. His frigid dignity turned them into children.

Dinner began under a pall. Memory served Wapaha Jim, reminding him of the uses of knife and fork, which he manipulated with slow and scrupulous care. It was easy for him to eat in dead silence; it was the natural

Indian custom. The table had been drawn up to the couch to accommodate West.

Nervous and ill at ease, West repeatedly failed to kindle conversation. He was furious with his sister. "I'm afraid the bread is a little heavy," he remarked, with a vengeful look at her. "My sister has not yet learned the art of making the best of Army rations."

Wapaha Jim munched slowly and swallowed before passing any comment, and that was Indian habit, too. Also, it gave him time to make mental search through the little shagreen book. "'Charm needs no art,'" he quoted dryly, and astonished them both.

He saw a hot flicker in the eyes of the girl, and correctly read it as a sign of rebellion. She had taken all she intended to take of subtle rebuke. She was gathering up her weapons. He respected her for that. To accept punishment in a humble and cringing spirit—even just punishment—had never appealed to him, either in himself or in anyone else. He prepared to meet a counter-attack.

West, sensing conflict in the offing, did what he could to head it off. He frantically sought inspiration, and found it when his gaze lighted on the mandolin hanging on the wall. "My sister will play for you later," he blurted rapidly. "She's queerly a right—uh—really a quite accomplished musician. Very. Plays everything. Sings, too. I mean, everything on the mandolin."

"Not everything," Tally corrected him modestly, and smiled innocently across the table. "I don't know any Indian songs. Perhaps Mr. Warbonnet will teach me some, and I'll sing them to him."

Wapaha Jim glanced solemnly at the mandolin and back to the girl. "Will you also dance for me?" he murmured, and held her eyes with his own.

She bit her lip, but it began to tremble, and her eyes grew very bright. She struggled visibly for control, but lost. Suddenly she was laughing helplessly, richly, her face glowing and her lips apart, and she looked like a lovely child.

Her laughter sprang a release in Wapaha Jim. It unloosed a rush of freed emotions that lifted him up, swept him along into laughter as abandoned as hers. He had not given way so boyishly to mirth in years, and he did not understand it, and did not try. It cleansed him of all resentment, and the sheer and unexpected joy of it ran through him like a sparkling flood. In this moment he was a white man sharing the gay humor of an attractive white girl. Their laughter filled the small house, overflowed into the dark and empty parade ground, and desultory talkers outside along the galleries hushed to listen to it. West gazed back and forth at them, blinking, befuddled, but vastly relieved. He didn't know what exactly had brought on the happy explosion, but he caught the infection and laughed with them.

Later, clearing the table while the two men smoked, Tally caught Wapaha Jim's eye. Both smiled without reserve. "I'm glad I couldn't keep from laughing," she confessed. "I suppose it was nervous reaction. You know now I didn't mean what you heard me say about you, don't you? I was just teasing West because he was being so serious and . . . What's the matter? Have I said something?"

"West?" Wapaha Jim picked up his lighted cigar from the floor. "Is that your name, Hathersall?" He had jerked badly. Now he held himself steady.

West had noticed nothing amiss. He nodded. "Short for Weston. What's yours?"

"It's . . . Jim."

"Oh, grand! Favorite name with us. We once knew a Jim. Didn't we, Tally?"

Wapaha Jim sat very still. The cigar split between his

fingers. It was cautious instinct rather than reason that held him mute. Tally was regarding him questioningly. Her susceptibilities were more acute than those of her brother.

"Yes, we knew a Jim," she said. "Jim Aherne—a boy. He was with us when Indians attacked us on the way to Oregon, years ago. West and I were the only ones who escaped. Do—do Indians always kill prisoners, Mr. Warbonnet?"

"Of course they do!" rapped West. "The treacherous, black-hearted murderers!"

Wapaha Jim tossed his ruined cigar into the fire with a quick flirt of his hand. The old angry resentment came crowding back, and he was Indian again. "Not always!" He looked straight at West. "Not all Indians. And they do not kill women on sight!"

West winced at the unexpected thrust. "You heard about that? It was a mistake. I've been sick about that ever since it happened." He shook his head at Tally. "You shouldn't hear about such things. But troopers do talk, and stories get around. We fired on two hostiles who came to spy on our camp, and killed one. We learned later it was a woman."

"Oh—how dreadful!"

"The man—a perfect devil—got away and took the body with him," West went on hastily. "We found a pistol that the woman dropped. It belonged to a man of ours, a deserter we found murdered. The Indian with the woman put up a terrible fight. Actually charged a party of ours and smashed it up, all alone."

"Perhaps," suggested Wapaha Jim roughly, "he loved the woman."

West nodded uncertainly. "Uh—yes. I've thought of that." He changed the subject. "You're putting up here in my quarters with me, you know. I insist. Plenty enough room. Tally is staying with the Chittendons, but she comes in and cooks for me. Very nice sister, I may say."

Tally continued her searching regard of Wapaha Jim. "Have you ever heard of that boy?" she asked. "I mean the boy we spoke of—Jim Aherne. I can never quite make myself believe that they killed him. Don't they sometimes adopt captive boys into their tribes? I've heard that they . . . Oh, hello, Captain. Shouldn't you be in hospital?"

Captain Vaugant, entering in the informal fashion of a brother officer, slumped into the nearest chair and touched his bandaged head. "I slipped out for awhile. What were you saying as I came in? Wondering if your old childhood love might have become a red brave with feathers in his hair, eh?"

"Your sense of humor is a little warped tonight, Captain," observed Tally.

Vaugant laughed shortly. His mood was not pleasant. "What's your opinion, Warbonnet?" he drawled. "Isn't that what the boy would be now, if they let him live? Most men are savages at heart, anyway, regardless of color. I once met a squaw man who'd lived with the Indians so long he was practically one of them. He even offered his pipe to the sun every time he took a smoke. Why, I wager you do that, yourself, when nobody's looking! And that ugly knife of yours—you don't carry it just for cutting plug tobacco, do you?"

Wapaha Jim let his gaze drift to the captain's head, to the patch of wavy brown hair not covered by the bandage. "I have used it to cut fur from animals," he said, and Vaugant narrowed his eyes dangerously.

"Play something," West said muffledly to Tally.

Ordinarily, Vaugant would have sprung to his feet and brought the mandolin, but his pain and temper drove courtesy out of him. "I heard some loud laughing going on here awhile ago," he remarked. "Could hear it right over at the hospital. Did I miss a good joke?"

"A very good joke," replied Tally, settling down with the mandolin. She sent him a steady look and said no more.

His jaw went tight. "Was it about your Jim Aherne? That reminds me—a rumor has cropped up that there's a white renegade among the hostiles. Two of our men swear on oath that a red fellow who charged our camp was really a white man in paint and feathers. He had grey eyes, they say. He may be your old girlhood flame, who knows?"

He levelled a stare at Wapaha Jim. "God help him when we catch him, no matter who he is! A renegade is . . ."

Tally struck a loud chord, began singing, and more company came drifting in to sit around and listen. They greeted Wapaha Jim, the officers and ladies alike, and he shook hands with several. But he was not one of them. Vaugant's words echoed in him. Regardless of their ready friendship, regardless of Tally and West, this was a camp of enemies who would pounce on him and kill him if ever they discovered who and what he was. Loneliness swamped in on him, as black as it had come to him when he parted from the Sioux on the bank of the South Fork.

He listened broodingly to the singer, and wished that she were not lovely and not Tally Hathersall.

★

THE BUCKSKIN POUCH

IN THE SAME WEEK THAT COMPANY A ANNOUNCED PREPA-
rations for a ball to be given the following Friday night,
the commander of the Department of the Platte arrived to hold inspection of the garrison. However, being
an understanding man, and knowing that this might be
the last dance before the campaign got under way, he
let it be known that he would cut short his visit and
leave on that Thursday. The whole regiment went out
on mounted parade, displayed its maneuvers and glittered its best on the flat stretch of plain outside the
fort.

Glossy horses marched through their paces, guidons
fluttered, the regimental band played "Garry Owen,"
and the trim cavalrymen showed the stern invincibility
of well-trained and spirited troops who took pride in
their calling. The department commander complimented
them, told them that they were the flower of the Army
—which they already knew—and afterward asked to
meet the remarkable Scout Warbonnet of whom he had
heard so much.

"Any civilian able to take command of a detachment
and take it through a successful action, as you say this
man did, is certainly worth meeting," he remarked.

He said much the same to Wapaha Jim when he
met him, and by inference implied that he had not pre-
viously entertained a very high regard for untrained

121

civilians as compared with Army regulars. He inspected the new scout from moccasins to long hair, all the length of him. His quick eyes said here was a piece of splendid material fashioned by nature to fit into a double-buttoned blue coat and a wide campaign hat.

"I shall recommend you for brevet rank," he promised, and the officers grouped behind him took notice. The commander had the reputation of being a swift picker of the right men.

West had to explain later to Wapaha Jim the meaning of brevet rank. "It's honorary. Your scout pay isn't affected, but your rank will be recognized as that of an officer. Shake, old man. Congratulations!"

Others added their congratulations, and Major Chittendon offered some advice tinged with dry cynicism. "Getting brevetted can be a short-cut around West Point," he said. "This seems to be an age of short-cuts. I can't say I approve, but you might as well take advantage of opportunity. Stay with it, and you'll probably wind up with a sword and regular commission. These Indian campaigns offer as many chances for quick advancement as the Civil War. Humph! I think I'll retire next year and write that book on cavalry tactics. Not that it'll ever be read. All a cavalry officer needs these days is a good horse, a hard head, and an eye for shooting!" He was always vowing to retire and write his book.

Wapaha Jim lived with a state of mind that became more torn and divided as time went on. Hard as he tried not to, he couldn't help liking practically everybody with whom he came into contact around the fort. They went out of their way to be friendly. The older ones included him in their conversations, and the younger ones sometimes embarrassed him with their frankly respectful regard. They voted him a natural-born cavalryman, than which there could be no higher compliment, and welcomed him into their select caste. He was a novelty, a source of curiosity, and they never tired of speculating about him.

Unwillingly, he was drawing close to them, and he could not rid himself of the sensation that he was among his own kind. It grew upon him, and he found himself changing his attitude and many of his opinions. Often he came to reality with a start, to find that he had been relaxed and smiling with some group, wholly forgetful of the coming campaign and the part that he must play in it.

No thought of rootless impermanence had ever troubled him when moving constantly about the country with the Sioux, but now insecurity plagued him whenever he recalled unyielding facts and the cause for which he secretly stood. He wondered if this was an omen. Warriors, when they received such forebodings, accepted them for what they were and knew that they were soon to die. He thought of his war-charm, the little shagreen book in the beaded pouch, lost in the Comanche fight. With it, perhaps, had gone his luck. He considered it likely that all things would end for him soon.

He pondered a good deal over the puzzle of the soldiers. They were not malignant, not as vengeful as he had imagined them. Hatred played little part in their attitude toward war. When they spoke of hostile Indians it was in a mood of tolerant condemnation, much in the same impersonal language that they used in speaking of bears and mountain lions. A lion could be admired for his savage fighting ability, and so could an Indian.

"I tell you, gentlemen, old Red Cloud could've taught us a few tricks. That red rascal knew his trade. And those fighting fools who rode with him! Finest light cavalry on earth, if they'd been properly trained, y'know."

"Sitting Bull has a thousand or so of that same kind, so they say. They'll put up a fight."

"Not a doubt of it, not a doubt of it. But we'll break 'em up and be back in time for summer furloughs."

A nodding of heads. These men were more than confident. They were certain of themselves. And then somebody would bring up the old subject of misinformed folks back East.

"On my last trip home I tried to correct some of their notions about Indians, but they went right on with them. Yes, the newspapers. Gentlemen, there's no more bloodthirsty animal than a penny-a-liner, but some of our politicians run them mighty close, mighty close. I heard more grisly yarns about Indians on that trip home than I ever came across in all my years of fighting 'em here in the West! I finally gave up. Couldn't convince anybody that Indians do fight like men once in awhile."

"Oh, the Indian is an ugly customer in a scrap, all right," somebody else would grant. "But give me any two companies of the Seventh, and I'll ride right through the whole Sioux nation. What's your opinion, Mr. Warbonnet?"

"Yes, Colonel. But the real fighting would not begin until you tried to ride back."

They laughed, regarding that kind of remark as a quiet joke. "Never turn your back on an Indian, eh? Right!"

And then the ladies would join them, and by an unwritten law all reference to war immediately became taboo. Music, cards, and light conversation from then on. Feminine ears must not be distressed by violent subjects. The world must be kept a pleasantly colored bubble for the ladies. The ladies subscribed to the gallant deception, maintained a delicate horror of swords

and guns, and rarely let slip their surprising comprehension of the grimmer side of Army life. They knew
what their men were here for, but one never mentioned
such things during the mixed social hours.

Strangely enough, it was soured old Major Chittendon who more or less unwittingly analyzed Wapaha
Jim's problem for him and did much to clarify his understanding, in a talk they had one night when they
came upon each other down by the river. It was a few
hours after the department commander left, and Wapaha Jim wanted solitude in which to think things out.
The major, a chronically solitary soul, was none too
pleased at this invasion of what he considered his own
private promenade.

"G'even'," he grumped shortly, and stopped to let Wapaha Jim pass on, so that he wouldn't have to share his
evening walk with him. But he had come out without
matches, and his desire for a cigar got the better of his
austerity. "Got a match with you? Thanks. Hum . . .
smoke?"

So they walked on in the same direction, smoking,
the black old Missouri rolling noiselessly by them. The
major was mollified by his companion's silence, but
after awhile it began to irritate him. Taciturnity was his
own prerogative; he did not care to have the initiative
thus taken from him. "Getting cold," he said, and that
reminded him to look up at the small infantry post on
the bluffs above the fort. It stood alone against the
night sky, a few tiny lights in a setting of square black
buildings. "Why they ever built that place up there
I'll never know. Like an icebox in winter. The poor
devils catch every wind. Why an infantry post, anyway? Huh! This country's for mounted men."

Wapaha Jim roused from his reverie. The cigar was
good. He had developed a taste for them. "I've heard

Indians say, 'If you have no horse, find a hill,' " he mentioned.

"Huh? Not bad, that. You've had a good deal to do with Indians, I take it. Queer people. We'll never understand them. No use trying. Only thing is to force them onto the reservations and govern them with a strong hand till they learn to behave themselves according to our standards. Should've been done long ago. All that shilly-shally with treaties—pah! What's it led to? More war. More dirty work for the Army. It's a thankless job we've got, but it's got to be done right this time of we're ever to have peace on the plains."

"I saw peace on the plains before I ever saw soldiers," returned Wapaha Jim.

The major glanced aside at him and puffed his cigar to a glow. "Hum! Maybe so, maybe so. I begin to suspect, sir, that you're some kind of idealist. Well, that's not to your discredit. Every man to his creed. The Army has its ideals, too."

"To kill or capture the Indians and take their lands?"

"That's a blunt way to put it." The major looked about him. "Let's sit a spell. Damned boots hurt me. New. Forgot to change 'em after parade." He settled on a hump, pulling his greatcoat about him and stretching his feet. "The Army's ideals, sir, don't necessarily run to killing. This is a police job we're doing. We're out here to put this country under protection."

"It needed no such protection before the white man came," Wapaha Jim reminded him.

"True," agreed the major. "But we did come. Young man, the history of the world is a long story of shifting peoples. Frontiers are never permanent. Remember that, in your idealism. Primitive races have always had to give ground to the more progressive peoples. It's an inevitable process. Would you have a few thousand savages hold onto half an empire for a hunting ground, when it could probably support a million fairly civilized white people?"

"The Indians have a right to keep their land," insisted Wapaha Jim.

"True again—in a legal sense," the major conceded. "They were here before us. And a couple of thousand years ago they probably chased out somebody else who was here before them. So it goes. When it's a matter of the greatest good for the greatest number, legality has no standing. Your Indians are fighting a lost cause. It was lost a million years ago, when the first thinking man reared up on his hind legs and brained his backward neighbor with a stone club because there wasn't enough meat for both of them. It's their misfortune that they've remained backward savages while the rest of the world grew a bit more civilized."

"Sometimes the savage brains the civilized man, Major."

"That's merely a slip-back. Sometimes the wrong kind of white people run amuck, too, and raise hell for a time. But civilization always recovers and goes on— pin your idealism to that. The Indian is a tough little man trying to hold back time and the world. He may get in a lick here and there, but he can't win." The major rose, rubbing his thin fingers. "Chilly. I'm going in. Hum . . . I wouldn't advise airing your broad views on the Indian question around the fort. Soldiers have only one opinion on the subject, otherwise they wouldn't be good soldiers. G'night. Damn these boots."

★

Considering the narrow resources at hand, Company A made fine work of the ball, everybody agreed. It was held in the barracks, that being the only building large enough to accommodate dancing, and the soldiers' bunks were removed to give more room. Arms had been stacked, the proud guidons and silk standards—blue and yellow—hung from their lances in groups, and flags bloomed from the ceiling and walls of the long room.

There was only the sutler's store to draw upon for ornamental materials, and the sutler was not equipped to provide much help, but ingenuity flourished mightily on colored paper and cracker-boxes. The large picture of President Grant was wreathed in green-paper laurel leaves, and the cracker-boxes, when carved, made excellent chandeliers and side brackets for oil lamps and candles. The big fireplaces, one at each end, threw out a cheerful warmth from the burning logs. Fiddles and a guitar supplied the music. An enormous sergeant with the best voice in the regiment sang out the dance calls.

"Oh, swing those girls, those pretty little girls. . . ."

The officers and their ladies formed a set at one end of the room and gave themselves over to fun. The enlisted men raised a swirling racket with their wives and the maids and the women of Laundress Row, all dressed in their best, and a proper decorum surviving in spite of ebullient gaiety. Uniforms and braid added a sparkling smartness to the quadrilles, and by contrast enhanced the soft feminism of demure chintzes and silk gowns brought out specially for the occasion. When the quadrilles gave way to the waltzing, all combined to effect an illusion of slow grace and beauty.

Wapaha Jim felt completely out of place, as conspicuous as a bull buffalo in a pasture of sensitive thoroughbred horses. Yet he was captivated by it, and had never seen anything like it. This he conceived to be the high mark of white culture, so high that it left him giddy and gazing up hopelessly at it. But it challenged him, too, because it placed him upon an inferior footing and offended his healthy ego. At first the waltz looked intricate to him, but he studied the steps while he stood

obscurely in a corner, and soon he caught onto the
rhythm. Dancing was an integral part of Indian life,
and many times he had danced for hours with brother
warriors to celebrate a coup.

He was moving his feet experimentally when he
found Tally gazing at him oddly from across the room,
and he stiffened, flushing. Tally was dancing with a
young pleb who seemed in a trance, and the eyes of
every disengaged young officer followed her wistfully as
she swayed by. She was dressed in a highwaisted gown
of flowered foulard silk, tight in the bodice, full and
long in the skirt, that somehow made her look as small
and dainty as a grave little girl wearing party dress for
the first time. Her gaze on Wapaha Jim was direct and
reflective, and it took no deep perspicacity to divine
that she was contemplating something for his benefit.
Before she and the entranced pleb could circle around
to where he stood, Wapaha Jim beat an orderly retreat
along the wall and got outside. He was scared. There
was no telling what Tally might have in mind, he had
learned.

It was dark outside, and when he moved out of the
radius of the lighted windows he had a comforting
sense of invisibility. He could still hear the music, and
the rhythm was still in his feet. Seriously, he took up
his tentative experimenting where he had left off. Three
little steps on the toes . . . one, two, three—and turn.
Why, this was easy. And the hands—now, where did
they go? Oh, yes, he had it. Right hand lightly—oh, so
lightly—around her waist. Left hand . . .

"That's splendid, Jim! You'll be a marvellous dancer!
Only don't hold that left hand so high—I never could
reach it without jumping."

He froze, feeling utterly foolish, his right arm curved
around empty space, his left up in the air. Tally stood
in a consciously demure pose, her hands clasped before

her, her head cocked to one side, gravely regarding him. She stepped closer to him, her skirt sweeping the ground. "Yes, Mr. Warbonnet, you may have this dance," she murmured graciously, while he stood tongue-tied, and then he had to go on dancing again, for she reached up and got possession of his left arm, moved into the curve of his right, and led off.

They danced. "The waltz is beautiful," she said. "Don't you think so, Jim?"

Jim did. He forgot his feet, and they behaved very well without his supervision. He looked down into her tilted face, and it was misty in the darkness, only the eyes shining and clear, and her small teeth white as she smiled. A new kind of wildness flowed through him, and an aching gentleness. He wanted to pick her up and take her away with him to some lovely land.

"You're . . . you're very light on your feet, Jim."

"You are on wings."

They danced on, saying very little, frankly looking into each other's eyes, unaware that they were now dancing in the light of the windows. The swirl of the flowered skirt threw shifting patterns of shadow on the ground, long shadows that ran into the outer darkness and were lost. A growing silence made itself known to them.

"Jim, the music has . . . Oh!"

She looked past his face, over his shoulder, and her dismayed little exclamation caused him to look around. Earth returned under his feet, and reality came in the form of laughing voices—many voices, belonging to many people who stood packed in and outside the open doorway of the barracks watching them. And a man was striding slowly across the patch of lighted parade ground, coming from Officers' Row; a man whose uniform showed a captain's double line of gilt buttons, and whose head was white with a bandage.

Mrs. Chittendon, the major's wife, was a lady of sympathy and some tact. She called from among the group in the doorway, "Imagine being able to dance so beautifully on that gravel! Now do come in, both of you, and show us what you can do on the floor."

The double row of gilt buttons advanced steadily, and the face of Vaugant emerged above them in the light. The captain had a small bundle under one arm, wrapped up in his full-dress sash. He fell into pace alongside Tally, ignoring Jim on her other side. The crowd fell back and drifted on in, smiling and exchanging glances, and they walked into the barracks.

"Was I mistaken in believing that you had promised me that dance, Miss Talitha?"

"You were not mistaken, Captain. You merely forgot to come and claim it in time." Tally's voice sounded a little breathless.

"I was coming for you when I saw you go out," retorted Vaugant. "I thought perhaps you were tired, and I hoped to join you outside." His eyes had much the same look of hurting strain in them as they'd had when he sat in the hollow nursing his injured head.

"Did you look for me?"

"Not at once. I thought it a good opportunity to bring you a small gift that I have for you, so I went to my quarters and got it. Coming back, I . . . perceived that you were engaged and obviously didn't wish to be interrupted."

There was color in Tally's face, and it heightened. "I'm sorry, Captain. Sorry that you are offended. There is no need for it." She touched his arm and smiled placatingly. "Don't be so grim. I'll promise to obey orders henceforth, if you'll tell me what you have there under your arm. My gift? Now don't keep me on tenderhooks. It isn't nice to be cruel to a girl." She was being nice to him, charming him out of his sullen temper for the sake of harmony.

Suspicious, but partly mollified, Vaugant took the bundle from under his arm. "One of the men had it and I bought it from him. He found it in that Comanche camp. I think it'll interest you. Hope you'll like it." He began unwinding the sash.

Jim walked away. He and the captain, he was sure, were about due to have trouble. He didn't want it to happen here. West called to him, offered him a drink from the punch bowl, and he joined him. He heard Tally exclaim, "Oh, how pretty!"

"You'll never guess what's inside," said Vaugant.

"Not a scalp, I hope!"

He sipped his drink, tried to keep his back toward them, but yielded to temptation. He looked to see what manner of gift it was, and, catching a look at it, he set down his glass with a bang and brushed past West. The gift was a small buckskin pouch, intricately decorated with beadwork and fine colored quills.

"That's mine!" he rapped, and reached for it.

Tally backed a step, her eyes wide, and people wheeled to stare. Vaugant, as surprised as the girl, gripped hard on the porch. "What the devil d'you mean? Why, you long-haired barbarian—!" His angry eyes narrowed. "Yours?"

It would have made for a scene and trouble, to try to prevent him from untying the string of the pouch and pulling out the stained and battered little shagreen book. Vaugant held it up. "Yours? This? If it is, then . . ."

He was interrupted by a cry from Tally. "It's—it's . . . I know that book!" Her face was white. "West! West —look!"

West came hurriedly to her, saw the book in Vaugant's hand, and stopped dead. "Good Lord—that was

Jim Aherne's! I'd know it anywhere. Where did it come
from? George—for God's sake, where'd you get it?"

Vaugant regarded their faces. "So that's what it is!"
he muttered. "Well, I'll be—! You mean the kid you've
talked about? His? Why, one of our men picked it up in
that Comanche camp. This fellow says it's his. Ask *him*
where he got it!"

He looked around at all the faces. "This, see it?" He
held it up. "This belonged to a white boy who was
killed by a band of hostiles years ago. You've all heard
about what happened to the Hathersall party on the
Oregon trail. The boy was with them. This was found
in that Comanche camp that we broke up. You can see
by the pouch that it's been carried around for a long
time by some Indian—or somebody the same as an Indian. And that fellow there—Warbonnet—admits it's his!
What's the answer to *that*, gentlemen?"

The significance was obvious. Faces, at first puzzled
and inquiring, sharpened startledly. Some of the ladies
gasped.

"It begins to look queer, doesn't it?" Vaugant pursued
relentlessly. "It begins to look as if our precious scout
is what I've suspected him of being from the first. He's
been living with hostiles—raiding with them—sharing
their loot! How did this come down to him? Why did
he guide us against those Comanches? Because he knew
we were after the Sioux, and he's their renegade friend!
He's been living with the same band of Sioux who wiped
out the Hathersall wagon-party!"

Wapaha Jim saw horror on Tally's face and on the
others'. Some of the men were almost glaring at him,
and West looked numbed. He said, looking at Vaugant,
"You lie! They were not Sioux who attacked the wagons!"

A trooper came limping on crutches from the far end
of the hushed room, after Vaugant searched him out

and called to him. Those able to leave hospital had been given permission to attend the dance. The injured man peered at Wapaha Jim's dark face and coldly reckless eyes.

"Ever see him before?" Vaugant demanded. "Think of him with a feather in his hair—on an Indian pony—a rifle in his fist! You saw that fellow. You saw him up close when he charged you and the others on the slope. You swore then that he was a white man, and I said you were crazy. Well? Speak up, man!"

"He—he could be," stammered the man. "Yeah, he could. His eyes . . . But his face was painted, sir. I dunno."

"Jim!" Tally stood before him, trying to make him look down at her. "Jim—say something! Tell them they're wrong!"

"They're not wrong," he said, and she shrank back. "I have lived and fought with Sioux. I have seen a Sioux girl shot dead by soldiers. I attacked those soldiers." His eyes glittered at Vaugant. "But he lies when he says Sioux killed your parents. Comanches did that."

"Then—what happened to the boy? Do you know?"

"He was saved by the Sioux. They cared for him and treated him well, and he became one of them. He is grateful to them."

Her eyes were big, incredulous but eager to believe. But she could find nothing to say, and it remained for somebody in the crowd to call out a challenging query. "How does *he* know all that?"

Seconds of silence dragged by. Wapaha Jim kept his gaze on Vaugant, who had the look of a man who had raised something bigger than he had expected. "My name was Jim Aherne. The Sioux call me Wapaha," he said at last, and paced swiftly out of the building before anyone could gather purpose to stop him.

He heard Tally cry after him, and West shout something. And then a storm of voices, Vaugant's the most penetrating and harsh. "What does it matter who he once was? He's a dangerous renegade now, and he's admitted it! If he gets away he'll take information back to the hostiles! General—!"

Wapaha Jim raced lightly across the deserted parade ground for the stables. His chances of quitting the fort without a fight were slim, and he was unarmed, but his rifle and pistol hung with his saddle in the stables, above the stall given to him for his pony. He was all through with this brief span of the white man's way of life. It had almost got him, but the break had been bound to come sooner or later and leave him running for his life.

A patter of steps brought him up alert in the dark stables, and he snatched out his pistol. He already had the skimpy Indian saddle lashed onto his pony, and was ready to go.

"Jim!"

Tally ran full into him, and he caught her. "Jim—oh, Jim, don't go away!" She tugged at him, trying to pull him out of the stables, all her reserve and restraint flung away. "Don't make us lose you again—after we've found you. Oh, Jim, darling, I've always felt that you were still alive! And something inside me must have guessed it was you, the first minute, I saw you. . . ."

"I've got to go," he said, but he didn't want to, and he held her to him.

"No—you can't!" She caught at his hair, drew his head down, kissed him fiercely. His urgency and his peril were lost upon her. Her wish to be near him drove out all thought of caution and circumstances, and of modesty. When he lifted her off her feet and kissed her, she laughed softly in her throat, and her arms were warm against the smooth brown nape of his neck. Then they were quiet, and with all his Indian training Jim failed to hear the quick, light crunch of more feet converging upon the stables. He didn't see Vaugant and the armed troopers, was oblivious of their presence, like Tally, until Vaugant spoke in a high and strangled voice.

"Miss Talitha! I must ask you to . . . to move away from that man. I have orders to arrest him. Take your hands off her, you cursed renegade!"

CHAPTER 11

★

THE GUARDHOUSE

THE FORT LOOKED NORMAL. SENTRIES PACED BACK AND forth. A squad of men marched with brooms and rakes to fatigue duty in the stables. And General G. A. Custer was putting his favorite mount, Dandy, through its morning workout on the parade ground.

A splendid and spectacular horseman, the general always had an admiring audience when putting a horse through its paces, although he was seldom conscious of it. The task and pleasure of handling a responsive horse absorbed him. His officers knew it, knew that compliments were not wanted, and contented themselves with an exchange of nods and head-wags. There was Second-Lieutenant Hodgson, rather short but a dashing figure, twirling his fine mustaches; and fair Captain Yates with his hat on straight and giving the impression of always standing to attention; and Lieutenant McIntosh, that dour-faced Scot with a humorous eye; and rakish-looking Lieutenant Calhoun; and handsome Tom Custer, brother of the general. . . . All watching "Autie" do tricks with Dandy. All worshipping the man.

For once Tally didn't so much as glance at the general. She kept her eyes on the tray that she carried, to see that the coffee did not spill over onto the cake that she had made, or ruin the cigars that West had contributed. Ladies along the galleries of Officers' Row, warmly clad for the cold morning, shook their heads and sighed, seeing Tally and West making their way over to the guardhouse. The ladies were making up a riding party. Fresh air was a cult among them, and they'd freeze before they'd admit it was indoor weather. The young wife of Lieutenant McIntosh whispered sympathetically that it was a great pity, that man turning out to be what he was.

"A pity indeed," boomed the large wife of the commissary captain. "I'm so sorry for dear Talitha. She's so foolishly loyal. I do think her brother should discourage her. After all, that man's a renegade. He'll probably be shot."

West said to Tally, "Let me carry that."

She refused. "You're an officer. It wouldn't look right. I don't mind carrying it. I want to. That cake—I do hope it isn't as heavy as it looks. I tried awfully hard."

"Cakes don't turn out the same in this country, they say. It's the altitude or something. You have to change the recipe. But that one looks fine to me."

They had to talk of something inconsequential, to keep from talking about Jim. On the subject of Jim they had said very little, but they understood each other. Anything that he could do for Jim, West was ready to do and take the consequences. His only fear was for Tally. He had little doubt that she was quite capable of blowing up the guardhouse on her own initiative and stealing the general's best horse for Jim to get away on, if she wasn't watched. Her mood was more than merely reckless, and he marvelled that he was the only one to perceive it. Everybody else thought Tally was reduced to a subdued sorrow. They failed to detect the calm lawlessness in her eyes.

The sentry at the guardhouse apologetically barred their entrance. "No ladies allowed inside, sir."

"This lady is. She has permission from the general. Call the sergeant of the guard, please, and . . . Ah, there you are, Sergeant. My sister and I wish to see Mr. Aherne. General's permission."

"Yes, sir."

The cell door was of heavy timber, with two bars of strap iron over the square peephole. The sergeant unlocked the door and withdrew. West knocked before entering, but Tally was already gazing through the peephole. "Hello, Jim!" she called. "Mind if we come visiting? Look! Cake, hot Santo, and cigars. And matches. I didn't forget matches. I think I'm thoughtful, don't you?"

Jim didn't say what he thought. He met them at the door, and West thrust out his hand. They shook hands, and stood looking at each other until Tally inserted a cup of coffee between them. "Drink it before it gets cold, Jim. If the cake isn't just right, blame the altitude —West thought up that excuse for me. Turn your back, please, West. I'm going to kiss him. Thank you. And . . . thank you, Jim. You're both very . . . You're both . . ."

"Saints and sinners, Tally, are you crying?" West wanted to know, turning around.

"No. A little emotion sneaked up on me and . . . Oh, lend me your handkerchief and stop staring at me. Light a cigar, Jim. No girl can cry over a man when he's smoking a cigar."

West, blinking at such shocking candor, attempted to bend the conversation with an I-remember-when. "I remember when he smoked one of his father's cigars behind the wagon, and got so white we thought he'd die. Seems to me you cried then, Tally."

"That's right. I did, didn't I?" Tally wiped her eyes. "That was way back when I first fell in love with the infamous scoundrel. I cried, and he laughed at me—white face and all. Then I hated him. You were a heartless young blackguard, Jim. Always lifting me up to high heaven with your lovely smile, and then letting me drop with a hateful grin. I hope you've changed your ways. I'm a big girl now, and I don't think I could survive the fall. Do you mind stepping outside for a minute, West? I . . . there's something I want to ask Jim."

"Certainly," said West, but he hesitated at the door. "I ought to mention a certain matter. Jim, last night I learned from the general that you could walk out of here and everything would be forgotten—if you'd agree to one thing."

"What thing?"

"Help us against the Sioux."

Contempt hardened Jim's eyes. "You expect me to save myself by betraying my people?"

"But they're *not* your people. They're Indians."

"I have friends and blood-brothers among them."

West gave up. "All right, all right. I can see your side of it. If I'd been the one to stay behind at the wagons that time . . ." He flushed at the old memory. "Well—perhaps I'd be the one in this cell, but for you and the grace of God."

"And I would be dead," returned Jim, "but for the grace of the Sioux."

"I think you'd better go, West," put in Tally. "Let me talk to him."

After he had gone, she sat on the narrow bunk and gazed at Jim with that same level look of critical pondering that he remembered her having as a child. She

began on a diffident note. "Jim—that girl. The Indian
girl. Did she die?"

"Yes. She smiled and tried to speak when I picked
her up, and died. Then I rode at the soldiers."

"You must have loved her very much."

"Yes. Luta-ho-ota was my sister."

"Your . . . Jim, how—?"

"She was the daughter of Yellow Eagle, who calls me
his son. She never harmed anyone. Comanches stole
her. Two friends helped me get her back. We were going home when we came to the soldiers. She was
happy."

Tally saw more than the bare picture that he outlined. "She was happy," she confirmed him, and nodded. "Of course she was. I'm sorry, Jim. I just wanted
to know about her. But it wasn't just woman's curiosity,
or—or anything like that. It wouldn't have made any
real difference if you'd said she was your wife. Or one
of a dozen wives. I suppose I'm shameless, and I ought
to have more pride. But I'd be your thirteenth bride,
and welcome—as long as you turned loose the others
after you got me!"

She rested her head on his shoulder, and they sat side
by side on the hard bunk. "We've got to get you out of
this place, Jim. If you won't listen to West's suggestion,
then I've got to do something. I don't think we have
much time."

"Are they going to shoot me?" he asked.

He felt her quiver a little against him. "They may. I
heard them talking about you last night."

She had heard them from upstairs, when she started
down from her room, and at the sound of Jim's name
she had listened with no twinge of conscience. The men
were downstairs in the major's room, and she recognized the rapid speech of the general.

"I understand his father was of good family. If only

for that reason, I'd be reluctant to make it a public case. The Eastern papers would get hold of the story, once he's stood up for trial. Treason always makes a big sensation. It's too bad. Personally, I liked the man. Had a high regard for him."

"He's a very fine man, sir," came West's voice, and Tally could have hugged him. "When he was a boy he sacrificed his own chances so that my sister and I could escape those raiders. And you are correct about his being of good family. His father was a gentleman, a man of culture. Jim would be a gentleman, too, but for circumstances. As far as that goes, he *is* a gentleman!"

And then Captain Vaugant, cold and precise. "It's natural and understandable that you should be disposed in his favor, Hathersall. And I grant he's something of an extraordinary character. Strong personality, brains and—yes—courage. But for just those reasons he's the more dangerous. We can't blink the facts. He's listed as one of the leading Sioux warriors—Wapaha. He's a member of a hostile band. He has fought against us and caused casualties. Why did he hide his identity when he came here? I tell you he came here as a spy for the hostiles! He's a renegade, and the circumstances which encouraged him to become such a thing have no bearing in the eyes of the law. Am I right, General? What about you, Major?"

"You have stated the case correctly from its—ah—purely unprejudiced angle, Vaugant," answered Major Chittendon dryly, and Tally could imagine Vaugant's ready-tempered flush. "But we shouldn't lose sight of the man's undoubted usefulness to us. I believe, General, you have that same thought?"

"Quite right, Major. I'm not writing any official report of the matter until we learn whether or not our man is willing to help us. Hathersall, you might be of some assistance there. Tell him that I'd like to reinstate

him as special scout. All I want is his word of honor. I
imagine he'd keep it. We could forget and overlook his
—er—past career, in return for valuable services. Strict
legality is all very well, Captain, but there are times
when it may be improved upon for the good of all concerned. Agree?"

"Yes, sir. But suppose the man refuses?"

A chair scraped the floor. "Then I'm afraid he'll have
to stand trial as an incorrigible renegade, and probably
die before a firing. . . ." The door of the major's room
closed, cutting off the rest.

Tally went back to her room, shaking, and sat in the
darkness.

Downstairs, the general returned to his chair, remark-
ing that he didn't like a draft on his back. "If Aherne
agrees to work with us," he said, "I'll want him to leave
at once to locate Sitting Bull's camp and gather all information possible concerning their strength, arms, and
disposition. Cigar, Major?"

"Thank you." The major accepted it, switched it deftly for one of his own, and spoke a thought while lighting up. "I'm distrustful of our 'friendly' Indians. There
are some Arapahoes camping with our Crows. They
come and go. They come in for powder and tobacco,
and go back on the warpath, in my opinion. Arapahoes
are generally at peace with the Sioux and Cheyennes,
remember. We couldn't keep them from finding out that
Aherne had left the fort, and they'd be suspicious.
Might ride ahead of him and warn the Sioux. They
know who he is now. It's all over the fort, of course.
Those Crows know now that Aherne is Wapaha. They
appear to recognize that name, too, incidentally. Appar-
ently he's been something of a terror, and they hate him.
That's a problem."

"It is, but there's a solution," said the general. "Not a
unique one, but good enough. We could rig a false es-

cape. Let him break out of the guardhouse, chase after him—and make sure we don't catch him. He'd be in on it, of course, and we could give him a gun so that he could blaze off a few shots and make it look convincing. I'll arrange it, if he agrees to the bargain and gives me his word. You put it up to him, Hathersall. If you can't move him, then I'll talk to him. Gentlemen, it's time for my wife to come looking for me, so I'm going home. G'night."

A guard passed the open door of the cell, but refrained from looking in, and Tally kept her head on Jim's shoulder. "Is it any use trying to coax you into accepting the general's terms?" she asked.

"No."

"I didn't think it would be," she admitted. "Then it's up to me. I'm not going to let them shoot you."

He tightened his arm about her shoulders. "Don't try. You'll only bring trouble on yourself."

She raised her head and tossed back her hair. "I don't care. They're not going to shoot you. I'll get West's gun and make them turn you loose, first! And you'll take me with you. I don't care where—down to Mexico, or back to your Indians, or anywhere. I'm going with you!"

Walking back to quarters with her, West said, "Not so long ago you told me that you were incapable of love, Tally, and I almost believed you, but I should have known better. I'm worried about you."

"Don't be. I'm very happy and I hope to be happier."

"Yes, I know," West observed moodily. "You've got that mad streak in you that doesn't care a rap, and you're giving it its head. I suppose you inherited it from Mother's side of the family. Not that she was wild, but she did have a strong mind and some spectacular ancestors. Great-grandfather Mathius Blake, for instance. Blockade runner, privateer, and heaven knows what else on the shady side. Be careful, Tally."

"This is no time to be careful!"

"That's probably what Mathius Blake said, when he tried to out-do Decatur and take two British ships. But the war was over, only he didn't know it, and the ships turned out to be armed frigates. He drowned."

Left alone in his cell, Jim listened to the sergeant turn the key in the lock and walk off down the corridor to the guardroom. He did not go up close to the small outside window of his cell, but he placed himself where he could look through it and see the log huts and tepees of the Crow scouts and their families. The Crow camp stood well away from the garrison proper, off to one side of the level plain behind the guardhouse, on a rise of land near the river. One particular tepee held his interest.

Its flap was open, and it was that which had caught his attention earlier in the morning. The triangular entrance looked directly down on the rear of the guardhouse building. The morning had been cold, yet the flap remained rolled back and no fire showed inside the tepee. Also, a blanket had been thrown over the smoke-hole at the top, where the poles joined, so that it stayed dark in there. These were details that meant nothing to the casual eye of any soldier who might glance up that way. To the man in the cell they were facts of significance. He studied the dark triangle, and did not move. After a full minute he let his gaze range side to side away from it, slowly and meticulously searching, and at last he found what he sought.

There it was, a metallic pinpoint that caught a tiny reflection of the sun, shining from a low ridge of snow that had banked against a long tuft of grass-roots, part way down the slope of the rise and below the Crow tepee. The snow was crusted, not new, a patch that would melt later in the day if the sun remained as warm as it was now. Jim watched the pinpoint. Crows seldom learned the precaution of blackening the muzzles of their guns when stalking prey. The man had sat in his tepee this morning, but the cold had caused him to move, and it was then that Jim had seen him. Now the man had crept down to the snowbank where he could lie hidden with his back warmed by the sun, keeping vigil, waiting for a face to appear at the cell window. Other Indians moved through the camp. None of them glanced down at the snowbank, not even the children.

The pinpoint shifted ever so slightly and lost the sun's reflection. Jim ducked, and went and sat on the bunk. He contemplated the window from that angle. It was a small square, set high in the wall, strongly barred on the outside, the single glass pane hinged on the inside. He had opened it wide during the night, for fresh air, and it still was open.

The Crows were out to get him and settle some old scores while the opportunity offered itself. One shot, and it would be done. They would present wooden faces afterward to the investigating soldiers, deny all knowledge of it, and next day blandly hold a dance to celebrate the coup, privately regretting that they were not able to take his hair. It did not occur to Jim to speak of it to his captors or to anyone else. This was a matter strictly between himself and the Crows. He sat and considered it. The Crows were not a patient people. He gave them one day to keep up the profitless vigil. When they tired of it they would undertake a more direct course or abandon it entirely. They knew he was Wapaha, son of Yellow Eagle, and they knew he was in this cell, agreeably unarmed. They had their ways of finding out such things.

When taps sounded that night, a trooper of the guard came to the cell door and looked through the peep-hole. "Turn in," he called, and watched the prisoner make his brief preparations for bed.

"He's a cool card, that," the trooper reported to the sergeant when he returned to the guardroom. "Got in his bunk an' went right off to sleep like he ain't got a damn care in the world. Just like an Injun. They don't never worry till the time comes—then they're dead an' it don't matter anyhow."

CHAPTER 12

★

THE ANGRY SHADOWS

THERE WAS NO MOON, AND SO THE NIGHT WAS BLACK WITH all the spirit-shadows of those restless dead who, unaccepted by the Great Mysterious and banned from the happy afterland because of their shortcomings, sinisterly roamed the earth to take sullen vengeance on the living.

It took rash nerve to be out on such a night, away from the safe refuge of the painted tepees, but the pair of creeping Crow men had fortified themselves from an illicit bottle.

One carried a short-bow and arrows, the other an old Colt revolving rifle holding five heavy percussion charges in the magazine. They wriggled their way past the granary shed, and after that they had to keep lying motionless because of the sentry. Wearing his greatcoat and muffler, the sentry paced his routine beat around the granary and along the rear of the guardhouse and cells. Head bent, ruminative, he vanished around the northern corner of the building, and after awhile he would appear again coming around the granary. His appearance could be timed, and the Crows watched him make the rounds twice before rising for their last noiseless advance.

They had about three minutes in which to do what they had come to do, and that was ample. The one with the short-bow glided to the little barred window at the end, while his companion stood watch. By standing on his toes he could look into the cell. He spent a few seconds, straining his vision to locate the bunk and make sure that it held a tenant, and he fitted a bright new arrow to his bowstring. The deed, and the prestige of the recipient, demanded a fine clean arrow.

But the angle of flight was bad and his position was awkward, standing on tiptoe and his hands having to be up in line with his ears. He wanted force and accuracy. No man could be sure of his aim, shooting from above shoulder-height with his right hand behind his head, and muscles had no real power in that position. And the iron bars were inconvenient; a feather might brush against one and deflect the arrow from its target. But his desire refused to allow him to give up, now that he could see the enemy.

He beckoned to his companion and exchanged his bow for the Colt rifle. His companion shook his head uneasily. That gun made an enormous noise when fired; they would have to run away very fast. But it was dark, and perhaps the spirit-shadows would approve so of this fine killing that they would help them get away.

Inserted between the bars, the rifle barrel tilted at a downward slant in the hands of the Crow. The muzzle drifted an inch or two, like a blind eye guided by sensory instinct, and its aim steadied to a point near the head of the bunk, just where the blankets followed the outline of a shoulder. The rifle roared like a cannon in the enclosed space, and it had a vicious kick and a back-flash of fire from the breech. The Crow had been prepared for the kick and flash, his shoulder braced to the butt and his eyes shut at the instant of squeezing the trigger. He knew the gun, knew its virtues and faults; the Army had discarded that model years ago when standard cartridges began coming into use.

But he was not prepared for the thing to rebound from the kick and jerk violently out of his hands into the cell. There was something *wakan* about that, and he had no time or inclination to look into it. It had felt almost as if an unseen hand snatched the weapon away from him. He fled with his companion.

It was terrifying to hear his lost gun boom a second explosion behind him from the cell window. His companion threw bow and arrows into the air, spun half around, and collapsed. From the cell window came another flash and boom, and in his last instant of life the Crow knew that it had been foolish to dare the spirit-shadows of the moonless night.

The uproar of the fort had an orderliness to it. Being accustomed to living on the edge of emergencies, troopers and officers automatically controlled their first impulses, and the reaction of the garrison followed a military design. Shots in the night could mean a raid on the stables, or an attempt to burn the fort, or even an attack in force. Anything.

Lights went out everywhere. The sergeant of the guard barked his commands. Doors banged along Officers' Row. Men poured from the barracks, few of them fully clad, but all armed. The calm voice of the general could be heard above others, calling for a trumpeter.

"Guards—turn out! Double-quick, there!

"Where did those shots . . .

"Captain, take some men and guard the stables!

"Sentry, where did those shots come from? Behind the guardhouse, you think? Sergeant—oh, sergeant of the guard! Check your prisoners!"

A trumpeter sounded a fast general alarm, every note clear and sharp, and then the stand-to.

The sergeant and a trooper of the guard hurried along the corridor of the guardhouse, calling to each prisoner as they passed the cell doors. "Daubert—you there? Good. Waymire? All right. Aherne—hey, Aherne, wake up! Aherne don't answer, Sergeant! Say—there's smoke in his cell!"

"Get the keys and take a look at him, while I go . . . Who's callin' me?"

"Sergeant!" a sentry shouted outside. "There's a dead Injun layin' out back here! He's been . . . Holy Saints, there's another'n!"

The sergeant went off at the double to report to the general, devoutly hoping that he wouldn't be held to account for it and struggling to figure out what kind of hell's prank could have happened. There'd be a big hullabaloo over this, if that Aherne renegade was dead in his bunk, as appeared all too likely.

The trooper got the keys from the guardroom and groped his way back through the darkness to the end cell. After some trouble he found the right key and pushed open the door. He took the precaution of striking a match as he entered, and left his carbine outside, but drew his dragoon pistol from its holster. With his pistol he hooked back the blankets of the bunk. He saw that he had uncovered nothing more than the straw-filled mattress, rolled up into a bundle, and his eyes bulged, but he was a little slow in turning and the match burned down to his fingers. He let go of the match, and so he never saw what it was that hit him.

It required only one long step for Jim to reach him from his still crouch against the wall alongside the door, and he brought down the butt of the Colt rifle in a single stroke that crushed a black campaign hat and drove the trooper under it to the floor. He bent over the felled man and worked fast, and when he left the cell he locked the door after him and dropped the keys back through the peephole.

"Hell!" swore the sergeant half a minute later, peering through the barred window at the rear of the building. "He's fell off his bunk an' layin' on the floor now. Oh, General! This way, sir!"

Somebody in the guardroom, fetching up heavily against a tall man in a hurry, recovered his balance and wanted to know where the devil the fellow was going.

"Doctor," came the muttered response from the tall man, as he rushed on out. He wore an Army great-coat and his hat was pulled down over his face, and he kept his right hand in his pocket. But he struck for the stables after leaving the guardroom.

There were troopers at the stables, inside and out, and every door was guarded. Some of them called queries to him through the darkness. He shook his head, entering, and passed along the stalls. To choose his Indian pony would invite notice, and it was too conspicuous to ride out on. He located a large grey, one of the best mounts of the Grey Horse Troop, but saddling it gave him some difficulty. He was unaccustomed to the McClellan saddle, and he had to work in silence and in the dark. The horse, resenting being called upon for service at such an unusual hour, squealed a complaint and stamped a hoof.

"Who's meddling with that horse down there?"

The demand rang through the stables in a voice of curt authority, unmistakably that of Vaugant. "Hey, you—that man there! Who gave you orders to saddle? Damn it, answer me!"

★

Vaugant was more irritated than angry. He liked to be informed on what was going on, liked to feel in touch

with all details and to possess a comprehension of any
moves. It was in this one respect that he privately
found fault with the general. The general had a way of
keeping many of his plans to himself and not imparting
them to his staff until the last minute, and not always
then. In this case Vaugant felt that he had a right to
know. He was guarding the stables on the general's direct order, and was responsible for the horses.

He reached the man at the horse, and tapped him on
the back. "Who gave you orders to . . ."

The man turned. A hard and blunt object prodded
Vaugant in his stomach, and he didn't need any light
to know that it was a pistol. He heard a low-toned
warning. "Don't try to stop me, Vaugant!"

There was the whisper of death in that warning, more
potent in the voice than in the pressure of the pistol
that gave it tangibility. It chilled Vaugant. "Damnation!" he said. "You!" And now his irritation became a
bitterness forked at this man and at the general, and he
felt fooled.

"If I were the general I'd never have taken the word
of a damned renegade!" he vowed. "Why the devil
didn't he tell me what to expect? Got that saddle
cinched? Those stirrup straps are too short for you. No
time to let 'em out now, though. All set? Well, get going,
then, damn you!" He looked to the nearest doorway.
"Make way for this man and let him through. Hey, you
two men coming in . . . Oh, is it you, Major? And you,
Hathersall? Huh!"

So they were in on it, but he had been left out. But
perhaps the general had paid him the compliment of
assuming that he would know what to do at the right
time. The general expected initiative from his best officers.

"How're things here, Captain?" asked Major Chittendon.

"He's leaving right now," answered Vaugant.

"Eh? Who's leaving?"

"Aherne, of course."

"Oh—!" The major swallowed his surprise. It wouldn't do to admit that the general hadn't taken him into his confidence. "Er—good," he said, but he wondered. He had heard the sergeant of the guard shouting something about two dead Indians. The sergeant had sounded very convincing. But then, the general had a knack for bringing out hidden talents in a man. He had evidently gone to considerable lengths to dress this thing up right for the benefit of the Crows.

Jim, bewildered but grateful for the unexpected aid and abettance, backed the grey out of its stall and swung up into the saddle. West caught his hand as he passed. "Good luck, Jim!" he whispered. "Don't worry, we'll shoot in the air."

They let him get a running start before firing off their pistols. The major knocked down a carbine that was being aimed carefully by a trooper. "Nobody gave you orders to fire!" he snapped.

A sentry ran out at the riding man from the far end of the stables. He shouted a command to halt and brought up his carbine. The rider bent low and veered straight at him. A thud, another shout, and the sentry rolled over and over, scrambling for his weapon. The rider angled off across the plain, slapping his mount. The beat of the hoofs could be heard for a little while, changing rhythm as the horse got into its top stride, then was lost in echoes and the noises of the fort. Some Crows came running down from their camp.

Vaugant went looking for the general and found him behind the guardhouse with a group of officers and men, staring off across the plain. Men were pounding on a cell door inside the building. "Do you happen to know who rode off on that grey, Captain?" he asked. "And that shooting we heard just now—?"

Vaugant saluted. "Yes, sir. It was—er . . ." He lowered his tone. "Our man. Everything went off all right."

Major Chittendon came hurrying up. "Aherne managed to get a horse, General," he reported, his face wooden. "Got clear away before we could stop him."

The general stared at them queerly. He swallowed, and beckoned to Captain Yates. "Get after Aherne—he's escaped! Take the Crows with you. I want that man back, Captain!"

He motioned to Vaugant and the major to follow him, and in the privacy of his quarters he mentioned that he would make no report of the affair. "If I did," he pointed out, "you gentlemen would be in trouble—grave trouble."

Vaugant smiled. "Quite so, sir."

The major, for his part, did not smile. "I don't exactly understand why the Crows were put on his track," he said slowly. "They're good trackers and may catch him. We gave him a good horse, but . . ."

"I take the responsibility for giving him the horse, Major," cut in Vaugant pleasantly. "And you may be sure that Yates is wise enough to keep those Crows from catching the fellow. Eh, General?"

The general eyed him reflectively. "On the contrary, I picked Captain Yates for his ability as a soldier, not as a guesser," he remarked. "It may surprise you to know that I had nothing to do with Aherne's escape. I'd have given a year's pay to prevent . . . H'mm. Are you sick, Captain? You may retire to your quarters. You too, Major—you don't look well, either."

When they were gone, the general penned a message to Fort Fetterman. He avoided details, but strongly advised that the campaign against Crazy Horse be pushed as soon as possible, regardless of the weather conditions.

He had reasons, he wrote, that caused him to believe
that the hostiles might soon obtain information concerning the coming campaign, and it would be well to press
action against them before they could prepare for it.

He sighed when he wrote that. It was a devil of a
thing that Chittendon and Vaugant had done. Ah, well
—he smiled wryly—he had made a slip or two of his
own in the past. But no mistake had ever affected him
as this one had affected Vaugant. The man had looked
positively insane.

CHAPTER 13

★

POWDER RIVER

THE INDIAN CAMP ON POWDER RIVER LAY IN A SNUG LITTLE
valley, protected from the winds and well provided
with water and fuel. Young cottonwood trees and underbrush gave shelter and forage to the large pony-
herd that pastured in the valley, and back of the hundred lodges grew a thick fringe of willows, oak, elm,
ash. Beyond the trees rose the high and rugged bluffs,
their bleak crests standing as eternal ramparts against
the northern howlers.

It was more than a camp. It was a winter village,
rich and luxurious for its kind, the home of many families. The tall lodges, painstakingly bulwarked against
the entrance of wind and cold, held the lives and
gathered possessions of an active and wayward people.
Warmth and comfort were here, and with them their
corollary illusion of safety. Enemies never had ven-

tured to penetrate this far north in winter, and never would. Summer was the season for war and all sports. The village slept while morning and death approached.

The troops from Fort Fetterman advanced along a deep ravine that led into the valley, and extreme caution was the order. They had come two hundred miles through bad weather and difficult country without betraying their advance, and nobody wanted to upset the surprise in the last mile. Advance scouts had located the site of the camp last night, and the attack was planned and timed for the dawn hour.

General Sheridan, hero of the Civil War, had supervision of all military operations between the Missouri and the Rockies; to Brigadier-General Crook he had issued instructions to move out from Fort Fetterman against the hostiles. General Crook, having whipped the Idaho Piutes ten years before, and the southern Apaches three years later, was conceded to be the most skilled Indian fighter on the plains—except by the Seventh Cavalry at Fort Lincoln, who solidly backed another nominee: Custer—General George Armstrong Custer—who had played hob with the wily Cheyennes on the Washita eight years before. There was nobody else like Custer. If those folks back in Washington had had any sense they'd have handed the whole campaign over to him, said the Seventh.

Crook had started out with an expedition big enough to eat up anything that got in its way: ten full troops of his cavalry, two companies of infantry, eighty-six wagons, four ambulances, a four-hundred-mule pack train, and a herd of beef cattle for rations. He headed northwest, finally hit an Indian trail, and sent six cavalry troops forward under Colonel Reynolds with orders to attack if he found the hostile village. The main column had to follow more slowly because of the infantry and wagons, but it was felt that the six troops of cavalry were more than 'enough to handle the matter and stood a better chance of approaching the enemy unseen.

Holding to the Indian trail, Reynolds made an all-night march, hoping to strike the village just before daylight. He got his wish, but the rough country and the cold night did his men and horses no good. When his Ree Indian scouts reported the village ahead, he followed the approved military plan of attack against Indians. He divided his six troops into three battalions, each to approach and charge the village from a different angle to prevent the withdrawal of the hostiles.

The advance battalion moved quietly down the ravine, not a bridle-bit jingling, not a whisper from the sleepless and squinch-eyed troopers. Nobody knew exactly what to expect when they made the sharp turn in the ravine that brought them into the valley. Then they saw the whole village spread out silently before them—and one slim Indian standing alone in the snow, not fifty yards ahead of them, motionless, gazing alertly at them. Just that one Indian, that single bit of human life, placed there by a millionth chance to see them and to wreck at the last moment all the careful preparations for a smashing surprise.

Men swore softly. An officer covered the Indian with his pistol, and signed a warning by placing a finger to his lips. His action set the example for others. Half a dozen guns threatened the Indian. "One yelp an' you're a cold turkey!" breathed a sergeant.

★

Long Mane looked at the guns, the hard and stubbled faces, the uniforms and big horses. He had come out because he could not sleep, because he was haunted, and because solitude was preferable to the crowded, sleeping lodge. He thought of Wapaha, whom he had left in that lodge sleeping with the rest. Wapaha had tried to convince Crazy Horse and the sub-chiefs, when he rode a dying horse into the village a few days ago, that soldiers would be coming before summer and that it would be wise to break camp and move farther north. But they could not believe that, and thought him mistaken. Even his friends, and Yellow Eagle, caring for him after his terrible journey to find them, thought hardships had affected his judgment. But Wapaha had been right in his guess. Here were the soldiers, come to attack a village that had been too comfortable to abandon in bad weather to avoid a questionable peril.

Long Mane wished he had his gun with him, or even a spear or knife. It was galling to die without striking a blow. But the happy land would not refuse him entrance on that account, and Luta-ho-ota would be there to speak for him. He filled his lungs with the crisp air.

The pointing guns roared as he threw out his long, ringing cry, but he carried it on to its end—a penetrating call to arms, a wild and prideful greeting to death, and a scornful defiance of the enemy. It rang out above the sudden thunder of the punishing guns, giving point and premise to their noise, and then his task was done. He fell in the snow, shot through and through, and the battalion charged the awakened village to the blare of a trumpet.

Afterward, the soldiers remembered how like a hornets' nest the village became, every lodge spilling its quota of darting figures, every figure coming out shooting. And they remembered the king hornet, that vindictive hero, that unsurrendering demon of violence— Crazy Horse, war-chief of the Sioux. He was everywhere, bold, undaunted in the face of annihilation, his hoarse bellow constantly encouraging the warriors.

The warriors took to the fringe of trees. They had to retreat and abandon the village, but they were not defeated, and they concentrated their shooting on the big horses, knowing from their long war experience that a dropped horse meant also a rider half out of the fight. They dashed in and out, oblivious of the cold that numbed the fingers of the troopers, cutting off a man here, another there, and keeping up their shuddery yells that scared the horses. While they fought, their families fled to the frigid shelter of the underbrush and open ice-wastes down the valley. The element of surprise, far from causing panic, had lighted a blaze of ferocity that incited mad daring among the red men.

They saw their pony-herd captured, and that was a disastrous blow. Wapaha Jim, wearing only leggings and an armless elkskin shirt, fired with savage concentration at the Ree scouts who ran off the herd. "*Hiyupo!* Save the ponies!" he shouted to Bad Buffalo, and Bad Buffalo joined him in the attempt, but it was hopeless. The Rees had been thinking about those ponies for a long time, and how to get them.

While the Rees stampeded the ponies, a string of troopers galloped between them and the village, cutting off pursuit and getting cut off in return. The maneuver was sound insofar as original purpose went, but the command was breaking up under the sharpshooting tactics of the highly mobile tribesmen. The soldiers, losing touch with one another, and looming up too plainly as targets on their big horses, began dismounting and fighting on the defensive from cover. Wapaha Jim heard a white man shout an order, and he guessed it was the voice of an officer.

Colonel Reynolds was worried and had reason for it. The two supporting battalions had not yet arrived. He had the village, but he didn't know how long he could hold it and had no way of keeping track of his casualties. He had to do something to take the tribesmen's

minds off victory. "Destroy the village!" he ordered.
"Burn everything!"

The other two-thirds of his command came charging
in at last, and rode into a hail of fire from the fringe of
trees. Flames rose and licked high into the air, and
tepees became pointed torches. A store of powder went
up with a mighty flash that lighted the whole valley and
dispelled the early grey of the morning. It lighted up
the riding squads of troopers, too, and the warriors took
advantage of it with their muskets and smoothbores.

Reynolds conferred hastily with such of his officers
as he could gather about him. The men were drunk
with fatigue and loss of sleep, so worn out that even
their instincts for self-preservation were blunted. Last
night, during short halts on the march, some of them
had had to be kicked awake. Their horses were slug-
gish from scanty feed rations and hard riding, and
scared of the yelling going on around them. In the face
of the stubborn Indian resistance there seemed only one
reasonable course to take, and the colonel took it.
Neither he nor anyone in the command had expected
such unconquerable hardihood, such astoundingly desperate counter-attacks. It was like trying to beat off a
flock of enraged hawks. They were up against Crazy
Horse and a die-hard Sioux gang big in courage. Reynolds ordered a retreat from the hornets' nest.

The retreat told on the morale of the exhausted
troops. It came dangerously close to being a rout, and
the Sioux never let up for a minute. Crazy Horse led
the harrying pursuit, a hot musket smoking in his hands
and venom in his hating eyes. Wapaha Jim darted along
near him, around the burning village to the mouth of
the ravine, as venomous as the great chief. He looked
upon the attack and destruction as a crime to be pun-
ished in the same coin. The tepees had been homes,
furnished with robes beautifully worked and decorated

by women's patient and clever hands; couches of fine pelts; parfleches crammed with warm clothes. And the stores of food, the jerked meat and pemmican; the carefully preserved herbs for the sick and the hurt; the weapons and traps and powder; the thick blankets for the women and children and aged. All gone in flames. The people were left destitute and half clad in bitter weather.

At the mouth of the ravine he turned aside and stopped. Crazy Horse growled at him, "Come! Let nobody hang back. Why do you stop?"

Wapaha Jim looked up from a slim body that lay stretched out in the trampled snow. "I have found a friend who needs me," he said, and the chief nodded and stalked on. Friendship came first in peace or war. No man must be left to die alone.

"I die, Wapaha," whispered Long Mane. He added proudly, "It was I who called out, and they shot me. Wapaha . . ."

He choked, recovered. "Bad Buffalo . . . your blood-brother. And Tatanka Hinto. And Running Bear. Many more. But not Long Mane. My heart was bad against you. Yet we played as boys. Now that I die . . . Wapaha, I would be your brother."

There was little time left. Wapaha Jim slashed his own forearm with his knife. He held the cut against Long Mane's chest. "Long Mane, my brother. . . ."

Bad Buffalo and four others found him still kneeling there, long after there remained no need to hold the limp body. "We go to get our ponies back, if we can," said Bad Buffalo after a steady look at the dead man. "You will lead us, Wapaha." He looked away. "Yellow Eagle died a little time ago, charging the soldiers."

Wapaha Jim stood up slowly. "My father . . . dead?"

"Yes. The old man's couch and fire were not for him. His heart was always young, and he was a warrior. He had to die this way. We look for another chief and we see you, Wapaha. The ponies . . ."

"Must I fight for ponies while I cry for my dead?"

"Without our ponies we will soon all be dead," said Bad Buffalo truthfully. He laid a hand on his friend's chest. "Now you are our chief. You must lead us, or it will be said that our chief has a little heart, and so shame us."

Prestige. Always prestige, first consideration, taking prominence even above death and disaster. But they were right about the ponies. "*Hopo*—let us go," muttered Wapaha Jim. He picked up his gun, and they trailed after him at a trot up the ravine.

The soldiers never forgot Powder River. They were plagued through the ravine and harassed for miles over the plains by recurrent raids and sniping. Dog-tired, hungry, disgusted, they were no match for the infuriated tribesmen. And they never forgot nor forgave the crowning insult of all, when—after they had joined Crook's main column—a tall hellion in ragged elkskin leggings and armless shirt led a swooping raid on the ponies and recaptured them. As an added touch of daring impudence the hostiles ran off with the Army beef-herd, too, to make up for their destroyed supplies. The half-naked Indians didn't appear to feel the cold. Their hearts were hot. The hungry soldiers nearly perished in their bearskin greatcoats, flannel shirts, blanket jackets, merino underware, buffalo boots and lambs'-wool socks.

It was three days before the Sioux tired of tormenting the struggling column and vanished, leaving the expedition crippled, short on rations, and with a trek of two hundred miles back to Fort Fetterman in Wyoming. The impossible had happened. A strong and confident Army force had been driven back, outfought and worn down by a gang of wild hostiles who didn't know when it was time to surrender and quit. The stunned officers of the expedition cursed Crazy Horse and his sub-chiefs, but with a new respect. Those untrained, ill-equipped red devils possessed a temper and a power beyond ordinary human scope. The soldiers ate horse-meat on the way home, the ambulances were crowded, and General Crook had sixty-six disabled and frost-bitten casualties to report when the column at last limped into Fort Fetterman.

When the news reached Fort Lincoln in Dakota, the men of the Seventh knew that they would very soon be called upon to go out and show what they could do. They were ready and willing. All those hostiles needed was a healthy taste of Custer's Cavalry, and they'd pull in their horns and be good. Custer was of the same opinion. There weren't enough Indians in the world to stand up against his unbeatable regiment.

Word came that General Crook was taking to the field again from Fort Fetterman with another expedition against the Powder River stronghold. By that time the Seventh was ten days out from Fort Lincoln, riding westward toward the Big Horn Mountains to search for Sitting Bull and his warrior army. They were to be joined along the Yellowstone by a Montana force under General Gibbon. With the Seventh marched three companies of infantry and a platoon of Gatling guns. General Terry went in command of the column, and under him Custer commanded the cavalry. Now it was early summer, and the snow was gone. No halfway measures this time. The hostiles must be subjugated and forced to live peaceably on the reservations, and the Army marched out to do the job.

The women hid their fears, as usual, and admired the gallant flash of buttons and spurs, the martial splendor of blue-clad fighting troops and groomed horses winding off through the sun-sparkled dust to the tune of "Garry Owen." Such superb men as these could surely never know disaster, and it was foolish to worry about them.

Earlier they had spoken their forcedly cheerful good-byes, their bravely frivolous send-offs, their whispered intimacies.

"Got your pipe, Tom? Matches? Well . . . good-bye, dear."

"John, don't you dare bring back any Indian belles—!"

"Marty, darling. Every night at ten o'clock . . . You'll remember?"

"Of course, sweet. I'll whisper my good-night to you. Don't forget to answer me."

"We'll be back in time for furlough, Grace. Write and tell your mother we'll be visiting her in the fall."

" 'Bye, Tally."

" 'Bye, West. If—if you should see him . . ."

"Sure. Be good. I'll take you East when I get back."

"*Trumpeter! Sound 'boots and saddles.'* "

The gay lilt of the band faded out, and when there was nothing more than the long line of dust to be seen the women drifted back to quarters. The fort seemed very big, very quiet, very empty. It would be a long, long summer.

CHAPTER 14

★

ON THE LITTLE BIG HORN

ON THE WIDE FLATS ALONG THE BANK OF THE LITTLE BIG Horn River stood the lodges of the Sioux and the Cheyennes, forming a dotted arabesque of circles that decorated the flats for a distance of some three miles. The forces of Crazy Horse had combined with those of Sitting Bull and Chief Gall, but not without another encounter with General "Three Stars" Crook.

With his second expedition, Crook had run into them on the Rosebud River—and been turned back again after a bloody fight. He had known, as did everyone else, that Crazy Horse was making his way to join Sitting Bull, and he and his troops did their utmost to prevent the juncture of the two great hostile forces. But the Indian fortunes of war were riding high, and every warrior tasted victory. Unable to break the advance of the feathered men, Crook withdrew with his wounded to the Goose Creek supply camp and out of the campaign for the time being.

Crazy Horse and his followers, now regarding themselves as unconquerable, pushed on toward the Little Big Horn. One prong of the triple-tined Army was crumpled. The Sioux and the Cheyennes were perfectly willing to try conclusions with the next.

It was rumored that Long Hair Custer might be coming next, and that suited the warriors very well. They had it in for Long Hair and his pony-soldiers. Only three years ago he and the Seventh had protected the men who came to build the railroad through Indian territory. The following year it had been Long Hair and the Seventh again who went up into the Black Hills, heart of the Sioux country, and indirectly opened the way for the white mobs that came later to dig out yellow metal and ruin the hunting. And there was that old grudge arising from the crushing defeat and death of Chief Black Kettle on the Washita, eight years before. Decidedly, the Sioux and the Cheyennes wanted to meet Long Hair Custer. They were gathered in one strong force, for once. They were in a tough and disputatious mood, arrogantly sure of themselves after handing two beatings to a very surprised Three Stars Crook.

Wapaha Jim drove his ponies to water, and while he waited with the picket ropes he looked over the great allied camp. This was a hot and windless day, a lazy day not fashioned for war and effort, the kind of day to tempt any man to stretch on the grassy bank and reflect pleasantly upon past coups. A lot of his friends were doing no more than that. A man needed rest between fights, and time for contemplation. The fight with Crook on the Rosebud had taken place only a week ago. Three Stars was eliminated as a menace. Other soldiers would be coming, but nobody expected them today. When they did come, they would get all the fighting they wanted. Meantime the camp rested.

Wapaha Jim thought of many things: of Fort Lincoln and the cavalrymen, of Tally and West, of Custer and Vaugant and Major Chittendon. He recalled his talk with the major that night beside the Missouri. Perhaps the major had been right in the broad sense, when he spoke of primitive races always having to retreat before the march of civilization. *"It's an inevitable process. . . . Frontiers are never permanent."*

Ah, but not in this case. Not in the case of the Indian. *"Sometimes the savage brains the civilized man, Major."*

Yes, the soldiers could call themselves the sharp edge of civilization's advance. The major had put it correctly in accordance with his own viewpoint. But the red man was hard enough to blunt that edge, and was proving it. The soldiers were patriots, the major had intimated. True. The red man was also a patriot, fighting for his land, his right to roam over it at will and to keep out trespassers. Jim revolved it all in his mind, arguing with the major's contentions, arguing with himself.

"Your Indians are fighting a lost cause. They can't win."

No? What do you think now, Major? Have you heard about Crook? You will. He can tell you about Indians and whether they can win. Not Piutes and Apaches, but Sioux. Twice he's had to quit. *Twice!*

Well, the soldiers had called for it, and got it, and it had to be a fight to the death. They had to accept the penalty for failure that they themselves had set. There could be no surrender, no mercy asked, expected or given.

Jim tightened his lips. Foolish to let this sick and brooding depression take root in him. Foolish to allow himself to be haunted by the thought that he was in arms against men of his own blood-people. *These* were his people, these around him. Their cause was his, win or lose. And he was a chief. He must lead, not look on. Nor look back.

The shallow, winding stream of the Little Big Horn coursed north and south, lined with tall cottonwood mottes along here, and on the eastern side towered the ravine-scarred bluffs. The site was well chosen for such a large camp, but the camp would soon be breaking up for the summer hunting, if the soldiers didn't come first. Hunting was best done in small parties. Neither Sitting Bull nor Crazy Horse would be able to hold this great host intact for long. There were jealousies, too, and rampant individualism that rebelled at sustained control. Jim put the ropes on his watered ponies and started back to camp with them. The title and prestige of chieftainship in no way relieved its possessor of everyday work, but only added duties and responsibilities to it.

Somebody raised a sudden alarm. "Look—soldiers!"

It was just before noon. By the time Jim got his ponies to camp, riding one and lashing the rest, the whole camp had turned out to see the dust boiling up in the south. Soon they could see the blue shirts, the gilt glints, the shimmer of sunlight on gun-barrels, and then the formation of the coming cavalry.

The soldiers came on, not fast, but steadily. Then they spread out into skirmish line, put their mounts to the gallop, set up a cheer, and opened action with a spattering of pistol shots. This was at the extreme upper end of the camp, and the soldiers had to come up a rise in the ground. Their bullets pierced holes through the tops of some of the outlying tepees.

The Ree scouts struck from a slightly different angle at the same time, yelling and shooting, and made a rush to drive off and capture the vast pony-herd of the camp.

Confusion did not last long. The women and children fled northward in a stream. Chiefs shouted commands, and the warriors gathered around the tall headdresses of Sitting Bull and Chief Gall. Crazy Horse and his personal clique were living down at the other end of the camp, and hadn't had time to get here yet. Wapaha Jim, with better than forty of his own band behind him, headed a prompt counter-charge at the Rees. A huge mass of warriors advanced to meet the cavalry. The fight was on. This hot and lazy day was made for war, after all.

★

There was much said afterward concerning the question as to whether or not Custer disobeyed the instructions of General Terry and kicked the whole strategy of the campaign to ruination by his premature attack. And about Major Reno, who failed to break through to Custer's aid when desperately needed. And about the Army carbines which fouled after a few shots. And about the amazing military genius attributed to the hostile chiefs, particularly Sitting Bull. But when most of the elaborate constructions of technical theorists had crumbled to a conglomerate rubble of profundities, there remained the immutable laconicism of the frontiersmen: "There was just too many Injuns."

Three strong Army columns had started out to find and quell the hostiles: one from Fort Shaw in Montana, under General Gibbon; one from Fort Fetterman in Wyoming, under Crook; and the Dakota column from Fort Lincoln, under General Terry, with Custer commanding the Seventh United States Cavalry.

But Crook got thrown back at the Rosebud, Gibbon got tangled in the Yellowstone badlands, Terry was slowed up by his infantry and wagons, and the impatient Custer rode to disaster with exhausted men and wornout horses.

They thought the hostiles would try to run away. Custer was convinced of it, so he used his own initiative after he left the main Terry column at the Yellowstone. He was expected to circle wide around the Little Big Horn camp, unseen, and be ready to cut off escape when the column moved down to the attack. But he didn't circle. Maybe he thought the hostiles had spied him and guessed his maneuver, and that if he failed to attack at once the chance might never come again. So he didn't wait for the now combined forces of Terry and Gibbon to show up. He didn't know about the Rosebud battle, didn't know that Crazy Horse had made his junction with Sitting Bull, didn't think there would be more than a few hundred warriors to attend to. His men were seasoned soldiers. Fresh or weary, well fed or hungry, they could handle any enemy set up against them. The Irresistible Seventh. He was proud of his crack regiment, eager to add one more victory to its record. And cavalrymen never did consider any military maneuver so altogether satisfying as a rattling good cavalry charge.

After crossing the ridge between the Rosebud and the Little Big Horn valleys he split up his force in accordance with the accepted tenets of military strategy. One troop he detailed to escort the ammunition pack train. Three troops, as well as the Ree scouts, Major Reno commanding, were to follow the plain Indian trail to the river and the camp. Three more troops, under Captain Benteen, were to swing over to the unknown terrain beyond the bluffs and come in that way if feasible. He retained the five remaining troops for his own command, and forked off from Reno's course to strike the enemy from behind a long spur of high cliffs on the east bank. The pack train followed in the rear.

The camp was still several miles away. The going was easy for Reno, for he had only to follow the trail. But Benteen's troops ran afoul of rough ground beyond the main bluffs, and had to work back toward the trail, while Custer himself had to make a detour or two around ravines. They couldn't all converge upon the camp at the same time.

So it was Reno's battalion that got there first and opened the fight, while the Ree scouts made their try for the Sioux ponies. Reno had had to cross the river to get at the camp, but he never quite reached his objective. A thousand Sioux and Cheyennes changed his mind for him. The closer he got to the camp, the bigger he could see it spreading out before him, and the bigger the horde confronting him. More and more warriors came swarming forward, armed with everything from bows and arrows to old Sharps military rifles, and they fired as they came. The Indians weren't running away today.

Reno halted his deployed force and looked around for some sign of Custer, but Custer was as yet nowhere in sight, nor Benteen's column, either. He gave the order to dismount and fight a defensive action, pending the arrival of Custer and Benteen and the ammunition packs. The warriors came at him. He saw the Rees flee before a furious band of Sioux, and that left him exposed on his left flank. Now his total force was reduced to little more than a hundred troopers. He was terribly outnumbered. To avoid being surrounded and shot to pieces, he withdrew his troops to a strip of timber farther back along the river bank.

Wapaha Jim and his Minniconjous tore headlong into the Ree scouts, counted their coups on the run, and chased them far up the valley.

"*Hiyupo*—kill them all!"

"*Onhey*—this one I mark for mine! And this!"

The Rees were attached to the Army, but not to its iron creed. They regarded themselves as free lances. Recognizing signs of catastrophe, they fled.

Somebody in Reno's command set up a guidon. The little blue-and-yellow pennant immediately took on the nature of a challenge and a target for the tribesmen. It was shot to ribbons. Some horses broke loose and bolted. Men were falling. Reno looked to his rear.

Vaugant, serving under Reno, saw the hasty backward glance. "No!" he protested, and had to shout to make himself heard in all the screaming noise. "Hold fast—we can stand 'em off till Custer comes!"

He was in a cold military rage. Had he been in full command, in Reno's place, he would have carried through with the charge and tried to split the opposing force by sheer dash and drive. To halt a cavalry charge and dismount on the defensive, to him was the blackest kind of error. Horses then became liabilities, and cavalrymen were never at their best on foot.

But Reno had command. The pack train was somewhere out of reach, and he feared running out of ammunition. Many of the carbines were getting fouled. He couldn't go forward. The howling horde had him backed up. He thought it suicidal to stay here. Bullets and arrows were creating havoc among his men and remaining horses. He shouted a command to retreat across the river to the nearest bluffs, and Vaugant cursed him but was not heard except by a veteran trooper who'd fought through the Civil War on the Confederate side.

The veteran snatched up the remains of the guidon. With his right hand he spaced revolver shots at the oncoming red men. "Neveh tu'n youah back on an Injun, suh, eh?" he commented companionably, and headed after the others. He was lying dead on the river bank when Vaugant passed him, the guidon in the mud. He was one of thirty-two others.

Vaugant saved the guidon and started across the river. The water was all a-splash from bullets, and dead horses and men lay half submerged in it. Only two-thirds of the battalion had got over. He barely got one foot wet when a paralysis struck his legs. He rolled on the muddy bank, half in and half out of the water. "Got me in the spine, reckon," he thought calmly, and it brought to him a recollection of the South Fork and how he'd nearly drowned in it when the raider's bullet chipped his skull.

"Damnation, rivers are my bad luck," he muttered aloud, and with his hands he clawed his way into the nearest clump of brush. The last few troopers went plunging across and joined the rest who were scrambling up the bluffs. He heard hard breathing close by him, and discovered it came from a young pleb lieutenant who had also crawled into the brush.

The lieutenant grinned faintly at him. "Cursed hot day, Mr. Vaugant," he remarked, but his voice was weak and shaky. The front of his blue shirt was darkly wet. "I s'pose they'll take our hair. Before or after they finish us . . . do you happen to know?"

"Can't say," said Vaugant. "Never thought about it."

The lieutenant had a nice singing voice, had often sung to Tally Hathersall's mandolin accompaniment, and had thought himself a hot rival of Vaugant. "Cursed hot," he said again, and began moving off on his hands and knees.

"Where're you going? Don't move or they'll spot you. They're right above us."

The lieutenant's reply came back, weaker. "I know. River. Going to get cooled off. S'long."

He got as far as the river. A group of Cheyennes, watching from the cottonwoods higher up the bank, let him get that far. They even let him suck up some water. Then they shot him and turned their attention again to the bluffs on the other side, where Reno and his remnant command were digging in to make a stand.

The valley had all the excitement of a battlefield, shooting sounding constantly along the river, groups of warriors riding over the flats. Wapaha Jim, returning from chasing the Rees, lost touch with his band. Everything was in a turmoil. Grim old Sitting Bull and his chiefs were trying to organize a grand attack on the bluffs, but most of the warriors were too busy seeking trophies and captured horses.

A Cheyenne came tearing up on a sobbing pony. "More soldiers coming!" he yelled, and pointed toward the other end of the long camp, three miles off. "More —many more!"

Wapaha Jim headed a wild race down-river. Chief Gall caught up with him, and Jim let him pass, a courtesy due the war-chief. He looked back and found hundreds following, but enough were staying to keep things hot for the soldiers on the bluffs. They thundered through the camp in a smother of dust, crossed the river to the big ravine at the foot of the spur of cliffs, and found hundreds more gathered there under Crazy Horse. Some men had set fire to dry grass in the hope of blinding and confusing the coming soldiers, and smoke rolled in clouds up the broken cliff-walls.

The Indian mob waited below the cliffs, those ahead

up the ravine watching and signalling every move of
the Army column. The mounted troops came at a trot
along the high bluffs, and for a moment were outlined
against the sky before they began the descent toward
the ravine and the river.

The watching Indians breathed noisily. Some of them
whined softly in their throats, eyes blazing. Chief Gall,
dour and dominant, growled to them to restrain themselves until he gave the word. But there was no actual
need for his injunction. The warriors knew what they
were doing. They were following a simple and direct
course that contained no element of inspired military
genius. With Reno's troops blocked and besieged three
miles up-river, and the Rees routed, natural reaction to
the new danger sent them to meet it in its turn. It was
due to the peculiar nature of the terrain, rather than to
Indian cunning, that Custer failed to see Chief Gall
lead his hundreds racing down-river to set the ambush.
Their dust mingled with the smoke of the burning grass,
and noises were largely cut off by the high cliffs.

Custer, leading his five troops of cavalry, reached a
point where he could overlook part of the valley and
the lower end of the camp. From that position, he saw
through the smoke what appeared to be a medium-sized
camp, almost deserted, and his only fear was that the
hostiles must have fled before Reno. He couldn't see
the horde waiting below the cliffs in the crooked mouth
of the ravine which he had to traverse in order to come
down to the river. He had heard the shooting, could
still hear some of it going on in the distance, and he
reckoned that Reno must have a bunch of the enemy
holed up somewhere.

He brushed back his fair mustaches, gave the brim
of his hat a tug, and motioned his troops to break into
a gallop. There was no time to lose. The Indians could
not have got far in their flight. He glanced back, ran a

professional eye over the column. A pity the horses were so done up. They had been without water for eighteen hours. The men had been in the saddles for almost a day and a half—and looked it, he had to admit. All bearded and grimy with dust. Nobody had shaved since leaving Fort Lincoln, thirty-nine days ago. Fagged out, all of them. Only one meal since leaving the Terry command. Well, he'd led men and horses in worse shape than this into action, and never been beaten yet. They'd perk up when they contacted the enemy.

Damn! But if those Indians got away . . .

He led his column into the ravine, down toward the river. All was quiet, save for the steady beat of the hoofs and the muffled popping of that distant gunfire.

Then hell exploded a thousand reports that blended into one long roar, and he found himself facing more Indians than he had ever faced before. Two thousand armed warriors full of fight. He had less than three hundred men with him.

The numbers of hostiles, the sudden fury of their attack, amazed him. Soon he was ringed in, troopers falling with their killed horses, the focal point for two thousand hammering and twanging weapons in the capable hands of the most warlike and dangerous Indians on the plains. The Panther of the Washita had ridden full into a death-trap. His charge was halted, smashed like a rock against granite.

He kept his head: For all his impetuosity he was seldom anything but cool, retaining a mastery of mind over chaos, able to estimate accurately the depth and extent of any emergency confronting him. He saw the Indians rising up everywhere about him in ever increasing numbers, hundreds slipping around to his rear, flanking him, blocking his escape up the ravine. Forced into it, against all his code and instincts as a cavalryman, he rapped a command to his trumpeter.

The hurried call blared out. The troopers dismounted to fight afoot on defense, trying to beat off the storming tide with their carbines and dragoon pistols spurting over saddle rests. Most of the mounts of the Grey Horse Troop broke away, and were soon followed by bays and sorrels. The tide closed in. Another sharp command and the retreat was made to higher ground, to a hilltop, pressed hard by the shouting tribesmen. The rest of the horses became unmanageable.

The Indians swarmed up the hill, blurred shapes in the blinding smoke and dust, advancing behind reddish flashes that boiled the thick haze in eddies. Then the carnage of the hand-to-hand struggle, and another hurried trumpet call that was chopped off short and never completed. . . .

CHAPTER 15

★

THE BLUE AND THE RED

AGHAST, HYPNOTIZED BY THE ENORMITY OF THE CATASTRO-phe, Jim could only look on from the bottom of the ravine. It was a nightmare. He could not believe it a reality, yet there it was happening before him—Custer defeated and wiped out with five troops of the peerless Seventh. Incredible! His mind refused to accept the monstrous fact. These could not be men of the Seventh who were dying.

He had been ready with his rifle to fire with the rest as the column rode into range, fully prepared to help fight off the enemy. But he had caught sight of the familiar head of Custer in the lead, the fair mustaches, the black slouch hat with its gold cord, and eyes that even at that distance could be seen as a dazzling blue. And other heads, the heads of men whom he had known and liked in Fort Lincoln. He could not shoot, and he had sat there on his restless pony while the rest swept forward. For the first time he grasped the full meaning of what they had implied when they had branded him a renegade. He could no more hammer bullets into them than he could have fired upon his Sioux friends. To shoot into that column of the Seventh Cavalry was like shooting at West, or Major Chittendon, or Tally. They were his people. They were not his enemies, and could not be. These were men of his own race and kind, dying in a trap.

A sick revulsion at the Indians rose in him, and with it a senseless desire to aid the defeated men. The soldiers were no longer the implacable hunters, the Indians no longer the persecuted prey. The soldiers were now the underdogs, beaten, and the Indians were on top, giving no mercy.

But there was nothing that he could do here. The soldiers were overwhelmed. Bodies littered the ravine, trailing the course of the retreat to the hill where they lay thickest, and their slayers had got to the business of stripping them of weapons and clothes. Even the runaway horses had been shot down in the blazing passion of the fight. The saddles were being taken; their leather could be cut up for straps and the binding of lance-shafts.

He turned away, unable to stand any more sights of such sacrilege, and wheeled his pony back into the valley. Some shooting still sounded spasmodically up the river, and he rode that way. He met Bad Buffalo leading two captured cavalry horses that had belonged to Reno's party, a troop guidon and spear stuck upright as an added trophy in one of the stirrup straps.

"Are you wounded, Wapaha?" Bad Buffalo queried concernedly.

"No. . . . No, I am not wounded." Jim rode on and left him staring and puzzled.

★

Benteen and his three troops had joined Reno on the bluffs, and the ammunition train a little later. Crossing a rise in the distance, Benteen had seen Reno's broken command plunging across the river and up the bluffs, and then he saw the size of the enemy force. To continue on to the camp with his small force and strike that huge tribal army would have been suicidal. He headed directly for the bluffs, keeping to his own side of the river, got there before they were cut off from him, and the pack train followed at a run. None of them knew what had happened to Custer, for the fatal ravine lay out of sight three miles away, but from the sounds that reached them they guessed that he must have run into a hot fight somewhere.

They entrenched on the bluffs, besieged from all points, and when the distant firing died down they didn't know what to think. Maybe Custer had been forced back. Maybe he had got through to the camp and was coming to lift the siege for them. But this last was a thin hope. The lack of firing along there was not encouraging.

More Indians, belonging to the mob that had ridden off down-river with Gall, came trickling back, shouting and exultant. The besieged men decided Custer must have been forced to withdraw. They thought of the main Army command, advancing down from the Yellowstone under Terry and Gibbon. Custer's Cavalry

was paying a high price for being too quick to fight.
Terry had planned his grand attack on the camp for
the twenty-seventh, and he'd know of no reason for al-
tering his plans. Today was the twenty-fifth.

"Where's Vaugant?" Benteen asked.

A huddled-down trooper sent a shot across the river
at a Sioux galloping through the cottonwoods, and swore
when he missed. "Somewheres yonder, sir, I reckon," he
responded. "Him an' a helluva lot more."

West Hathersall crawled over. He had come up with
Benteen's force. "Who's that officer lying down there
with his head in the water?"

"That's Lieutenant Wheeler, sir," said the trooper.
"Dead. I been keepin' 'em off from his scalp. Some of
'em hanker for his hair. It's light an' curly, y'know. There
goes 'nother'n to try for it. Watch me drop him." He
aimed carefully and fired.

West cocked his pistol. "That fellow's too quick for
you. I'll get him." He blazed three shots, and the hammer slapped on an empty shell. "Quick, all right.
Where'd he go?"

"In the brush," Benteen told him. "Let's smoke him
out."

"Better not, sir," put in the trooper. "I got a notion
there's a wounded man or two of ours layin' in there,
God help 'em. I'll watch for that devil to poke his head
up, if he ever does."

Jim was relieved when more bullets didn't begin
screaming down into the brush where he lay flat on his
stomach. That pistol shooter had got off his three shots
fast and close, whoever he was. The bullets had spattered through the foliage, one tearing a groove in his
back en route. It made a painful wound and he felt himself bleeding. He lay still, figuring out his near sur-
roundings from the mental image he had taken of them
from among the cottonwoods higher up the bank. That

dead lieutenant must be lying a little way ahead and to the left.

He raised his head a fraction and peered through the brush. Yes, there he lay. He could see the booted feet, toes sunk in the mud. Vaugant, then, must be over toward the right, in line with the dead man.

He had spotted the captain without at first knowing it was he, when he rode through the cottonwoods to get a nearer look at the dead lieutenant on the lower bank. Seeing the fair hair, he had thought at once of West. But it wasn't West, he'd found on hasty inspection. It had to be a hasty inspection on the lope, because somebody up on the bluffs was shooting at him. Then he saw the other officer, partly hidden by the overhanging brush, lying on his back with his eyes open and alive. He slid off his pony and let it go, and tracked back on foot for a better look.

He saw then that it was Vaugant, and right away he had to take a long leap down to avoid catching some fast pistol-shooting. He edged on toward Vaugant.

★

Vaugant said levelly, "Hello, renegade! Come for my hair?" He held his pistol cocked in his right hand.

Jim pulled himself nearer. "How bad are you hurt?"

"Not so badly that I can't pull this trigger!"

"Good. You can use your hands. Be ready when you hear me coming with horses. Try to signal the soldiers not to fire on me. We'll have enough trouble, getting away from the Indians."

"What the hell!" muttered Vaugant. "What's your game, damn you?"

His face was sunken with pain and from loss of blood, and now a black rage brought the lines of his features into sharp prominence. It was his position and his helplessness that enraged him. It cut his stiff pride and ego. The hardest blow that Jim could have dealt him he was dealing now—quietly stating his intention to save him. To be saved by this man was intolerable. Vaugant cursed him. "Hell take your damned renegade soul, get out of my sight or I'll shoot!"

Jim had never been able to figure out why Vaugant aided him in his escape from Fort Lincoln. It had not been from sympathy or anything like friendship, that was certain. But Vaugant had done it, no matter for what reason, and it was a debt to be paid. Also, he was a white man and a captain of the Seventh. "You helped me escape, once," Jim said. "I do the same for you, if I can."

He slipped on through the brush, and Vaugant spent most of his failing energy in sending more curses after him. For Vaugant it was irony of the most biting kind, but after awhile, white and exhausted, he thought of the Terry column. Somebody would have to get word through to Terry and hurry him. If Aherne could get horses, if he could break out of this valley with the man . . .

Up on the bluffs West wiped his smoke-stung eyes after helping repel another attempt by a hostile party to rush the high position from the south side. He crawled back to his spot overlooking the river and found the same trooper still there.

The trooper was cutting his boot away from a badly swollen ankle. "I swear I saw that feller again, skulkin' off awhile ago," he complained. "But my damn gun's fouled. Heard any word about Custer yet, sir? Wonder where he is?"

All the command was asking that same question, aloud or mentally, but nobody knew the answer. West cleaned the trooper's carbine for him. It occurred to him that he did it quickly and efficiently. His hands did not blunder; they were steady. He realized that he was not nervous. He remembered that only a few minutes ago while repelling the rush, he and Benteen had exchanged grimy grins when they collided while diving for the same shallow rifle-pit. "I'll make a good soldier yet," he thought, entirely without conceit, and was a little annoyed to find that the revelation surprised him. "Hell, I *am* a good soldier!"

The trooper banged away with his cleaned carbine. He was a fair marksman, but slow in finding his sights. "Look at that cuss—same one!" he exclaimed exasperatedly. "Ridin' two ponies this time, damn'f he ain't! What's that movin' down there in the bush?"

"Don't shoot at that waving arm, man—it's got a blue sleeve!" West had his field glasses out. He swept their focus up from the brush where the arm waved, to the rider threading at a mad gait down through the cottonwoods, riding one pony and leading another. "Jupiter's ghost! Hey, don't shoot at that man, either! *It's Jim . . . Jim Aherne!*"

"What? The renegade?"

"Renegade be damned! He's going down for a wounded man, can't you see? *Come on, Jim—make it, old man!*"

The rider shot out of the trees. The two madly racing ponies bumped, sliding down the bank, their flying hoofs gouging out chunks of loose earth, and it seemed certain that they must tangle and spill together, but they kept their footing. The lean rider bent far over, punched and kicked the led pony away from his side, and swung both animals crashing full into the brush. A group of Cheyennes showed up on top of the bank, all afoot and shouting in angry surprise. But none of them shouted louder than West on the bluffs.

"Look out, Jim, they're after you! Oh, you—you wild-headed son . . . Oh, you Jim! Damn it, you men, drive

those turkeys back! Shoot, damn it, shoot! Oh, God, they got him!" The Cheyennes were firing. The rider tumbled between his ponies.

★

Jim was hit, but his tumble was voluntary and fore-designed, although almost ruined by the sickening punch of the Cheyenne bullet that smashed through his ribs. He had one arm over the neck of his pony, a hand tight in the mane of the other, holding both animals apart while they dragged him through the brush. He did what he could to hold them to their course when they wanted to swerve aside from the man lying in their path, and at the last instant he threw his legs forward and spread them apart, putting all his weight on the ponies.

From his expression, Vaugant thought he was going to be trampled, but as he stroked up his pistol he saw and comprehended Jim's maneuver, and he raised both arms and tried to sit up. The moccasined feet came forking at him, hooked under his armpits, and he clamped his arms around the legs.

It was a rough kind of rescue. Years later the cavalry were to perfect a slightly gentler method of picking up a disabled man on the run—the "monkey drill." But that required a pair of expert horsemen working together, not one, and some said it was a modification of an old Indian trick. The violent wrench brought a smothered groan from Vaugant, but he hung on, and then he and Jim were locked together, towed between the ponies.

In a sheltered sag of the higher bank farther up-stream, Jim hauled the ponies' heads together and forced the animals to halt. He staggered, boosting Vaugant onto the back of one, and mounted the other.

"Hang on, best you can," he said, and took the pistol. "How far to the rest of the column—and where?"

"Toward the Yellowstone. Fifty miles or more. Are you hit, too?"

"Yes."

"Too bad," said Vaugant bleakly, getting a grip on his mount's mane. "Too bad if you die. Some day I want the pleasure of killing you, if I get out of this. Where's Custer?"

"Dead, and all his men. Come on!"

They rode up-river and crossed it before the Indians besieging the bluffs realized that one of them was a soldier. Both were tattered from the clawing brush, smothered with mud, unrecognizable now. Even then the watching Indians did not shoot, thinking the soldier a captive, until the band of Cheyennes came racing along the bank in pursuit. Jim lashed both ponies with his belt, keeping Vaugant before him, and took to the first opening in the long wall of bluffs.

On the plains beyond the bluffs they halted again. Vaugant could not hang on any more. His eyes were still open, but that was his only sign of life when Jim held him from sliding off. But he cursed when Jim touched his useless legs, cursed with his teeth shut.

"I've got to tie you on," Jim told him, and stumbled against his pony. "And myself." He made use of Vaugant's belt and his own. He strapped Vaugant's feet together under the belly of his pony, and managed to do the same task for himself.

Vaugant's greyed face twitched when his mount took a step, the agony of his strapped legs almost overpowering him. He squeezed his eyes shut, and when he opened them they were glassy and seemed of a different color. "I think you enjoyed doing that," he gasped. "You damned savage, you're grinning at me!"

Jim's grin stemmed from pain and the effort to hold onto consciousness, and he said nothing. Half his body

felt hacked to broken bones and torn flesh, and the premonition of death touched him again as it had in Fort
Lincoln. With such a wound, a man could not expect
to ride fifty miles and live. And he was no worse off
than Vaugant. But perhaps the ponies would keep on
the move, after they got well away from the camp.

He weakly slapped both ponies, and they settled to
their steady lope. Vaugant moaned and lolled over. Jim
rode up close to him, held him from dangling head
down, and they rode that way, hanging on to each
other, knee to knee.

Early next morning a mounted infantry lieutenant,
scouting the trail ahead of the marching column, sighted
two lonely objects far ahead. He adjusted his field
glasses and inspected them. Two horses, he made them
out to be, played out and just standing there droop-
headed, each with a bundle on its back. When he came
up to them they didn't even pretend a show of shying
off. The bundles, he found, were two men. He raised
the head of the one in tattered blue, saw the sunken
face and cavalry buttons, and got the shock of his life.

"Goddlemighty!" he gulped, and jumped to his horse
and spurred hard back to the column.

CHAPTER 16

★

BISMARCK

A BRIGHT SUN WARMED THE MUDDY STREET, AND THE
plank sidewalks were already drying although it was
not yet noon. Winter had tapered off and now it was

early spring again. Carpenters were at work, the pounding of their hammers distinct in the clear air, building another frame house to add to the town of Bismarck, but the essential quietness of the street and the morning were left undisturbed.

This was still a new town, a frontier town only sixteen miles from Fort Lincoln, but it had early taken a strong hand with the lawless element and driven it out. Here a young matron could wheel her new baby in its new bassinet along the boardwalk for the morning stroll to market, serene in the knowledge that the most reckless horseman would take to the far side of the street to avoid splashing her. Saturday nights had their riotous hours, but that was to be expected and condoned, and respectable people knew when to stay home. It was fundamentally a town of sober citizens who attended to their businesses, of young married couples who had come West with some capital and ambition, and many children. Where there are families there is responsibility, and where there are children there is law. The houses were neat, small, most of them new, each with its frilled curtains, its bit of garden, and generally a baby carriage out in front when the sun shone. Bismarck was growing fast, and had passed quickly through its wild period of frontier adolescence.

Jim Aherne finished reading the *Bismarck Gazette,* looked up, and for a moment felt as if he had been whisked back here from a long journey and deposited into a cool pond, a sanctuary untouched by the slightest ripple of harshness. It was unreal and monstrous that he should be here, sitting in a neat little garden before a neat little house on a quiet street, while men still starved and fought and died elsewhere.

He put a hand to his side and dug his fingers under his ribs to feel for pain. There was very little. He was well. Well enough, at least, to ride a pony, and that was recovery according to Sioux standards.

The months had passed, some of them lost to him because of his drugged senses and terrible weakness, others intolerable when the wracking pain tormented him night and day. He had no memory of being borne back to Fort Lincoln, or of anything thereafter except clouded snatches of semi-consciousness, until one cold morning he discovered that it was Tally who seemed always to be beside him. The hospital was crowded with the wounded of the Reno and Benteen troops, and a civilian doctor had been engaged to help the overworked Army surgeon.

"Tally . . . Did—the rest—get there?"

"Yes, Jim. The same day they found you and Vaugant."

"And Vaugant—?"

"Alive. They say he'll recover."

Then the long torture. An aching body tightly taped —"To hold you together," said the doctor. A wound that healed too fast, and the burning, bursting agony of inflammation. The Bismarck doctor lanced it open again. He probed for more bone splinters. "Must be you're the Lord's pet," he said. "That nasty bit of lead did damage enough to kill a buffalo. You lost a pow'ful lot of blood."

They fed him cautiously on liquids, and were interested to find that he could hold them. When he could roll over and feed himself they moved him into Bismarck to the little house on the quiet street. Tally's house, so new that it smelled woody, and a woman servant so old that she ran the household as her own.

"Uncle Philip left everything to West and me," Tally told Jim. The major had died with Custer. "I couldn't stay on at Fort Lincoln very well, with Uncle gone and West away on campaign, so I had this little house built for me. You're to stay here till you're well, Jim."

It did not occur to either of them that the arrangement might not be in accordance with the best proprieties as seen through the eyes of respectable Bismarck. Tally's standards were forthright and independent, and Jim's followed the strict but simple probity of the Sioux. Neither required more than a purely personal moral code of conduct, with little need for obeisances to the dictates of convention.

Tally came out of the house and joined Jim in the patch of garden. She sat and regarded him, as she sometimes did, frankly and with a gravely humorous curiosity. "I should be used to you by now, but I'm not," she said thoughtfully. "Not quite, that is. I mean, I can't quite get used to seeing you as a white man."

His dark tan was gone, bleached out, leaving only the natural darkness of skin that she remembered his having as a boy. She recalled that his father had had that same kind of fine dark skin, same high cheekbones, same hint of seeking in his wide-apart eyes, same black hair. She smiled, thinking of how she had played Delilah and sheared off that long hair while Jim lay helpless. He had hardly known himself when she held a mirror before him, and she had laughed outright at his expression.

"But you're decidedly a white man, and you don't need those civilized clothes you're wearing to prove it." She nodded at him, still smiling. "And yet there's a difference about you. I can't place my finger on it, but it's there. Perhaps it's because you lived with savages so long."

"Perhaps it's because I *am* a savage," he said somberly.

"No." She shook her head slowly. "Underneath, you're as civilized as your father ever was—as far as that went. You're a most presentable white man, too, I might add. Handsome. But you probably know that. Oh, I've seen

some of our fair lady neighbors eyeing you as they
tripped by—the coy sweets, darn 'em. You're such a
tall and striking sort of animal, Jim. You make most
other men look tame. Yes, it must be some of the old
wildness in you."

He didn't smile. He dropped his gaze back to the
newspaper, and said, "I'm what I always was, Tally."

Her own smile faded. "Another battle?"

"Yes. At a place called Red Water. The Sioux were
defeated again. Sitting Bull is said to be trying to retreat up into Canada. He hasn't many fighters left."

★

After Custer's disaster, the thoroughly aroused government had poured soldiers into the Indian country,
column after column.

The high tide of war's fortune receded for the Red
Man. There were so many out to crush him—General
Terry, General Crook, Colonel "Bear Coat" Miles . . .
Cavalry and infantry, Gatling guns, light artillery, Crows
and Rees. They were all after him. A price had been
placed on the feathered head of old Sitting Bull. The
remnants of the Seventh were out with the rest, craving to avenge Custer. Winter had not stopped the relentless pursuit.

The Yellowstone—Slim Buttes—Cedar Creek—half a
dozen other places of battle, and each a defeat for the
Sioux. The great army of Sitting Bull had broken up.
The crippled old chief had tried to hold the plains
tribes together, but there were too many feuds, too much
ancient animosity and arrogant individualism dividing
them. Fragments of his forces broke away, went hunting; or, being hungry, and tired of fighting on the run,
rode into the Indian agencies for rations and traded
their independence for something to eat. The Cheyennes

quit and gave up. Crazy Horse, after wintering in the Big Horns and nearly starving to death, finally surrendered with three hundred warriors. Chief Gall swallowed his pride and ate agency rations.

But not Sitting Bull. Not that irreconcilable old hater. With the dregs of his once mighty legion he was fighting his way to the land of the Red Coats, burdened with aged patriarchs and crones who stayed with him because of old faith, and children too young to desert him. But his remaining warriors were the die-hards, the toughest of the crop; they'd stick as long as there was action and something left to fight for. Through the severe winter they had kept on the move, dodging, fighting, losing their tepees, food supplies, spare ponies. Hunting was poor. There was little meat. The starving survivors of a wild empire pushed on toward exile, harried from all sides, turning to fight off the pursuers and dragging wearily on again into the north.

The *Gazette* carried an account of the latest fight, this one on Red Water. A few prisoners had been taken, among them a wounded warrior who had stayed behind to fight a rearguard action while his people got away. But that night he knifed a trooper, stole a horse and gun, and escaped despite his wounds. Crow scouts said his name was Bad Buffalo.

It meant that some of the old band, at least, were sticking it out to the end with Sitting Bull and retreating with him to the north. Jim, knowing the hardships of such a retreat, could see it in all its stark misery: women trudging ahead with their hungry children, the old men hurrying them; the lean warriors half-clad and shivering, riding in the rear on thin and spent ponies. A stubborn, unsurrendering mob of outlaws, led by a crippled old wolf who could not forget that he had been the mightiest chief of the Indian nations.

"They're whipped—why don't the soldiers let them

go?" Jim exclaimed, and his skin grew whiter. He stared at Tally, but he wasn't seeing her, and she knew his visions.

"It's Sitting Bull they want," she said. Fear crept into her face, a fear that was not new. "Don't think about it, Jim. If he surrenders . . ."

"He'll never surrender! And there are others like him. If they had kept together—if so many of the chiefs hadn't deserted him . . ." He crushed the newspaper in his hands. "I deserted, too!"

They were silent a long time. Tally rose suddenly, with a look in her eyes that would have disturbed West. She came around and stood behind Jim, and rested a hand on his shoulder. "Jim . . ." Her voice had a breathless quality. She paused for better control. "Jim, I've been told it's time I married. West said so a year ago. Do—do you think . . ."

She had to pause again. This pretense at casual coquetry was too hard to keep up, too false, and she could not go through with it in that vein. She said levelly, "Jim, I know you love me. Why don't you ask me to marry you?"

He came to his feet. "Tally, I . . ." He faced her, looked down at her, and she met his eyes and searched them. "I can't. What am I? A renegade—a white savage. I shouldn't be here. I should be up there with Bad Buffalo and the rest. Why should I be here, safe and well fed, while they starve and die? I have friends and blood-brothers among them. Many of them would risk their lives for me, if I needed help and they could give it."

"But you love me, don't you?"

"I'm Wapaha," he said. "I'm a Sioux. My color doesn't change that. These clothes don't change it. I'm one of them. I believed in their cause, and they believed in me. They made me a chief. Don't you see I can't just turn my back and forget them, now that they're beaten? As long as I'm alive, they look for me to come back to them. Perhaps I could help them. God knows they need help now!"

"But you love me, don't you?"

". . . Yes, Tally."

She stood on her toes and kissed him. "Well, at least I got you to admit that," she said shakily. "I know you'll do whatever you feel you have to do, Jim. Stubborn, just like your father. Won't listen to anybody, will you? But—Jim—whatever you do—please don't get yourself killed. Maybe the world needs white savages like you— foolish champions of lost causes and the beaten. And if the world doesn't, then I do. Oh—here comes Martha with lunch. Thank you, Martha. . . ."

Two days later a familiar figure came walking up the quiet street. Captain George Vaugant had been on sick leave, and didn't yet look any too well. He was thinned down, and it brought out all the brittle hardness of his features. He walked stiffly, with not much of the cavalry swagger, his knees bending very little and his heels clomping solidly on the boardwalk. No spring to him.

Jim met him at the little picket gate, and the two men regarded each other. "Is Miss Hathersall in?" Vaugant queried curtly.

"No. Shopping."

"Good. No, I'll not come in. What I've got to say I can say on my feet. I've been to Washington. They're still holding an investigation on the Little Big Horn affair, and I was called. Your name came up. I found that West Hathersall had cleared you in his report. He didn't actually say so, but he had intimated that you were privately working for Custer all along as a government special scout in the hostile camp."

"West didn't have to do that."

"No, and I don't thank him for it," Vaugant snapped stonily. "Naturally, I had to back up his statement. Custer never reported your escape, because it would have involved some of us. West Hathersall and I are the only ones left alive who know the truth about what happened, and we can't tell it, if only for Custer's sake. The commander's old report on you was read, too. Also, Terry mentioned you in his account. Yes, they held you up as a hero for saving me and being the means of hastening the column to Reno's relief. The fools!"

He thrust a hand under his tunic and drew out three long envelopes. "Yours. They were given to me to deliver to you personally. One contains your back pay as a scout, and another your brevet commission. This last one"—he almost gagged at the words—"is an official commendation on your conduct. 'Extraordinary valor and devotion to duty . . .' by Judas! And the suggestion that you take officer's training for regular rank. Here, take 'em. They've been burning my pocket long enough! And now I've a personal matter to discuss with you, Aherne—or Warbonnet, or Wapaha—or whatever you call yourself."

"Either will do," said Jim. "They're mine." He fingered the envelopes, hardly knowing what to do with them. When he thought of Vaugant's having to be the one to bring them to him he couldn't restrain an appreciative grin at the irony.

Vaugant saw the grin. Muscles bunched about his mouth. "You're living here in this house, and so is Miss Hathersall," he said, and his voice had a tinny ring. "Any man of ordinary perception would realize that such a situation is not to the best interests of a lady's good name. But you could hardly be expected to possess such perceptions, so I am taking it upon myself to . . ."

"What are you trying to say?" Jim interrupted.

Vaugant shifted his weight from one stiff leg to the other. "For your benefit I'll use blunt language that you may understand. You're doing Miss Hathersall no good by living in her house. Oh, we all know she's a lady and pure as sunlight, we who really know her. But there are others who don't know her, and they're whispering behind their hands. While you were an invalid I presume it was all right, but now you're as sound as I am, and it's getting to be a scandal. Why, I heard of it ten minutes after I got here, and I came near shooting the smirking blackguard who spoke of it in the hotel bar."

Jim said softly, "I could shoot another."

Vaugant's eyes gleamed readily. "I'd be happy to meet you any time, any place! But get out of her house first. You're wrecking her good name. Leave ladies alone and go back to your damned savages—you don't belong here! I'm not speaking merely for myself. I'm speaking as a white man for all white men." He really believed that, and it was evident in his black scorn and anger. It was not in his iron character to descend wittingly to accusations for purely personal motives.

He moved to go, and looked back. "Brevet commission! Lieutenant Aherne—*alias* Wapaha, the renegade! You'll never get away with that while I live. Don't try to change your eagle feathers for the spread-eagle! Go and take your licking with the rest of the savages, if you're the man you think you are!" He stamped off down the quiet street.

Jim Aherne stood for long minutes at the gate, staring unseeingly at the muddy street, and when he turned back to the house he shivered a little, but not from anger.

That afternoon he boarded a supply boat bound northward up the Missouri for the Buford Landing on the edge of Montana, and left behind him the brevet commission with a message to Tally scrawled on the envelope. The pay-drafts he cashed, and he used some of the money to buy tobacco, and when he reached Buford five days later he bought three horses and loaded two of them with dried beef. Then he struck on toward the northwest. The Sioux would be thankful to get the dried beef, if he could find them, and tobacco was a solace for tired warriors. He hoped he wouldn't run afoul of any Army detachments on his way. He didn't want to have to make his farewell to his country over a smoking rifle.

CHAPTER 17

★

SURRENDER

SITTING BULL HAD A HARSH DECISION TO MAKE THAT BORE heavily upon the fate of himself and his people—to return south and surrender, or stay here and starve. He was hard pressed. He retired alone up the slopes of Wood Mountain and earnestly prayed to *Wakan Tanka* for guidance.

"*Ho, Tunkansila wankanta.* . . . O, Great Father, I come to you. I—*Tatanka Iyo-ta'ke*—chief of my people, come to you as a small boy crying. I cry for help. *Tunkansila*, tell me what I must do for my people. The old ones are homesick, and they die. Our children go hungry. My warriors talk against one another . . ."

Here in the land of the Red Coats he had hoped to find a regeneration of the old freedom, and time and opportunity to rebuild the power of his nation around the meagre core of its remains. Defeated, his prestige at its lowest ebb, a poverty-ridden fugitive in exile, still he had held on to his hope of some day gathering the fighting tribes again under his command and sweeping the white men from the Indian country.

For a while he and his people had found here in Canada the peace and rest they needed. There was hunting and food. The Red Coats had been tolerant of their presence, though firm in their demands that the exiles obey the laws of the land. He had risen to new heights of tact and diplomacy, and made friends of the surrounding Canadian tribes, sternly punishing any of his unthinking young braves when they poached on forbidden territory or yielded to impulse and stole horses from the French Slotas. "Be good," he admonished them. "Obey the laws of the Red Coats. Be happy. Make friends."

But it was too good to last. His luck had deserted him when he needed it most, along with the bulk of his fighting men. Fires burned away the prairie grass, and the game vanished. Mange sickened the famished ponies. The young men were forced to cross furtively over into Montana for their hunting, braving the Army patrols on one hand and the Crows and Hohes on the other. Each time they brought back more casualties and less meat. Sometimes, failing all else, they stole cattle from the Montana settlements. Poverty roosted in the camp of Sitting Bull.

The French-Canadian traders began giving the Sioux the cold shoulder, and finally refused the old chief any more credit. Once they would have been glad to honor his promise to pay, but that was when the expert Sioux hunters had been rich in furs. Now they were beggars, and their high chief shuffled around in a shabby blanket. *Le Roi est mort!*

The isolated white settlers of Montana, forever in fear of seeing a red horde come thundering down upon them from the north, petitioned Washington again and again to trap the old king-wolf and eliminate the potential peril. There was always the chance that discontented agency Indians might slip away and join the exiles for a marauding invasion; as long as that chance persisted, settlement was retarded and the homesteaders already on the ground worried for their lives and property.

The folks in Washington set the wheels moving. The first effect became apparent when the Red Coats flatly informed the Sioux that they could not be granted a free reserve in Canada, that there were United States reservations waiting for them south of the line, and that they wouldn't be too broken up about it if the Sioux went to them.

Then came dribbles of agency Indians—men who had given up with Crazy Horse and Gall and other chiefs. Well fed, these men, and smug with new virtue. Their visits were brief, but potent. They talked behind the old chief's back, talked of food and leisure in the reservations, and went away again, leaving discontent behind them. More followers drifted off, went south over the line, gave themselves up for something to eat.

The Black Robes came—the missionaries—and used their well-intentioned persuasion. And sometimes a grave Army officer, flanked by Red Coats, arrived and spoke reasonably to the people. More desertions.

It was a cumulative process, a corroding and a steady whittling down of the old chief's power and following, aided by Nature in a harsh mood. The faithful old people remained, but they were homesick, pitifully homesick for their own land. This was alien soil. The young men, bound by the omnipresent Red Coats to keep the peace, hedged in by the exigencies of exile, and denied even the natural sport of stealing horses from the Slotas, soon grew dispirited and restless. The time came when the old champion had to choose between two bitter alternatives.

So he went alone up Wood Mountain and asked

Wakan Tanka about it. But *Wakan Tanka* had turned
his face away, so he came down, and after he sat for
three days in his lodge he called a council and announced his decision. "There is no place for us here. We
are not wanted. We will go back and give ourselves to
the soldiers."

He knew that he was proclaiming the final end of the
free Sioux nation; that when he crossed south over the
line it meant the death-blow to any last hopes for an
Indian renaissance. For himself it meant humiliation and
captivity, the termination of his prideful career. But his
people could hang on here no longer, and their fighting
edge was blunted. In this moment Wapaha Jim saw
the old chief as rising to his greatest height, divining
the best course for his people and grimly leading the
way against all his fierce instincts for self-interest.

The few sub-chiefs rose and gave their assents, each
in turn seconded by mutters from his followers. Wapaha
Jim rose last. He had nothing to gain and little left to
lose. "I go with the rest. Let my band speak."

Bad Buffalo hobbled forward. "We have kept together. We go back together."

He was hopelessly crippled. His right thighbone,
smashed by a bullet, had healed crookedly. He had
been near death when Jim rejoined the band, but he
had fought his dogged way back, and now he laughed
at the way he had to get around. Like a bear with an
arrowhead in its haunch, he said—one hip down, the
other up, all misshapen and grotesque. He rocked widely when he walked, and sat at an awkward slant when
he rode. Very funny. But Jim noticed that he didn't
turn on that ugly and engaging grin of his very much
any more. Laughed loudly and often, yes, but that was
not the same. Bad Buffalo had laughed aloud rarely in
the old days, but his grin had been a sincere and happy
thing to see.

They hadn't questioned Jim when he rejoined them. Where he had been was his own affair. His absence and reappearance was just one more tangled thread in a chaotic pattern where so many men and events had gone haphazard. The day of power was gone when they could afford to sit in judgment. They were glad he had come back, and were thankful for the dried beef and tobacco. When Jim had felt impelled to begin an explanation, Bad Buffalo voiced the general sentiment of the band.

"You were lost. You are with us again. That is enough, Wapaha," Bad Buffalo told him, and thumped him gently on the chest. "There are not so many of us now, but we still must have a chief."

There were not many in the melancholy procession that crossed the line below Willow Branch. Less than two hundred souls—all that was left intact of that untamed multitude that had spread its camp for three miles along the bank of the Little Big Horn. A trader—LeGare, a Frenchman—provisioned them for the journey, and accompanied them as far as Fort Buford with a caravan of wagons and Red River carts. He had to empty his warehouse to do it, and it was a total loss to him, but he was wealthy enough to afford a last generous gesture, and he was glad to get the Sioux out of his territory.

The old people grew more cheerful as the slow journey progressed farther south across Montana. They were coming home, and it was summer again and the wildflowers were blooming on the plains. They exclaimed in delight, pointing out to one another the dark fire of orange-lilies, the gorgeous cactus blossoms, the modest primroses. They had left many identical flowers blooming behind them just north of the line, but these were *their* flowers, the flowers of *their* land. Much better. Much brighter.

They said nothing about the buffalo bones that littered the plains everywhere, the skeletons left by the voracious white hunters. These were the gravestones of the great herds that had passed this way and would never return. The poorest fool in the plodding cavalcade knew that it was the slaughter of the buffalo that had rotted the foundations of the empire of the Indian. The loss of the buffalo had brought poverty and hunger, and hungry men had had to compromise and eat their pride along with agency rations.

They were met outside Fort Buford and given a camping place and rations, and time to rest. Little was said. The soldiers gathered around, curious. Officers walked through the camp. All stared constantly at Sitting Bull and his little coterie of head men. There he squatted, the notorious old wolf, with all that remained of his savage brood, in captivity at last.

The white men agreed that he didn't look so much. Just a shabby and tired old Indian, silently eating with the rest. Not a feather in his hair. Not a gaudy gewgaw on him. He was taking it hard, looked sick and broken. The officers discussed him among themselves.

"Well, he certainly gave us a dance for our money while he lasted, didn't he? I wonder if he's the actual man who put the bullet into Custer?"

"We'll never know. Any one of his crowd looks capable of having done it. That fellow with the bent leg, for instance. Did you ever see an uglier devil in your life?"

"Bad customer, all right. Say, look at that tall buck near him—the one with the red feather in his hair. I swear he's got grey eyes! What d'you make of him?"

"Got a nice build, eh? Could tear your head off, with those arms."

"But his eyes—!"

"Yes. I've seen a couple of northern Sioux with light

eyes, though. Somebody once told me that they've a legend about some golden-haired men who wandered into their country a long time ago and were taken into the tribe. Norse rovers, possibly, though only the Lord knows how they got this far inland. That fellow might be part throw-back. I've even heard of a Sioux with reddish hair. Think of that. Huh! Makes one suspect that those ancient rovers weren't Norsemen, but Irish, eh?"

In the afternoon they were lined up, and every Sioux sensed that the final step faced them. They were told to hand over their weapons. It was first a request, made mild so as to avoid friction. Some of the Indians complied before they fully realized what the act signified. Others held fast to theirs, glowering. The request was repeated as a peremptory demand. The troops were drawn up in formation, confronting the tribesmen.

Again the demand, and an answering silence. Then a sharp word of command that brought concerted movement from the soldier ranks. The defiance did not break. It looked like trouble.

A crippled figure slouched forward, ungainly, ugly. "I have fought many times with this gun," growled Bad Buffalo. "I have been a warrior. My coups are many. Now all that is finished. Take my gun."

It broke the tension. Others followed suit. Sitting Bull handed his own rifle to his youngest son, a boy, who paced over and laid it on the pile. Wapaha Jim tossed his own after it. The ponies were being led away by soldiers. The officers breathed easier, distributed more food, tobacco, small gifts.

"Phew! Thought for a minute they were all set to kick up one last explosion. Better get them started down-river as soon as possible. Telegraph news of the surrender to all posts and agencies. Colonel, be kind enough to arrange passage for these people on the *Sherman* before she pulls out."

On the *General Sherman*, river steamboat, the last of the Sioux nation was shipped off down the Missouri toward Fort Yates and the Standing Rock Reservation. The War Department showered blessings and thanks upon everybody concerned, and the Montana settlers invited their home relatives to come on out to a fine land of safety and plenty.

Ten miles or so above Fort Lincoln an Army officer on a sweating horse hailed the steamboat from an obsure landing, and boarded her. He was Lieutenant Weston Hathersall of the Seventh, he said, and he wanted urgently to talk to a Sioux by the name of Wapaha.

★

"Jim, for heaven's sake listen to reason. You can't throw yourself away like this—I won't let you!"

"You can't stop me, West."

"Oh, you—you madman! Haven't you sacrificed enough for these people? You stuck by them to the finish. Now it's all over. You're a white man. You can't go on with them and be an agency Indian!"

"I can. I'm Wapaha, a Minniconjou Sioux."

"You're a flaming idiot!"

West was baffled, frantic. He had used every argument at his command and got nowhere. It was dark on the river now, and soon he must notify the captain to pull in at the Fort Lincoln landing. He had been returning to the fort from routine patrol, and on the way had heard by chance of the surrender and the southbound boatload of captives.

"Be damned to this Wapaha business—you're Jim Aherne!" he reiterated, red-faced and vehement. They stood in the deserted stern of the chugging boat. "You've got a brevet commission in the Army. Lieutenant Aherne—that's you! You could take regular officer's training any time you chose. Why, you could rise to be a . . ."

"A white savage in uniform," Jim finished for him, and shook his head. "No."

"But you'd never have to fight Indians, Jim. That's all ended. The Army's got a different job now. Outlaws and bad characters of all kinds are drifting into the territories, heading for the gold camps. Until civil law comes, it's our job to keep the country in hand. Settlers will be swarming in next year. With all your experience and knowledge of the country you'd be a valuable officer. You'd be helping to—well—build civilization."

"I don't know that I care to help," said Jim.

West took a different tack. "What about Tally? I guess you know how she feels about you, don't you?"

A few lights came into sight ahead. Fort Lincoln. The boat would not put in to the landing unless requested.

"Yes, I know," Jim said. He turned his gaze away to the water under the stern, roiled black and white by the boat's paddles. "That's the reason—one of the reasons— why I'm going to stay Wapaha. She's what she is, and I'm what I am. I should stay with the Indians. It's where I belong."

"That," observed West, "sounds like George Vaugant."

Jim nodded. "He said it. He was right."

"You think so? He proposed to Tally a month ago. She turned him down. Listen, Jim. I've got to run and tell them to let me off at the fort. For the last time, will you get off with me?"

"I'm sorry, West. No."

West stared at Jim's turned head. "You—!" he began

chokingly, and then impulse caught up with him. He lunged at Jim.

Jim was taken completely by surprise. He staggered, the stern rail hit him behind the knees, and he went backwards over it. There was nothing to grab. He twisted, falling, and the noise of the ponderous paddles roared for an instant close in his ears, but it was blotted out when the cold shock of the water closed over him.

As he beat to the surface and got his head clear he saw West outlined against the night sky, diving after him. After West's splash he heard another, but by then he was swimming for the shore and couldn't see what it was that made it.

He waded ashore, angry, but with some laughter struggling in him. To be batted into the river was annoying, but there was something irresistibly funny in the fact that West had done it. Too, he could not help feeling glad at the impulsive act. He waited on the bank, soaking wet. West came plowing ashore, and another figure behind him.

"That was a fine trick on an old friend!" Jim grumbled. "What good do you think . . . Bad Buffalo, keep your hands off that soldier!"

They met on the bank. "I was watching. I saw him try to kill you!" Bad Buffalo's eyes glimmered in the darkness. "Let me break his neck, Wapaha! Nobody will know. Nobody saw us jump off the boat."

Jim grinned at them both. It was good to have friends who were ready to shove you into a river for benign reasons, or do murder for you. "This soldier is a friend, Bad Buffalo," he explained gravely. "No, he did not want to kill me. He would keep me from going to the reservation, and he thought he was doing good."

The Sioux gutturals meant nothing to West. "What's this rascal up to?" he asked. "What are you telling him?"

"He just wanted to break your neck for trying to drown me, is all, West. I think you'd better lead the way to a fire and some blankets, or I'll give him a hand!"

West looked at Bad Buffalo's face and gorilla shoulders. He was wet and cold. "Let's slip in to my quarters. I'll light a fire and make some coffee. What'll we do about this man?"

"He's with us, and as wet as we are, and he's a very good old friend of mine," said Jim. "His name's Bad Buffalo. He goes with us, and it's up to you to see that he doesn't get into any trouble for jumping off that boat. Lead the way to that fire. *Hopo!*"

Sentries, after challenging them and recognizing West, stared at them as they passed into the fort. It was long past taps. The only lights came from here and there along Officers' Row. A late sitter on a gallery called out a startled query to the dripping and bedraggled trio, but West led the way into his quarters without response.

CHAPTER 18

★

THE LAST CAMPAIGN

DRYING SOME OF HIS CLOTHES BEFORE A ROARING FIRE, JIM motioned to Bad Buffalo to remain still when a rap sounded on the front door. Bad Buffalo, draped in an Army blanket, went on swallowing all the hot coffee he could hold, but his eyes slid uneasily about him. All his life he had lived in open spaces, his home a flimsy and portable tepee of buffalo hide, when he had one. This place of permanent walls reeked of alien odors, and he distrusted everything about it.

West went and answered the knock. "Oh—er—good evening, Colonel. Eh? No—no trouble. Not at all. That is, not now. Had an accident. Fell off the boat. Yes, the *Sherman*. It just passed a little while ago. I was on it."

"Obviously, if you fell off. And your—hem—companions, Lieutenant?"

"Yes, sir. They fell off, too. I mean they jumped off to save me. We're drying our clothes. Got wet in the river, you know, when we fell in. That is, I mean when I fell in and they . . ."

"Yes, a reasonable consequence. You can tell me the details in the morning. I see you're not quite yourself tonight. A bit coolish in the river, eh? Goodnight. Ah, by the way . . ."

"Yes, sir?"

"The boat didn't stop? H'mm. Of course, you will accept responsibility for any consequences that may arise from this somewhat remarkable accident, eh? Goodnight."

West closed the door and returned wiping his brow. "Fine man, the colonel," he remarked. "He's not Custer, but we all like him. Got a lot of new faces in the regiment these days. You'd get along fine with them, Jim."

"Yes. What will you do in the morning?"

"First thing, I suppose, will be to have this Bad Buffalo escorted on down to Standing Rock."

"Both of us," Jim said. "I go with him."

"Oh, for the love of—! Jim, don't be a fool. You're here now. I'll cut your hair and give you some clothes, and I'll tell everybody you've been . . ."

"You'll tell them nothing. My hair and clothes will do to wear to the reservation. I wouldn't look Indian without them."

West began getting into his damp tunic. "Then I'm

riding down to Bismarck tonight to get Tally. She'll change your mind or nothing will!"

Jim shoved him into a chair and stood over him. "If you do, Bad Buffalo and I are starting out on foot right now for Standing Rock. West, don't you see? It's Tally I'm thinking of, and I've got to keep away from her. Vaugant was right. He hated me, but he spoke for all white men when he told me I didn't belong."

"Damn him!" West swore. "It's Vaugant who's put that poison in your mind. Poisoned you against yourself. Get rid of it, Jim. He's in love with Tally. I swear he was only talking for himself."

Jim shook his head. "I've never liked him, but he's a straight man. He told me the truth as he saw it. It was his opinion—and next to you, he's the only white man alive who really knows me. His eyes are clear." Unconsciously, he fell back upon Sioux figuratives. "He sees me. You are blinded by old friendship. You don't see me. You see Jim Aherne. He sees Wapaha, the Sioux—the white savage—the renegade."

"He's here in the fort, I believe," West muttered darkly. "I've a mind to call him in and demand an apology."

That was made unnecessary. Half an hour after the colonel paid his inquiring visit, the door opened and Vaugant walked in without knocking. He looked thinner than ever and walked as if on wooden legs, and something about him reminded Jim of Long Mane in his bitterest moods. His stare raked over them.

"So you're playing host to a couple of Sitting Bull's boys," he drawled, and West stiffened. "The colonel tells me you fell off the boat. The boat failed to stop, so you fell off. Quite a fortuitous accident. And what plans have you for your two guests, may I ask?"

He didn't wait for a reply. "Conspiring in the escape of government prisoners is a damned serious offense!" His brittle banter was abruptly discarded. "You can't get away with it. The colonel got a glimpse of these two when you brought them in. You can be broken for this!"

West said defiantly, "That's my affair!"

Jim made to speak. Before he got a word out, Vaugant stuck a finger at him. "Keep quiet till you're spoken to!"

It was too much. Jim caught him by the front of his coat and pulled him up close. "I could kill you and it wouldn't matter to me," he said muffledly, and the undertone of his voice brought a grunt from Bad Buffalo, who could detect menace in any language, human or animal. "It wouldn't matter, because I'm going to Standing Rock tomorrow and I'm finished. Be careful, soldier!"

West was releasing a stream of words, damning Vaugant for what he had said now and in the past. "You've done enough to him, damn you! You've poisoned him— told him lies about himself, and he believes them. He's throwing himself away, and I can't stop him!"

Vaugant did not move. For a moment he gazed impersonally at West, and then at Jim. "I think I told you once that I'd accommodate you any time, any place, Aherne." Some sort of cold humor put a slight downward droop to the corners of his mouth. "Step outside with me. Hathersall, you stay here and keep that damned ape with you." He waited for his coat to be released, turned on his heel, and led the way out.

On the dark gallery Vaugant's thinned face was a blurred mask. "I'm leaving tomorrow. Leaving the Army. Can't sit in a saddle any more, curse that Indian bullet. I've nothing to lose."

He paused. His eyes reminded Jim more than ever of Long Mane. The same inner pain and brooding thought were there. "I've nothing to lose," he repeated. "And neither have you. We're both finished. But there's this one last satisfaction we can have—one of us can have—

before we quit. One last campaign, eh? I'll meet you in the morning. I'll be up along the river, over the hill where the timber begins. I'll have two loaded rifles. Suit you?"

"Yes. And if I kill you—?"

Vaugant shrugged. "Does it matter what happens afterward? It doesn't to me. We'll meet in that clearing where the old Ree camp used to be. We'll put one rifle under the cut-bank where the river bends, and the other in that clump of willows farther up the river. We start action when we take our positions, and stalk each other. Clear?"

"Quite clear."

"Good. It ought to be an interesting little private campaign for us to finish up with. Be there before sun-up. Don't tell Hathersall. If you climb over that wall at the end of the granary, and be careful, nobody need see you leave the fort. But watch out for the sentries. I wouldn't want anybody else to shoot you."

They exchanged nods and parted. Vaugant went off across the empty parade ground, and Jim watched him march his stiff gait into the darkness, and walked back into the house. West eyed him worriedly without coming to the point of asking a blunt question, but with Bad Buffalo it was a different matter.

After they turned in to bed, Jim became aware of the scarred warrior bending over him in the darkened downstairs room. "Wapaha . . ." The name came in a crooning whisper. "When do you kill that soldier of the stiff legs?" It was useless trying to fool Bad Buffalo.

"In the morning, perhaps," Jim answered. "We meet with guns. When it is over, I want you to go on to the reservation. Tell our band that I want you to be the next chief, Bad Buffalo."

"But you are chief, and you will kill the soldier!"

"That may be true," Jim conceded patiently. "But we

have surrendered. To kill a soldier now is not war, but a great crime. Tomorrow I shall be dead, or in the prison-house, or perhaps running away to the north again. Old friend, take my feather and remember what I say. When you are chief, be a good chief. Forget anger. Keep the young men from trouble. There will be many changes that must be made by our people. Help them make those changes. Be patient. Remember always that the white men do not understand our ways. Make friends among them, and try to make them understand. You will need friends among them. They can help you. Now sleep."

"Yes, Wapaha. I shall remember. We have been good friends, haven't we?"

"We have been brothers."

★

The spot designated by Vaugant was well chosen—wooded enough to afford clever stalking, and a long rise of ground between it and the fort. The ground was still packed hard from its one-time use as a Ree camp-site, but weeds and low brush dotted it here and there. Trees partly surrounded it, thickest toward the river, but mostly young and spindly, for the Rees had used up the best timber.

Where the riverbank was low a depression had been formed by the overflow of the floodwaters each spring. It was dry now, but along here the dwarf willows were thick. Within seventy yards of it, the same spring flood-waters had carved into the face of the higher bank where the river bent, leaving a natural breastwork and a bare lower bank to stand on.

Jim had a sketchy recollection of the place, and his mind automatically pondered its points and possibilities as he approached it. He had come around the long rise to avoid any chance of being skylined from the fort while crossing it, but he thought he was early on the scene until he saw a buckboard and team in the clearing. It was not yet full dawn. He remembered Vaugant's remark last night about his not being able to sit in a saddle any more. Evidently the captain's stiff legs wouldn't allow him to do much walking, either.

Vaugant sat waiting in the buckboard, looking up at the lightening sky. He lowered his head as Jim entered the clearing, regarding him, but did not rise. Jim came up to the buckboard. Vaugant had evidently driven here by way of the lower riverbank and ran into deep mud in the dark. Mud caked the wheels, the body was spattered with it, and the team looked as if it might have had a hard time getting through.

"Good-morning," Vaugant greeted him, and climbed slowly to the ground. He seemed a little exhausted by his efforts in getting here, and under a strain that was at variance with his cool phlegm of last night. "The light will be better shortly. Shall we begin?"

Jim nodded. Unthinkingly, he reached out a hand to save Vaugant from falling. The captain had swayed badly, getting to the ground.

Vaugant brushed his hand aside and caught hold of the buckboard. He stood there for a moment until his legs were steady again. Some sweat gathered in the deep crease above his nose, and his lips were colorless. "I'm all right," he said harshly. "Damned legs. My arms are all right—and my shooting eye. Look out for yourself. I'll take those willows if it's all the same to you. Doubt if I could get down that cut-bank."

Jim nodded again. He noted a change of expression on the strained face, a flicker of dour triumph, and he wondered at it. But it didn't matter, and he let it pass. Nothing could make much difference to what was going to happen, and whatever happened could not greatly change the ultimate outcome. He walked to the cut-bank and slid down it, and on the lower bank he looked for the rifle. But there wasn't any rifle in sight.

Even now he suspected nothing against Vaugant. He thought that he might have made a mistake, that perhaps this was not the spot the captain had meant. It was inconceivable that Vaugant should have failed to set out the rifle for him. He moved farther on upstream, searching, keeping his head down. Vaugant could be expected to fire his opening shot pretty soon. It would be embarrassing to have to call him over to locate the rifle that he had placed . . .

Jim stopped, rounding a nose of the bank, all his thoughts suddenly jammed.

"Are you . . . are you looking for this, Jim?"

She sat in a hollow of the bank, her loose wrap splashed with mud and clay, and in her hands she held the little beaded pouch of buckskin. Her eyes were bright, gravely inquiring. "You left this behind you, Jim. I've brought it to you . . . for luck."

He could find nothing to say, except to mutter her name just once. "Tally!"

And then it was as he had known and feared that it must be, if he saw her. Reason and restraint were straws against his flood of hunger for her. She rose swiftly, and when he touched her she was trembling. The little buckskin pouch fell between them, and the weight of the shagreen book inside made it slap solidly on the ground, a cheerful and inconsequent sound in the silence.

After awhile she said, against his chest, "Jim, will they let a white girl onto the reservation? They'd better. I'll not let you get away from me this time—or any time. If you think . . ."

She uttered a muffled scream, staring over his shoulder, and Jim spun around. He could admit that there

was some reason for her scream. Grown men, catching
sight of Bad Buffalo creeping up on them, had been
known to yell out loud and flee.

Bad Buffalo came slithering around the bank, hideous
and ungainly, noiseless as a ghost, and he had West's
heavy revolver with him. He grinned at Jim, bobbed
his head up above the bank, and a happiness deepened
his grin. He raised the big revolver, taking aim at something in the clearing, and Tally screamed again.

"No! Jim—don't let him!"

Jim grasped the long brown arm, and Bad Buffalo
eyed him astonishedly. "What is wrong, Wapaha? I
followed you, and I have a gun. You have no gun. There
is the soldier. Let me shoot him."

Jim looked over the bank and saw Vaugant walking
slowly toward the buckboard, without a rifle and without any attempt at keeping to cover. Tally said, "He
rode into Bismarck for me last night. He rode a horse,
and he was fainting when he knocked at my door. The
doctors told him he must never ride again, months ago.
He asked me if I still loved you . . . and then he told me
you were here, and we rented the buckboard and drove
the rest of the night."

Bad Buffalo, knowing nothing of what was being
said, still wanted to shoot. Jim had to restrain him. "No,
Bad Buffalo, this one also is a friend."

"A friend? *Ma-ya!*"

Tally said, "He told me to wait here and help him win
his last campaign. I brought your brevet commission
with me. It's in the pouch with your little book. He
told me to bring it. Said you'd want it. 'I'm getting out
of the Army,' he said. 'Tell your man he can have my
sword and boots. I'll never need them again, and somebody ought to use them.'"

They climbed the bank, and Jim felt the way he had
felt when dying Long Mane asked to be his blood-

brother. Vaugant looked over at them, laboriously climbing up into the buckboard. He picked up the lines, straightened himself on the seat, and looked at them again. He didn't smile.

"Tell that red son of Satan to drop that gun and come here," he called curtly. "Doesn't he know he's surrendered? I'll take him down to Standing Rock. It's on my way. I'll tell 'em he jumped off the boat to save an Army man—God forgive me for a liar—and they'll probably make a hero of him!"

Watching the buckboard go trundling slowly off up the long rise, Vaugant and Bad Buffalo together on the seat, Jim experienced an aching sensation of loss. This was the real finality, the last small flourish of the Battles of the Plains—that mud-spattered buckboard carrying away two crippled fighters whose war was done and who would never fight again. They sat side by side, hunched, each with his own long thoughts. Gone the wild glory, the fierce hatreds, the fire and the martial gallantry. The early sun tipped no flaunting plume with brave light, glinted on no polished sword-hilt. Bad Buffalo sat huddled in his blanket. Vaugant wore his greatcoat and no sidearms; he was a retired and invalided officer on his way home.

Before leaving, Bad Buffalo had run his scrutiny over Tally, and given a grunt that could have meant anything. "*Wanna.* I go, Wapaha. You stay? That is good. You will have children. Tell them about us, about our people. Tell the white men why we fought. Last night you said we will need friends in the years coming. You will help make us those friends, Wapaha, and you will speak for us when we need you . . . ."

Jim felt Tally's hand tighten in his, and he closed his fingers over it. The loss remained, apart from this gain, for it had to do with a way of life that could never come back. The coming way would take its place, and he knew that in time the loss would belong only to memory, as with any loss created by death.

Yellow Eagle, old Pehangi—dead these two years—and Iron Breast, who fell at Slim Buttes. Long Mane, and Crazy Horse—killed in a guardhouse brawl—and Tatanka Hinto, and all the rest. And Custer, Major Chittendon, all the officers and troopers who had gone their way. They were all part of that loss.

Remembrance of the major trailed another remembrance in its wake, and Jim thought of that talk by the river. The major had been right. Frontiers were never permanent, and the Indian had fought for a cause that had always been lost. His wild and splendid reign, with its derivative virtues and faults, had to give ground before the mightier force of civilization. The tide was too high for an island of ancient barbarism to stand unswept by it. He had fought, lost, and now he stood face to face with the new regime. There would be those who would go down before it, baffled, unable to fit themselves into the alien pattern. The rest would learn, conform, and perhaps eventually become a living and vigorous part of it. Meanwhile, the land of their old domination would fill with the overflow of the world, homesteaders would farm the valleys and plains, and the bones of the buffalo would be plowed into the soil.

The Indian in the buckboard turned, just before the team plodded over the crest of the rise. He raised his right arm in the old familiar gesture that could mean peace or friendship, greeting or farewell. The invalid officer beside him looked at him for a few seconds. He twisted around and briefly made the same gesture to the couple in the clearing.

Jim kept his arm raised until the buckboard wheeled on over the hill. He was very quiet while walking to the fort, and he didn't see West come hurrying out and halt at sight of them. But Tally did, and sent him a signal, and West went striding off to the stables for horses.

Tally laughed a little breathlessly. "Your hair, Jim . . ."

"H'mm?" He brushed a hand over it, and grinned down at her. No brooding reverie could last long with Tally around. "I gave my feather to Bad Buffalo. Oh—long, eh?"

"Too long for Jim Aherne . . . for Brevet-Lieutenant Jim Aherne. I can see I'll have to play Delilah again."

"Who was she?"

"A certain lively lady with winning ways."

L(eonard) L(ondon) Foreman was born in London, England in 1901. He served in the British army during the Great War, prior to his emigration to the United States. He became an itinerant, holding a series of odd jobs in the western States as he traveled. He began his writing career by introducing his most widely known and best-loved character, Preacher Devlin, in "Noose Fodder" in *Western Aces* (12/34), a pulp magazine. Throughout the mid thirties, this character, a combination gunfighter, gambler, and philosopher, appeared regularly in *Western Aces*. Near the end of the decade, Foreman's Western stories began appearing in Street & Smith's *Western Story Magazine*, where the pay was better. Foreman's first Western novels began appearing in the 1940s, largely historical Westerns such as *Don Desperado* (1941) and *The Renegade* (1942). The New York Herald Tribune reviewer commented on *Don Desperado* that "admirers of the late beloved Dane Coolidge better take a look at this. It has that same all-wool-and-a-yard-wide quality." Foreman continued to write prolifically for the magazine market as long as it lasted, before specializing exclusively for the book trade with one of his finest novels, *Arrow in the Dust* (1954) which was filmed under this title the same year. Two years earlier *The Renegade* was filmed as *The Savage* (Paramount, 1952), the two are among several films based on his work. Foreman's last years were spent living in the state of Oregon. Perhaps his most popular character after Preacher Devlin was Rogue Bishop, appearing in a series of novels published by Doubleday in the 1960s. George Walsh, writing in *Twentieth Century Western Writers*, said of Foreman: "His novels have a sense of authority because he does not deal in simple characters or simple answers." In fact, most of his fiction is not centered on a confrontation between good and evil, but rather on his characters and the changes they undergo. His female characters, above all, are memorably drawn and central to his stories.